W9-BWN-000

"The cause is hidden, but the result is known."

—OVID

CASE PENDING

DELL SHANNON

Edited, with an introduction and notes,
by Leslie S. Klinger

Copyright © 1960 by Elizabeth Linington
Introduction and notes © 2020 by Leslie S. Klinger
Cover and internal design © 2020 by Sourcebooks and Library of Congress
Cover design by Heather Morris/Sourcebooks
Cover images © The Library of Congress

Sourcebooks, Poisoned Pen Press, and the colophon are registered trademarks of
Sourcebooks.

Cover image: *Dolls in a Rural Home in Madison, North Carolina.* Carol M. Highsmith,
1980–2006. Carol M. Highsmith Archive, Prints & Photographs Division, Library of
Congress, LC-DIG-highsm-15917

All rights reserved. No part of this book may be reproduced in any form or by any
electronic or mechanical means including information storage and retrieval systems—
except in the case of brief quotations embodied in critical articles or reviews—without
permission in writing from its publisher, Sourcebooks.

The characters and events portrayed in this book are fictitious or are used fictitiously.
Any similarity to real persons, living or dead, is purely coincidental and not intended by
the author.

Published by Poisoned Pen Press, an imprint of Sourcebooks, in association with the
Library of Congress
P.O. Box 4410, Naperville, Illinois 60567-4410
(630) 961-3900
sourcebooks.com

This edition is based on the first edition in the collection of the Library of Congress,
published in 1960 in the United States by Harper & Brothers.

Library of Congress Cataloging-in-Publication Data is on file with the publisher.

Printed and bound in the United States of America.
SB 10 9 8 7 6 5 4 3 2 1

CONTENTS

FOREWORD

Crime writing as we know it first appeared in 1841, with the publication of *The Murders in the Rue Morgue*. Written by American author Edgar Allan Poe, the short story introduced C. Auguste Dupin, the world's first wholly fictional detective. Other American and British authors had begun working in the genre by the 1860s, and by the 1920s we had officially entered the golden age of detective fiction.

Throughout this short history, many authors who paved the way have been lost or forgotten. Library of Congress Crime Classics bring back into print some of the finest American crime writing from the 1860s to the 1960s, showcasing rare and lesser known titles that represent a range of genres, from "cozies" to police procedurals. With cover designs inspired by images from the Library's collections, each book in this series includes the original text, as well as a contextual introduction, brief biography of the author, notes, recommendations for further reading, and suggested discussion questions. Our hope is for these books to start conversations, inspire further research, and bring obscure works to a new generation of readers.

In *Case Pending*, author Elizabeth Linington, writing under the pseudonym Dell Shannon, introduces us to one of the first

Latino detectives to appear in fiction. Independently wealthy and a snappy dresser, Mexican American homicide lieutenant Luis Mendoza faces skepticism from his colleagues in the police force. But he excels at his profession, and cracks case after case in more than thirty books in Linington's Mendoza series.

Early American crime fiction is not only entertaining to read, it also sheds light on the culture of its time. While many of the titles in this series include outmoded language and stereotypes now considered offensive, it's fascinating to read these books and reflect on the evolution of our society's perceptions of race, gender, ethnicity, and social standing. Linington's mid-century Angelenos face racial prejudice, economic disparities across neighborhoods, and other challenges that are still with us today. Her exploration of these issues adds a welcome dimension to an already entertaining read.

More dark secrets and bloody deeds lurk in the massive collections of the Library of Congress. I encourage you to explore these works for yourself, here in Washington, D.C., or online at www.loc.gov.

—Carla D. Hayden, Librarian of Congress

INTRODUCTION

Police procedurals, stories in which official detectives and their methods are featured, are not a new addition to crime fiction. Detectives star in some of the very earliest works of the nineteenth century, beginning with the memoirs of Vidocq, Emile Gaboriau's novels about the police detective Monsieur Lecoq, and the plethora of semifictional books appearing in America as the "experiences" or "recollections" of various detectives.* The first modern American police procedural is Lawrence Treat's *V as in Victim* (1945). In nine novels, Treat used actual law enforcement routines and extensive scientific evidence in showing police at work, usually interpreted by Jub Freeman, a police scientist.

The idea of focusing on the police in this way was taken up by Hillary Waugh, who wrote two series of procedurals, and in 1956, by the prolific Ed McBain, whose fifty-six novels and dozens of short stories about the fictional "87th Precinct" in a thinly disguised New York City continued until his death in 2005. The first woman to tackle the form, however, was Elizabeth Linington, who penned four different series (three under pen

---

*The earliest were "dime" novels, which began to appear in America in the 1870s. Allan Pinkerton, founder of the eponymous detective agency, jumped on this bandwagon with his own (probably ghostwritten) memoirs in 1876, with the first book to bear his name being *The Expressman and the Detective*, and more than a dozen additional titles before 1900.

names) and produced more than eighty titles of crime fiction. Linington's success paved the way for other women, such as Dorothy Uhnak and Lillian O'Donnell. More importantly, her blending of the personal lives of the police officers with their jobs and her unflinching portrayals of the victims and villains led to greater development of characters and the political and social issues of the day in crime writing. Later writers of cop-oriented crime fiction like Joseph Wambaugh or Michael Connelly, whose books give us rich pictures of the families of the police officers, clearly owe a debt to Linington's work.

Case Pending, first published in 1960, is remarkable in several respects. First, Linington develops detailed portraits of the police in the story, including Detective-Sergeant Arthur Hackett, the critically important investigator Dick Morgan, and, of course, her lead character, Lieutenant Luis Mendoza. In particular, Mendoza's relationship with Alison Weir, which has its flirtatious beginnings here, as well as Mendoza's friendship with Hackett, are developed fully in later novels. Second, we also get clear pictures of the victims and their families. Although Linington's portraits of the Ramirez family, the witness Agnes Browne, and the family of Carol Brooks suffer from racial stereotypes, she devotes more time and care to writing about their lives than was generally thought necessary for popular crime fiction. Third, Linington was among the first to weave together multiple story lines into a tapestry of police activities. Linington shrewdly recognized that unlike the amateur detective, the police deal with a multiplicity of crimes and victims and must juggle their investigations along with paperwork, rivalries among agencies, shortages of manpower, and other common features of modern government agencies.

Linington was well aware that the writer of police procedurals was under even greater scrutiny than the average mystery writer with regard to realism. To ensure reasonable accuracy, she not only researched the rules and regulations of the Los

Angeles Police Department, she also cultivated friendships with police officers, including one in Atlanta who often provided her with the true facts of unusual cases. Linington often based her fictional crimes on accounts from "true crime" magazines and newspapers and relied on friends and maps to provide her with geographical details after she moved away from Los Angeles.

It does not appear, however, that Luis Mendoza sprang from any sort of personal experience. In an interview, she addressed the subject directly:

[Interviewer]: "How did you pick up on the idea of Luis Mendoza? Did the Spanish theme come from living in this area [Southern California]?"

[Linington]: "Well, it didn't. I had this little idea for the plot of *Case Pending*, and introduced the detective on the scene—just in carrying out the plot. And he rose off the page and captured me alive, and I couldn't stop writing about him."

[Interviewer]: "Do you happen to know why he happened to be Mexican American?"

[Linington]: "I couldn't tell you—it just came."*

Linington certainly recognized that she was creating an artificial character. She admitted that her Spanish was poor, and no one would regularly say something in Spanish and then repeat the same phrase in English—a common occurrence in her Mendoza novels. More importantly, Linington seems to go out of her way to emphasize that Mendoza is a cut above the "regular" Mexican Americans who appear in *Case Pending*. Not only is he wealthy, well-dressed, and eccentric in his choice of cars, people with whom he interacts make a point to observe that he is of "true" Spanish blood and therefore a gentleman and aristocratic in bearing. Certainly many of the police—and many of

*Margaret J. King, "An Interview with Elizabeth Linington," *Armchair Detective* 13, no. 4 (Fall 1980): 301.

the other minor characters—look down on the "Mexes" with whom they interact in Los Angeles and are careful to distinguish Mendoza from that lot. Linington seems to have little sympathy for the families struggling in the neighborhood she depicts, whether they are Mexicans, black, Irish, or Scandinavian. Her real sympathy seems reserved for Dick Morgan and his wife and child.

Although Linington has Mendoza express disdain for psychological theories of sexuality and crime, it is very apparent that she understood those theories well and she uses them to great advantage in *Case Pending*. Her depiction of the dynamics of the Lindstrom family rings true, down to the details of the killer's obsession with dolls and the peer pressure felt by Marty. While Linington may have unkindly intended her story of Agnes Browne, who is convinced of her own culpability, as a sort of comic relief, it sadly also seems genuine.

Linington deftly captures the "melting pot" that was Los Angeles of the late 1950s, with masses of immigrant populations of all ethnicities crowded into the neighborhoods east of downtown, many of whom would soon be displaced by the development of Elysian Park and the Los Angeles Dodgers' new baseball stadium. Though the "zoot suit riots" of 1943—violent clashes between American servicemen and Mexican American youths in Los Angeles—were more than 15 years in the past, the city, with a population of almost 2.5 million people of widely diverse racial and ethnic backgrounds, had yet to have a mayor who was not white, and racial tensions still simmered throughout the region.

In a 1967 essay about her craft, Linington characterized the mystery-detective novel as exciting and the most challenging type of writing. She saw the detective story in political and philosophical terms, as "the morality play of our time," with the police procedural its purest expression. In this, she helped develop a new school of crime writing, in which the plots took backseat to the development of the characters. Linington wanted to show the police not just as instruments of detection or punishment but as individuals, with jealousies, failures, and personal struggles. Writers like Joseph Wambaugh and Michael Connelly embraced this approach, expressed by Wambaugh like this: "The best crime stories are not about how cops work on cases but about how cases work on cops."[*]

Although Linington was not the first to write police procedurals in America, the volume and popularity of her multiple series justify her coronation as the "Queen of Police Procedurals." *Case Pending* is not only her first effort in the field, it is one of her finest.

—Leslie S. Klinger

---

[*]Elina Shatkin, "Cop on Crime Writing: Joseph Wambaugh," *Jacket Copy* (blog), *Los Angeles Times*, April 26, 2008, https://latimesblogs.latimes.com/jacketcopy/2008/04/how-do-you-like.html.

One

When Gunn came down the hall to his office at half-past eight, he found Curtis waiting. Curtis was holding up the wall beside the door; he opened his eyes at Gunn's step. He looked tired and rather dirty.

"And a good, *good* morning to you too, Chief," he said. Gunn didn't like to be called *chief*.

"What'd you draw?" Gunn unlocked the door.

"Just what we expected. I won't come in—I'm going home to bed—I can give it to you in ten words. Williams showed up about eight, you'll get that on Henry's report. Went in, about twenty minutes later came out with our Ma Williams, and they went down to the Redbird bar on Third. Ten forty, shifted to the Palace.* Henry called me from there, and I took over at midnight. They drifted home about half an hour later and stayed. His car's still outside."

"Well, now," said Gunn, pleased. "Fancy that."

"And for your further information," said Curtis, "I damn near froze to death sitting it out in my car. Next time I'll take along another blanket and a portable radio."

---

*The Palace Theatre, at 630 South Broadway in downtown Los Angeles, was built in 1911. It was originally known as the "Orpheum" and housed the Orpheum Vaudeville Circuit, but it was renamed the Palace Theatre in 1926, switching to showing films. The theater remains in operation in 2019.

Gunn grinned benignly and told him to go home. He went on through the stenos' room to the center of three partitioned-off rooms at the rear, hung up his hat and coat, and sat at the desk. Henry's report was neatly centered, waiting for him there; Henry never missed getting in a written report immediately, however late his duty. *Williams in 7:57*, it announced laconically, and the rest of what Curtis had said. Very nice, thought Gunn.

So now they knew that Mr. John Williams hadn't deserted his wife and four children. The county had been passing over sixty-three dollars and fifty cents per month* to Mrs. John Williams for four months, on her claim of desertion and failure to provide. The kids had to be fed, had to be sheltered and clothed—after a fashion—by somebody. It appeared that once again the county had been rooked. Williams was a skilled carpenter, probably making good money on an out-of-town job. Gunn made a nota-tion on the report, *Morgan to see*, and sighed. Naughty, naughty, Mr. and Mrs. Williams, collusion to defraud the state—and maybe next time they'd think up something slicker.

He got out his file of current investigations, wrote a brief summary of the conclusions in the Williams case, and set the file page aside for refiling among cases completed. He flicked over the rest. He heard the girl stenos begin to drift into the outer office.

Rossiter. Brankin. Peabody. Prinn. Fraty. Kling. A new one, Lindstrom. There were follow-up reports to be typed in on six or seven of them; he took those out to the stenos. "Morning, girls." Morgan and Stack came in together.

"I want to see you about that Mrs. Gold," said Stack.

"What about her?"

Stack followed him back into his office. "I told you I finally

---

*About $706 in household purchasing power in 2019. Samuel H. Williamson, "Purchasing Power Today of a US Dollar Transaction in the Past," MeasuringWorth, 2019, https://www.measuring-worth.com/calculators/uscompare/. The maximum Mrs. Williams and her family could get in Los Angeles under the CalWORKS program in 2019 is $1,242, considerably more than in 1960. "CalWORKS Maximum Grant Levels," World Institute on Disability, 2019, https://ca.db101.org/glossary_item.aspx?item-id=6521.

caught up to the guy—the Reno D.A.'s office found him, he's working in some joint there as a waiter. I had it all set up to crack down on him, see, Reno says he ought to be good for seventy-five a month, and I went round to give the glad news to the missus. And then the rabbi puts the kibosh on it."

"What rabbi?"

"Mrs. Gold's rabbi. He was there. He says please will we just drop the whole thing and leave it to him—I guess he figures it'll be less of a disgrace or something if he can handle it—"

"Oh," said Gunn. "Well, he might have something there. If he can get it without any fuss, so much the better. Man'd feel better about it if he's persuaded instead of forced, the money'll come easier—less chance we'd have more trouble. It works out with ministers sometimes, but we can't let 'em stall forever. You tell him we'll give him a couple of weeks to try it his way before we crack down." Gunn went out with Stack and looked into the room next to his own; Morgan was sitting there at one of four desks, looking at some papers. "Oh, Dick."

Morgan looked up. "Yes, sir?" he responded dully.

"Little job. Henry and Curtis have tied up the Williams case. Another collusion, way you figured. Williams is weekending—they were at a bar until midnight and it's a good chance you'll catch him still in bed with her if you make it snappy. Here's the report."

Morgan got up. "All right. Williams—yes."

Gunn looked at him more closely. "You look a bit off-color."

"I'm all right," said Morgan. He did not look it. As he took his topcoat from the peg behind the door, Gunn saw his hand shaking. He was the thin, sandy type that doesn't change much between boyhood and old age, doesn't look much different sick or well. But there were lines around his mouth now that Gunn hadn't seen before, and his eyes looked tired, as if he hadn't slept. He had a little trouble folding the paper Gunn handed him, putting it away in his pocket.

"How's Sue?" asked Gunn casually. "And Jan?"

"Fine," said Morgan, buttoning his coat carefully. "Just fine, thanks."

"Must get together again soon, Christy was saying just last night—she'd like to kidnap that Janny of yours, kind of lonesome with our three grown and off."

"Oh—yes, sure. I guess so. We'll do that, thanks."

Gunn stood in the door of his office, absently jingling the coins in his pocket, and watched the other man out to the corridor. What was wrong with Morgan? He felt some responsibility for Morgan, unreasonably, for it had been his doing that Morgan got this job. Dick Morgan was the son of an old friend of Gunn's, and he'd known the boy most of his life. Boy, well, Dick was thirty-eight, but it depended where you sat: Kenneth Gunn was sixty-two. And good as he'd ever been too, once he'd got out of the hospital after that business last year; but the doctors wouldn't pass him for active duty again. Nearly forty years' service, and then a home-made bullet out of a punk's zip-gun* retired him. And Bill Andrews got the promotion to head of Homicide instead. Way the cards fell, and Bill was a good man; but Gunn hadn't known what to do with himself that six months. He'd jumped at this minor post in the D.A.'s office; and he could say now, a year later, he'd given Kelleher something to talk about at the next election, by God.

It was a new department, this little corps of investigators—the husband-chasers, inevitably they were called; and if Gunn couldn't claim their job was as important as the one he'd done for forty years in and out of uniform, at least the Scot in him took pride in reckoning how much they saved the taxpayers. He'd set up the organization himself, and it served as a model for those some other counties were building, here and in other states. He and his crew had tracked down over two thousand runaway husbands so far, to pry minimum child-support funds

---

*An improvised, usually homemade firearm.

out of them anyway. Authorities in other states had cooperated, of course, but it came out even: they'd picked up deserters for other D.A.'s offices from Maine to Oregon, too. Gunn had the exact figure whenever Kelleher wanted it; to date it was upward of half a million dollars this office had saved the county in support of deserted wives and children. There'd been a time a man could walk out and it was nobody's job to locate him, make him provide for a deserted family. These days, no. He couldn't go across the Arizona or Nevada line and thumb his nose at the California taxpayers.

Gunn himself hadn't had any idea what a staggering sum casual desertions cost the state, until he saw the figures last year. And he could have doubled the amount saved by now if he could have another dozen men, another dozen office clerks. This was the hell of a big town, and it attracted the hell of a lot of indigents and transients, as well as the usual shiftless ones any city had.

But he wasn't thinking about that as he looked after Dick Morgan. He stood there passing a hand over his jaw in a habitual gesture, a big hefty man with a round, amiable face and thinning hair, and for a minute he worried about Morgan. Dick had had some rough breaks: just out of college when the war came along,* and he was married and had a child by the time it was over so he never did go back to finish his law course, but like so many others went into a big-company job. Then they lost the child, one of those unnecessary accidents, a drunk in a car, turning down their street just at random. That had nearly finished Sue, because she couldn't have another... Sure, they put the drunk in jail for manslaughter, but what good did that do a six-year-old girl, or Sue and Dick?

Dick's father had been alive then and living with them, and

---

*This is the only clue to the year of the story: Dick was "just out of college when the war came along" (in 1941), when he was probably twenty-two years old. At thirty-seven (likely in 1956), Morgan lost his job, and he was hired by Gunn shortly after that. He doesn't seem to have been on the job long, so the year is likely 1957 or, at the latest, 1958.

Gunn used to drop in there. Hadn't done old Rob Morgan any good either, losing his only grandchild like that. After a while they'd put their names down with a couple of adoption agencies, but those places were so damn finicky; they'd waited almost five years before they got Janny—but Janny was worth it. And just about then had come one of those squeeze-plays, a company merger, a few new hatchet men from the front office, and Dick was out—at thirty-seven, with nowhere to go, a mortgaged house, and less than a thousand in the bank.

Gunn wouldn't have blamed him for feeling bitter. At the same time, being Gunn, he wouldn't have had Dick Morgan on his staff—old Rob, sympathy, or no—if he hadn't known Dick could handle the job the right way. It wasn't a job that paid anything like what Dick had been earning before, but it was a job and Dick had seemed grateful and certainly competent and reasonably contented with it.

To anyone who didn't know him, Dick's manner just now might suggest a touch of indigestion, or a spat with his wife at breakfast, or an unlucky bet on the ponies. But Gunn knew Morgan for a man of abnormally equable temper, and that little nervousness and bad color meant a lot more than it would with another man. Besides, Dick and Sue never had spats; Sue wasn't that sort. And Dick didn't bet—or drink, either. Not since eight years ago.

Gunn hoped the boy wasn't in for another piece of rough luck somehow. Janny, maybe—some illness? Some people walked all their lives with bad luck at their shoulders.

No good worrying about it now.

His phone rang and he stepped back into his office to answer it. The voice at the other end was the heavy bass of Captain Bill Andrews. "Say, Ken, among your little brood of wives you wouldn't have one Sylvia Dalton, would you?"

"Don't think so. Why?" Gunn riffled through the current file before him.

"Well, it was just a thought. Maybe you noticed by the papers that New York sort of misplaced Ray Dalton the other day. He was up on a three-to-five and got himself paroled, but he never did report in to his officer. New York thinks now— the usual information received—he lit out west, specifically to these parts, and'll be obliged if we can return the goods undamaged. Thing is, the party that said he headed west also said it was to see his wife. I came up with the bright thought that wives of crooks don't usually like to work very regular, and maybe this one was accepting our hospitality."

"Not unless she's doing it under another name. It's a thought, all right."

"Yeah. You might just check for initials. I can give you a make on her."

"I've got nothing else to do but your work," said Gunn. "I don't know every one of our customers personally, you know. Sure, somebody sees 'em all, but I've got eleven men on duty. Yes, sure, I'll check with them. Send over the make. Don't I remember Dalton? It rings a bell—"

"It ought to. The Carney job, five-six years back. Cameron and Healey were on it—liquor store knocked over and two men shot, proprietor and a clerk. We couldn't tie Dalton to it tight enough, but he was in on it. I guess at that we made him nervous enough to run back east, and New York put the arm on him for another job."

"I remember," said Gunn. He leaned back in his chair and regarded the ceiling. For a minute, with the familiar shoptalk, he almost had the illusion he was back at headquarters in a real job, not this makeweight piddling business, and under Kelleher too…but, damn, a job worth doing. "It's worth a try," he said. "Any kids?"

"One, a boy about twelve-thirteen."

"O.K.," said Gunn. "I'll have a look, might come up with something."

———

Morgan drove slowly down Main Street, not cursing at the traffic; he handled the car automatically, stopping for pedestrians, for red lights.

Mrs. Williams lived on a run-down street among those that twisted and came to dreary dead ends the other side of Main. He would surprise Mr. and Mrs. Williams together and deliver a little lecture on the dangers of conspiracy to defraud. Maybe it wasn't so stupid of them to pull the shabby little trick, the commonest one in the list, with scarcely any attempt at secrecy; until the formation of this new department, God knew how many people had got away with it for years.

The problem created, Morgan thought as he had before, went beyond the Williamses or any individual—or the amount of public money. In essence, a social problem, and not a new one. If it wasn't money from this county office, it'd be money from another: people like the Williamses didn't give a damn. Williams, letting himself be branded a wife- and child-deserter, getting a job and a cheap room somewhere out of town, sneaking back for week-ends with his family, all to cheat sixty-three-fifty a month out of the county—on top of the three hundred or more he could earn as a skilled workman.

At a bar last night with his wife until midnight. Last thing they'd worry about was leaving the kids alone: four kids, the oldest eleven. It was a shabby, cheap neighborhood, almost a slum, though there were worse streets. People like the Williamses didn't care where or how they lived: often they had more money than others who lived better, but their money went on ephemeral things—on flashy cars and clothes and liquor.

Morgan was driving a six-year-old Ford. He wouldn't be surprised to find that Williams' car was a new model, and something more expensive.

But all that was on the surface of his mind; he couldn't, for once, be less concerned. Deeper inside a voice was screaming at him soundlessly, What the hell are you going to do? *Ten thousand bucks. Ten thousand...* All right, so he knew what he ought to do: Richard Alden Morgan, law-abiding citizen, who'd always accepted responsibilities and stood on his own two feet, and where had it got him? So it was just the breaks: everybody had bad luck. But, God damn it, so *much* bad... And a damn funny thing to think maybe, but if he could blame himself (or anybody), some concrete way, reason he'd just brought it on himself, he wouldn't feel so bitter. Nothing like that with Dick Morgan, he thought in savage sarcasm: respectable, righteous Morgan who paid his bills and lived within his income, Morgan the faithful, considerate husband and father—how did the old song go, *everything he should do and nothing that he oughtn't-O**—and got kicked in the teeth all the same. You could say "the breaks," but it damn well wasn't fair that Sue should be dragged under with him—Sue hadn't done anything, neither of them had done anything to deserve—

Janny hadn't done anything. Except get born.

He coasted gently to the curb two doors from the apartment house where the Williamses lived, and sat for a minute, getting out the watchers' report, rereading it but not really taking it in. Parked smack in front of the apartment was a year-old Buick, a two-tone hardtop. That'd be Williams, sure; Henry had taken down the license.

All right, so he knew what he ought to do. Go to the police, tell the story. Honest citizen. Sure. The police would take care of the man with the pock-marked face and dirty nails and cold gray eyes and the rasping voice that said *Ten thousand bucks, see.* And would that be the end of it? Like hell it would. The juvenile court would have something to say then, miles of red tape to unwind, and in the end they'd lose Janny anyway—he knew

---

*Originally from a ballad sung no later than the nineteenth century, W. S. Gilbert and Arthur Sullivan adapted the lyric into the 1884 operetta *Princess Ida; or, Castle Adamant,* in which a character sings, "You're everything you ought to be / And nothing that you oughtn't, O!"

how those things went, how judges figured, how the cumbersome, impersonal law read. It was all the fault of the damned pompous law to start with: the silly God-damned inhumanly logical rules of the accredited agencies.

Suddenly his control broke one moment, and he pounded his fist on the steering wheel in blind, impotent fury. Not *fair*, after everything else—the panic in Sue's eyes, the panic he heard in his own voice telling her—*ten thousand*—what the *hell* could he do? The police. The money. No choice for him even here, it had to be the police; he couldn't raise money like that.

You had to be logical about it. Juvenile hall, a state foster home, an orphanage, still better than anywhere with that pock-marked hood, the kind of woman he'd—

Ten thousand. The car wouldn't bring five hundred. They still owed four thousand on the house, a second mortgage wouldn't—Sue's engagement ring, the little odds and ends of jewelry they had, maybe another five hundred if they were lucky.

He'd sat still to be kicked in the teeth for the last time. If he could get from under this by forgetting every righteous standard he had—But it wasn't so easy, it never was. So, go and rob a bank, hold up a liquor store, sure, get the ten thousand. It wouldn't cancel out: the threat would be just as potent, and in a month, six months, a year, there'd be another demand.

He straightened up after a while and took a couple of long breaths. It wasn't any good agonizing round and round in the same circle, they'd gone over all this a hundred times last night. He'd just have to play it by ear. Meanwhile he had a day's work to do—conscientious, methodical Morgan, he thought tiredly.

He got out of the car, slipping the ignition key in his pocket. See the Williamses and try to put the fear of God into them. The county wouldn't prosecute this time, on a first offense involving a relatively small amount: the courts were working overtime as it was. Morgan looked up Commerce Street to the corner of Humboldt,* where something seemed to be going on—he could see the tail end of a black-and-white police car, its roof light flashing, and the fat Italian grocer had come out of his corner shop with a few early customers. Whatever it was, a drunk or a fight or an accident, it was round the corner on Humboldt.

He started up the worn steps of the apartment. After he'd dealt with the Williamses he might as well drop in on Mrs. Kling, and that new one was somewhere around here too, if he remembered the address—he got out his case-notebook to look. Yes, Mrs. Marion Lindstrom, 273 Graham Court.

---

*Humboldt Street is just northeast of downtown Los Angeles and east of Elysian Park and Chavez Ravine (later the home of Dodger Stadium—the stadium opened in 1962); except as noted, the other streets mentioned in the novel are fictional.

Two

There were worse streets than Commerce, but it wasn't a neighborhood where anyone would choose to live, except those who didn't think or care much about their surroundings, or those who couldn't afford anything better. Ironically, only a few blocks away rose the clean modern forest of civic buildings, shining with glass and newness and surrounded by neat squares of asphalt-paved parking lots. Like many cities, this one sprouted its civic and business center in its oldest section, inevitably bordered with slums. It might look easy to change matters with the power of condemnation, the expenditure of public money, but it wouldn't work out that way if the city fathers tried it. There'd grow up other such streets elsewhere if not here; there were always the people who did not care, the landlords who wouldn't spend on repairs. Every city always has its Commerce Streets.

Commerce started ten or twelve blocks up, at the big freight yards, and dead-ended two blocks down from Humboldt. It was a dreary length of ancient macadam lined mostly with single houses—narrow, one-storey, ramshackle clapboard houses as old as the century or older, and never lovingly cared for: here and there was one with a fresh coat of paint, or a greener strip of grass in front, or cleaner-looking curtains showing, but most were a uniform dun color with old paint cracked, brown devil grass high around the front steps. About halfway down its length, the street grew some bigger houses of two stories, square frame houses not much younger and no neater: most of those were rooming houses by the signs over their porches. Interspersed with these were a few dingy apartment buildings, a gas station or two, neighborhood stores—a delicatessen, a family grocery; and in windows along nearly every block were little signs—SEWING DONE CHEAP, CANARIES FOR SALE, FIX-IT SHOP, HAND-TAILORING.

Agnes Browne lived behind one of the signs, that said primly, SEAMSTRESS, in the ground-floor right window of the house at the corner of Commerce and Wade, two blocks up from Humboldt. She worked as a waitress at a dime-store lunch counter; the sewing added to her wages some, and anyway she liked to sew and figured she might as well get paid for it. She didn't care much for going out and around; it still made her kind of nervous. She couldn't help but be afraid people were looking at her and thinking, Huh, kind of dark even for Spanish, wonder if—When the landlady said Browne didn't sound very Spanish, Agnes had told her it was her married name and she was a widow. But she was kind of sorry she'd ever started it now; it was like what the minister said for sure, about the guilty fleeing where no man pursueth. It hadn't been the money, she could earn as much anyway, maybe even more, at a dozen jobs colored girls got hired for; but there were other things besides money. Only she felt guilty at making friends under false pretenses, and as for Joe, well, she just couldn't. Joe was a nice boy, he had a good job at a garage, he was ambitious; he'd asked her for a date half a dozen times, but it wouldn't be right she should take up with him. Not without telling him. A lot of girls would have, but Agnes didn't figure it'd be fair. All the same, she liked Joe and it was hard.

She was thinking about it this morning as she started for

work; seemed like she couldn't think of anything else these days. She was a little late, it was ten past eight already, and she hurried; she could walk to work, it was only two blocks down to Main and four more to the store.

As usual she cut across the empty lot at the corner of Humboldt. There'd been a house on the lot once, but it had been so badly damaged by fire a few years back that what was left of it was pulled down. Now there was just the outline of the foundation left, all overgrown with weeds—devil grass and wild mustard. Agnes had tripped over the hidden ledge of the concrete foundation before, and skirted it automatically now; but in the middle of the lot she tripped over something else.

When she saw what it was she clapped a hand to her mouth and backed away without picking up the purse she'd dropped. Then she ran across to Mr. Fratelli's store where there was a tele-phone. Agnes knew her duty as a citizen, but that didn't say she liked the idea of getting mixed up in *such* a thing.

Huddling her coat around her, listening to Mr. Fratelli's excited Italian incoherence, she wondered miserably if the cops would ask many questions about herself. Probably so, and go on asking, and find out everything—maybe it served her right for being deceitful, the Bible said *that* never did anybody no good in the long run, and wasn't it the truth...

———

"I figured you'd like to take a look before they move it," said Hackett on the phone. "The boys just got here. If you want I'll put a hold on the stiff until you've seen it."

"Do that." Lieutenant Mendoza put down the phone and rose from his desk. Hackett was the one man under him who fully respected his feeling in such matters, though it was to be feared that Hackett put it down to conscientiousness. The truth was less flattering: Mendoza always found it hard to delegate

authority, never felt a job well done unless he saw to it himself—
which of course was simply egotism, he acknowledged it. He
could not do everything. But Hackett, who knew him so well,
had a feeling for the nuances; if Hackett thought he should see
this, he was probably right.

When he parked behind the patrol car twenty minutes later
and picked his way across the weed-grown corner toward the
little knot of men, one of the patrol officers there remarked *sotto
voce*, "That your Mex lieutenant? He don't like to get his nice
new shoes all dusty, does he?"

Detective-Sergeant Arthur Hackett said, "That's enough
about Mexes, boy.* For my money he's the best we got." He
watched Mendoza stepping delicately as a cat through the tall
growth: a slim, dark man, inevitably impeccable in silver gray,
his topcoat just a shade darker than his suit, his Homburg the
exact charcoal of the coat and with the new narrow brim, tilted
at the correct angle and no more. Mendoza's tie this morning
was a subtle foulard harmony of charcoal and silver with the
discreetest of scarlet flecks, and the shoes he was carefully
guarding from scratches were probably the custom-made gray
pigskin pair.

"My God, he looks like a gigolo," commented the patrolman,
who was only a month out of training and meeting plainclothes
men for the first time on the job. "What brand of cologne does
he use, I wonder. Better get ready to hold him up when he takes a
look at the corpse." He hadn't enjoyed the corpse much himself.

"Don't strain yourself flexing those muscles," said Hackett
dryly. "Like Luis'd say himself, *las apariencias engañan*—
appearances are deceiving."

Mendoza came up to them and nodded to the patrolmen at
Hackett's mention of their names. At close quarters, the young
recruit saw, you could guess him at only an inch or so under
your own five-eleven, not so small as he looked; but he had the

---

*A disparaging term for Mexicans in Los Angeles.

slender Latin bone structure, minimizing his size. Under the angled Homburg, thin, straight features: a long chin, a precise narrow black line of mustache above a delicately cut mouth, a long nose, black opaque eyes, sharp-arched heavy brows. A damn Mex gigolo, thought the recruit.

"I thought you'd like to see it," Hackett was saying. "It's another Carol Brooks."

Mendoza's long nose twitched once. "That is one I'd like to have inside. You think it's the same?" His voice was unexpectedly deep and soft, with only an occasional hint of accent to say he had not spoken English from birth.

"Your guess, my guess, who knows until we get him?—and maybe not then." Hackett shrugged. "Take a look, Luis."*

Mendoza walked on a dozen steps to where other men stood and squatted. The ambulance had arrived; its attendants stood smoking and waiting, watching the police surgeon, the men from headquarters with their tape measures and cameras. Mendoza came up behind the kneeling surgeon and looked at the corpse; his expression stayed impassive, thoughtful, and he did not trouble to remove his hat.

"When would you say?" he asked the surgeon.

"Oh—morning. Didn't hear you—you always move like a cat. It's a messy one, Luis, see for yourself. Between ten and midnight, give or take a little." The surgeon hoisted himself up, a stoutening, bald, middle-aged man, and brushed earth from his trouser legs. "I'll tell you what she actually died of when I've had a better look—strangulation or blows—my guess'd be the head blows. There was a sizable rock—"

"Yes," said Mendoza. He had already seen the rock, jagged, triangular. "She was cutting across from Commerce, so she knew these streets." A faint track made by foot traffic, just out from the corner of the house foundation, and the woman lay across the track.

---

*Although the first-name references may seem strange between sergeant and lieutenant, it will be seen that Hackett and Mendoza have a close relationship: Mendoza later calls him "Art."

"Daresay," grunted the surgeon. Hackett strolled up and the patrolmen followed, the recruit concealing reluctance. "No identification yet but you probably will have if she's local. Either she wasn't carrying a purse or he took it away with him."

"Never get prints off that rock," added Hackett to that. "You see what I mean, Luis. First off, it looks like any mugging, for what she had in her bag. I don't say it isn't. You take some of these punks, they get excited—Doc'll remember the ten-dollar word for it." Hackett, who looked rather like a professional wrestler, adopted the protective coloration of acting like one on occasion; possibly, thought Mendoza amusedly, in automatic deference to popular expectation. In fact he was—unlike Mendoza—a university graduate: Berkeley '50.[*] It was a theory that Mendoza did not subscribe to: he had never found it helpful—or congenial—to pretend to less intelligence than he had. "They're after the cash, but they get a kick out of the mugging too. Horseplay."

"Yes, I know," said Mendoza. "This doesn't look like horseplay."

"She wasn't raped," offered the surgeon.

"I can see that for myself. She's on her way home, at that time of night—maybe from late work, from a friend's house. There's a full moon, and she knows these streets—she doesn't think twice at cutting across here. But something is waiting." He sank to his heels over the body, careful to pull up his trouser knees first, and regarded it in silence for a long minute.

Before it had been a body it had been a young and pretty woman: in fact, a very young one, under make-up lavishly applied. The too-white powder, the heavily mascaraed lashes, the smeared dark-red lipstick, was a mask turned to the pitiless gray sky of this chill March day. The unfashionable shoulder-length hair, where it wasn't stiffened with clotted blood, was

---

[*]That is, the University of California, founded in 1868. Hackett is, therefore, between the ages of thirty and thirty-two, though he might be older if he enrolled after World War II on the GI Bill or had his schooling interrupted by the war.

bleached white-gold, but along the temples and at the parting showed dark. "Coat pockets?" he murmured.

"Handkerchief and a wool scarf," said Hackett.

"To put over her hair in case it rained," nodded Mendoza. "Then she had a handbag too."

"So I figured. Dwyer and Higgins are looking around the neighborhood." A bag-snatcher, whether or not he was also a murderer, seldom kept the bag long; it would be tossed away on the run.

Her clothes were tasteless, flamboyant—tight Kelly-green sweater with a round white angora collar, black faille skirt full-cut and too short, sheer stockings, black patent-leather pumps with four-inch heels, over all a long black coat with dyed rabbit round the collar and hem. Mendoza felt the coat absently, expecting the harshness of shoddy material: cheap, ill-cut stuff.

Two very different corpses, he reflected, this tawdry pseudo blonde and Carol Brooks. Carol Brooks, six months ago, had been an eminently respectable and earnest young woman, not very good looking, and she had died in the soiled blue uniform dress she wore for work. Otherwise, no, the corpses weren't so different.

"Yes," he murmured, and stood up. "He didn't intend murder, to start with—I don't think. He hadn't any weapon but his hands. And he didn't reach out to find one, blind, like that, and pick up the rock—it wasn't used that way, Art. He had her down, she was fighting him, trying to scream—he was strangling her, finding it not quick enough—and he slams her down on the ground, hard, just by chance on the rock. I can see it going like that. Unpremeditated violence, but once it unleashes itself"—he looked down at the body again—"insane violence."

"Here comes Bert," said Hackett, "with the handbag. Not that it'll maybe take us very far."

"That's a loaded question for the so-called expert," said the surgeon, looking interested over the flame of his lighter, "but

I'll say this, at least—he must have gone berserk for some reason. Nobody can say sane or insane just on *that* evidence—unnecessary violence. *That* sort of thing is apt to be vicious personal hatred, or a couple of other quirks."

"You're so right," said Mendoza. "You'll make a report all embellished with the technical terms, but to go on with for the moment?"

"Her neck's broken. Excessive laceration of the throat. Half a dozen head wounds, all but one on the back of the skull—the one that killed her, I think, is this here, on the temple. Maybe she turned her head in struggling and—The left shoulder is dislocated. She was struck repeatedly in the face with a fist. You can see the cyanosed areas,* there. Her right arm is broken just below the elbow. The whole torso has been damaged, kicked or maybe jumped on. Fractured ribs, I think, and internal injuries. It's on the cards some of that was done after death, but I don't know that it'll be provable—probably a very short time after, of course. There's some damage to the left eye, as if a finger or thumb had been—"

"Yes. It was Dr. Bainbridge who made the autopsy on Brooks," said Mendoza. "You wouldn't remember. That is the one thing of positive resemblance. Otherwise"—he flicked away the burnt match and drew deep on his cigarette, shrugging—"any mugger after a woman's bag, who used a little too much violence."

"So?" said the surgeon. "Ever catch that one?" Mendoza shook his head.

"Well, here we are," announced Hackett, who had gone to meet Dwyer. "In plain sight in the gutter a couple of blocks away." It was the bag one would have predicted she would carry: a big square patent-leather affair with a coquettish white bow cluttering the snap-fastener. "*Ya lo creo,*† as we might put it, huh?"

---

*Bluish in color, resulting from deoxygenation.

---

†"I think so," a phrase used colloquially here to mean something like "sure, just what I expected."

Mendoza lifted his upper lip at it. "Before you get a promotion and cease to be my junior in rank, Arturo, you will have perfected your vile accent. It may take years."

Very delicately Hackett delved with two fingers into the bag's interior and came up with a woman's wallet, bright pink plastic, ornamented all round the border with imitation pearls. Mendoza regarded it with satisfied horror: the very object this girl would have admired. "Lot of other stuff here—doesn't look as if he took a damn thing. Funny he put the wallet back after grabbing the cash, if—He might've figured the wallet alone'd be spotted quicker and picked up, but then again muggers don't think so far ahead usually, and this one, I don't see him in a state to think at all, after *that*. If—"

"*¡Basta!** One thing at a time."

"Her name was Elena Ramirez. No driver's license. Dimestore snapshot of herself and, I presume, current boy friend. Social Security card. Membership card in some club. I.D. card—address and phone—little change in the coin purse— that figures, of course, he'd take the bills—"

Dwyer said, "Prints are going to love you for putting your fat paws all over that cellophane."

"All right," Mendoza cut off Hackett's retort abruptly. "Give me that address, Art. I'll see the woman who found her and then the family—if there is one. Dwyer, you and Higgins can begin knocking on doors—did anyone hear a disturbance, screams perhaps? When we know more of the background, maybe I'll have other jobs for you. They can take her away now."

———

Hackett drifted over to Fratelli's grocery behind Mendoza. In two hours, tomorrow, Hackett would be the man nominally in charge of working this case; a lieutenant of detectives could not

———

*"Enough!"

devote all his time to a relatively minor case like this. The fact annoyed Mendoza, partly because he had an orderly mind, liked to take one thing at a time, thoroughly. Even more did it irritate him now because it was intuitively clear to him that this girl and Carol Brooks had met death at the same hands, and he wanted very much to get that one inside, caught in a satisfactory net of evidence and booked and committed for trial.

If one murder was more or less important than another, neither of these was important:* the kind of casual homicide that happens every week in any big city. This girl did not look as if she would be much missed, as if she had been a human being with much to offer the world, but one never knew. Carol Brooks, now, that had perhaps been a loss—yes. He remembered again the warm gold of the recorded voice, a trifle rough as yet, a trifle uncertain, but the essential quality there. However, his cold regret at missing her murderer had nothing of sentiment in it. The reason was the reason, in a wider sense, why Luis Mendoza was a lieutenant of detectives, and—most of the time—regarded fondly by his superiors.

There are people who enjoy solving puzzles: he was not one of them. But—probably, he told himself, because he was a great egotist, and his vanity was outraged to be confronted with something he did not know—once a puzzle was presented to him he could not rest until he had ferreted out the last teasing secret. It was not often that he was faced with a complex mystery; the world would grow a great deal older before police detectives in everyday routine met with such bizarre and glamorous situations as those in fiction. *Por desgracia,*† indeed: unfortunate: for complex problems inevitably had fewer possible solutions.

This thing now, this was the sort of puzzle (a much more difficult sort) that Mendoza, and all police detectives, met again and again: the shapeless crime that might have been done by

---

*Anticipating the catchphrase of Michael Connelly's iconic Los Angeles detective, Harry Bosch: "Everyone counts, or no one counts."

†"Unfortunately."

anyone in the city—mostly impersonal crime, this sort, with destiny alone choosing the victim. The shopkeeper killed in the course of a robbery, the woman dead at the end of attack for robbery or rape, the casual mugging in an alley—nothing there of orderliness, the conveniently limited list of suspects, the tricky alibis, the complicated personal relationships to unravel: criminal and victim might never have met before. Or perhaps it might be an intimate business, a personal matter, and only arranged to look otherwise—and if it were, so much the easier to find the truth, for one had then only a few places to look.

But so often it was the casual, shapeless thing. And there are always, in any efficient city police force, the policemen like Luis Mendoza, single-mindedly, even passionately concerned to bring some order and reason, some ultimate shape, to the chaos. Not necessarily from any social conscientiousness— Mendoza cared little for humanity *en masse*, and was a complete cynic regarding the individual. Nor from any abstract love of truth or, certainly, of justice—for all too often the criminals he took for the law evaded punishment, this way or that way; and Mendoza sometimes swore and sometimes shrugged, but he did not lose any sleep over that. Being a realist, he said, *Lo que no se puede remediar, se ha de aguantar*—what can't be cured must be endured. Nor from ambition, to gain in rank and wages through zeal—Mendoza desired no authority over men, as he resented authority over himself, and his salary would not begin to maintain his wardrobe, or a few other personal interests. Nor even solely from earnest attention to doing one's job well.

The only reason for such men, the end goal, is the contemplation of the solved puzzle: the beautiful completeness of the last answer found. It is so with all these men, whatever kind of men they may be otherwise. Having the orderly mind, they must know where every last odd-shaped small piece belongs in the puzzle, no matter if the picture comes out landscape or portrait or still life, so to speak.

Mendoza, in fact, forced to file away an unanswered question—as he had six months ago in the Brooks case—felt very much the way an overnice housewife would feel, forced to leave dinner dishes in the sink overnight. It worried him; it irritated him; and in every free moment his mind slid back to the thing left undone.

He said now absently to Hackett, "*Eso se sobreentiende,*" it's not so good that he's been loose for six months—one like that." With only a few people he didn't watch his tongue, or even let it drift into the Spanish deliberately; and that (as Hackett was fully aware) was a mark of affection and trust.

"Oh, I don't know, Luis. One dame every six months, pretty damn moderate, come to think." Hackett glanced at him sideways, "So you think it's the same joker too."

"That eye. It's a little psychological point, maybe—" Mendoza tossed away his cigarette and paused with his hand on the shopdoor. "Or am I being too subtle? In a fight with another man, anything goes—one of you may have an eye gouged out. But to do that to a woman, and a woman you have already made helpless—Well, what do we call insane? You and I have seen it, there are men whose lust turns sadistic, and they're not legally insane. But I don't think this is one of those, Art. I didn't think so with Carol Brooks. Because of that eye business. And Bainbridge says to me, *de paso,*[†] just what Dr. Victor says now—probably much of the damage is made after death. Only just after, but—*Dije para mí,*[‡] it's a wild one, never mind the doubletalk of the psychiatrists. A real, hundred-percent, guaranteed genuine wild one—*mucho loco.*"[§]

"Hell, I said the same thing. And you know what that means,

---

*"That's obvious."

†"On the way"—meaning, "in passing." Linington freely admitted that she didn't speak Spanish fluently, and her effort to include naturalistic Spanish-language exclamations and expressions in this and her other Mendoza novels often produced phrases (such as this one) that no native speaker of Spanish would ever utter.

---

‡"I said to myself."

---

§Linington's Spanish is at fault here; Mendoza should have said "*muy loco*"—"very crazy."

chico—work or brains don't count in catching him. He's got no sane reason for picking this girl or that. It'll be luck, that's all, if we do. My God, he might not know himself what he's done, and a hundred to one the only way we'll ever put a name to him is if he happens to have a brain storm in front of witnesses next time. Probably he's living quiet as you please, an ordinary guy nobody'd look at twice, maybe going to work every day, comin' home prompt at six to kiss his wife and look at the sports page before dinner—goes to church every Sunday—never done a thing anybody'd think queer. It'll just be the way the cards fall, if and when and how soon we get him."

"It isn't always," said Mendoza, "the hand dealt to you, so much as the way you play it."

"You should know. How much do you average a year in poker winnings, anyway?"

"Sometimes enough to buy my shirts."

"That ain't hay for you, at what, twelve bucks a throw...* You know something else? When we do catch up with him, he's going to be some guy who's got the reputation of being the kindest, mildest, sweetest-tempered *hombre* God ever put on earth. Everybody who knows him'll say, Oh, John couldn't be the one, he'd never do such a thing, officer! Want to bet?"

Mendoza laughed, abrupt and mirthless. "Don't I know it! I only hope he doesn't have another brain storm before we catch up to him. No one's ever accused me of being a sentimental man, *¡no, por Dios!*—but I don't care for his notions of how to treat women." He swept the Homburg off, passed a hand over the thick, Indian-straight black hair that grew to a widow's peak, and opened the door.

---

*More than $100 per shirt in 2019.

Three

The girl who had found the body was nervous, too nervous. Not a nice experience, but it had been over an hour ago, and if she had nothing to do with it, why was she trembling and stammering and eying the policemen as if she expected the third degree? Mendoza was mildly curious.

She was a rather pretty girl, about twenty-seven, neat rounded figure, modest and dowdy in a clean cotton house-dress. Fine olive-tan complexion, big brown eyes, minimum of make-up: a respectable girl.

"Her name was Elena Ramirez. I realize you wouldn't be likely to recognize anyone you knew under the circumstances—so, did you know Miss Ramirez?"

"Oh, no, sir, I never heard of her." She twisted her hands together and her eyes shifted away. "I'll be awful late for work, sir, I don't know nothing—"

Mendoza let her go. "Sergeant Hackett will drive you to your job and explain why you're late"; and to Hackett, "Conversation—find out what you can about her, and then see what you can pick up where she lives. I don't think she's got anything to do with it, but one never knows. I'll see the family. That takes us to an early lunch, maybe—Federico's at twelve-thirty, O.K.?—we'll compare notes."

"*Está bien*," said Hackett, and joined Agnes Browne outside. The Italian grocer, hovering to get Mendoza's attention, asked excitedly if he had said Ramirez—the family Ramirez over on Liggitt Street, would that be? Sacred name of God, what a terrible thing—ah, yes, he knew them, only to nod to, the *signor* comprehended—sometimes the wife came in to buy, not often—God pity them, to lose a daughter so—no, no, the girl he did not know at all—she was assaulted, assassinated by some madman, then?

"So I think," said Mendoza. The men from headquarters had dispersed; the ambulance was gone, the patrol car was gone. Across the street he saw Dwyer leave the first house next to the corner lot and head for the neighboring one. Mendoza crossed to his car and stopped to light a cigarette; he looked at the car thoughtfully, getting out his keys. He believed in buying the very best piece of merchandise obtainable of what one set out to buy, giving it loving care and using it until it fell to pieces. A thing like a car, that by this scheme was with you for years, you got acclimated to one another, it had personal individuality for you, it was more than a mere machine of transportation. The austerely elegant black Ferrari club-saloon was only thirteen years old,[*] just into middle age for a Ferrari, and it would be mad, extravagant, to give it up: he had no intention of doing so: but there was no denying that with the increase of traffic and parking problems, its size was a disadvantage, not to say a nuisance. The trouble was, if he did buy a new car, it would be one with less than twelve cylinders—unless he should buy one of the new, smaller Ferraris, which was piling madness on madness.[†]

---

[*]This is Linington's error: The first Ferrari road cars were not built until 1950, and the events of the story could not have taken place after 1960, when the book was published. While Mendoza's Ferrari could not be more than a decade old, Linington's point—that Mendoza valued expensive cars but used them "to pieces"—stands.

[†] The cars with "less than twelve cylinders" that Mendoza was thinking about were not Ferraris—Ferrari made only V12 engine–driven cars until the late 1960s. The "madness upon madness" that Mendoza is avoiding is presumably the cost, which was likely significantly more than he paid for the "thirteen-year-old" Ferrari saloon.

He muttered, "*Es difícil*," got in and started the engine. ("Now look, Mr. Mendoza," the mechanic had said patiently, "the number o' cylinders isn't anythin' to do with how good the car is! If you knew *anythin'* about engines at all—! I know it sounds to you like you're gettin' more for your money—facta the matter is, about all it means is it costs more to run, see? Sure, this is the hell of a great car, but you'd be just as well off, get just as much power and speed, with say something like that Mercedes six—I mean if you got to have a foreigner—or one of them slick hard-top Jaguars—")

Liggitt Street, a block the other side of Main and one down, was a bare cut above Commerce. Not so many signs in windows, and the houses, most as old and poor, better cared for. The Ramirez house was one of the two-storey ones; as he came up the walk, he saw that the curtains at the narrow front windows were clean and starched, a few flowers planted against the low porch.

He did not mind breaking bad news to strangers, and often it was of help to notice reactions: little things might tell if this was as impersonal a fate as it looked, or had reasons closer to home. But he fully expected that a good deal of time would be wasted, from his point of view, while they assimilated the news, before he could decently ask questions.

He was not wrong there. The family consisted of Papa, Mama, assorted children between three and sixteen, an older daughter perhaps twenty-one, and a stocky middle-aged man who bore enough resemblance to Papa that his designation as Tío* Tomás was superfluous. Mendoza waited through Mama's hysterics, the dispatching of a message to the parish priest, the settling of Mama on the sofa with a blanket, cologne-soaked handkerchief, glass of wine, and her remaining brood nested about her comfortably. He found a cracked pink saucer in obvious use as an ash tray and smoked placidly in the midst of the uproar, eyes and ears busy.

---

*"Uncle"—that is, Papa's brother.

Not native Mexican-Americans, these, not a couple of generations across the border. The kids, they had the marks of smart American kids, and their English was unhesitating, sparked with slang; but Mama, fat and decent in ankle-length black cotton, and Papa, collarless neck scrawny above an old flannel bathrobe, were Old Country. It was no different, Mexican, German, Lithuanian, whatever—always there was bound to be a little friction, the kids naturally taking on freer modern ways, the old ones disapproving, worried, and arguments about it. So? The man called Tío Tomás sat in a straight chair behind the sofa and said nothing, smoking tiny black Mexican cigarillos.

"You know I must ask you questions," said Mendoza at last, putting a hand on Manuel Ramirez's arm. "I'm sorry to intrude on your grief, but to help us in hunting whoever has killed your daughter—"

"*Sí*, yes, it is understood," whispered Ramirez. "I—I tell you whatever you want to know. *María Santísima*, my brain is not working for this terrible thing, but—excuse, mister, I don't speak so good in English—"

"Then we speak Spanish."

"Ah, you have the tongue, that's good. I thank you—pardon, mister, the name I did not—"

"Lieutenant Mendoza."

"Mendoza." He gave it the hard Mexican pronunciation that was ultimately Aztec, instead of the more elegant Spanish sibilance. "You are—an agent of police?"

"I am. I'll ask you first—"

"The gentleman's good to wait and be polite." It was the oldest girl, coming up quietly, looking at him with open curiosity; she was pale, but had not been weeping. She was not as pretty as her sister had been, but not bad-looking, in a buxom way. "Of course we know you got to ask questions, but look, Papa, no sense disturbing Mama with it—I guess you and me can tell him whatever he wants. Let's go in the kitchen, if that's all right, mister?"

"It is Lieutenant, Teresa," said Ramirez distractedly; he let her urge him through a shabby dining room. Mendoza strolled after: she threw him a glance over her shoulder of mixed interest, anxiety, and a kind of mechanical female blandishment. The kitchen was big, cold, reasonably clean. "Please to sit down, sir—if you would accept my hospitality, a glass of wine—it's only cheap stuff—" Ramirez was trying to pull himself together; the conventional courtesy was automatic.

"No, no, thanks. Tell me first, I believe your daughter lived here with you?—then you must have been worried that she didn't come home last night? Do you know where she was?"

The girl answered from where she had perched uneasily on the kitchen table. "Sure, we were worried. But she might've gone to stay overnight with a girl friend, or—well, you know how it is, we sort of talked back 'n' forth and kept waiting for her maybe to call one of the neighbors with a message—Mrs. Gomez next door lets us—"

"Where had she gone and when did she leave?"

"She was—she was just out on a date. I don't know where they were going. Ricky, he was here for Elena about seven, I guess, and they went right after." In answer to the query only begun, she added hurriedly, "Ricky Wade, he's a boy Elena's— Elena had been going with a lot. A nice boy he is, you needn't go thinking anything about him, see. I don't know where they were going, but they did go to the Palace rink* a lot—that roller-skating place, you know. Silly, I say, but Elena's—Elena was just a kid, she liked it."

"She would have had nineteen years only the next month," murmured Ramirez. "It was wrong, Teresa, I said so! We should have gone to the police at once, at once! Elena was a good girl in her heart, she was properly brought up, never would she have done such a thing—all the talk around and around, I should have let you and Mama talk and gone to the police myself—"

*The Palace Arena, featuring roller skating and roller hockey, was at 1712 Glendale Boulevard in the 1950s, about four miles away from the Humboldt Street neighborhood, west of Elysian Park.

"What would she not have done, Miss Ramirez?" asked Mendoza.

"Oh, well, I s'pose we got to say or you'll think it's funny we didn't seem more worried." Her mouth tightened. "We were going to do something about it this morning, don't know what, but—We *were* awful worried, you can see that, way Papa and I both stayed home from work—it wasn't as if Elena ever did nothing like that before, stay away all night and not call or nothing. But—well, we got to thinking maybe her and Ricky'd eloped—you know, over to Las Vegas or somewhere, to get married in a hurry—"

"It is not true!" exclaimed Ramirez excitedly, jumping up. The bathrobe fell open to reveal his spindly legs and unexpectedly gay pink cotton underpants. "It is a wicked lie, that Elena is got in trouble with this fellow and has to run away and marry quick! She is a respectable girl, never would she—oh, she does this and that Mama and I don't like, sure, but she's young, it's different times and ways now, I know that—she's impatient, she wants the moon like all youngsters, but never would she—"

"I never said she did, I never! But after they made up and he came back, she sure meant to keep him, she was set on marrying him someday, you know good as I do. All I *said* was, if he all of a sudden wanted to elope, she wouldn't take the risk of losing him, she'd say yes quick!"

"Did you disapprove of this Mr. Wade, then?" asked Mendoza of Ramirez casually.

"Disapprove—" He moved his thin shoulders wearily. "He is not of the faith. I don't know, if Elena wanted so bad, I—You don't have nothing to say about it any more, anyway, fathers. The kids, they go their own way. She wouldn't have been happy in such a marriage, that I thought. But it wasn't really serious, they were just youngsters—"

"Elena was serious, all right!" said Teresa. She turned to Mendoza. "Look, you might's well know how it was, an' weasel

round like I s'pose you got to, to be sure Ricky didn't have nothing to do with—with killing her. That's silly, he wouldn't. Elena
met him in school three years back, see—that's Sloan Heights
High,* where I went too. Only I had the sense to finish, and she
didn't—wanted a job so's she could buy a lot of splashy clothes
'n' all—soon as she turned sixteen, she got a work permit an' a
job uptown in a Hartners' store,† putting stuff on the models in
the windows, unpacking in the stock room, like that—"

Ramirez moved restlessly. "All this foolishness," he muttered,
"keeping girls in school so long—history and algebra, it don't
teach them any better to keep house and bring up the kids. And
Elena always give Mama her five dollars a week, regular, like she
should."

"I'm not saying nothing against her, Papa, only she should've
finished like I did, learned typing and all, so's to get a better job.
Sure she gave Mama money, and bought things for the kids too,
she wasn't stingy. All I—"

"Mr. Wade," murmured Mendoza.

"That's what I'm *getting* to. She saw I was right in the end, see?
Because the Wades, they reckon they're a lot too good for the
likes of us, they didn't like Ricky taking up with Elena. Mr. Wade,
he works for the city, they own their house and all that—you
know. Elena, she liked Ricky a lot, sure, he's a nice boy like I said,
but at the same time she saw it'd be kind of a step up the ladder
for her, marry into a family like that. She didn't want to stay on
Liggitt Street all her life, well, who does? But the time she had a
little fight with Ricky, 'n' don't go thinking it was anything serious, just a little spat like, she started thinking how silly it'd be to
really lose him—I know all this because she talked it over with
me, see, nights—we got the same room. I mean, she thought, he's
used to different sorts of ways and she got worried she wouldn't
know how to act right about things like that if they got married."

---

*A fictional school.

---

†There was no chain named "Hartners'" in California in the 1950s—this is probably a disguised
"Hartfield" store.

"It was foolishness," said Ramirez. "That school place for teaching the fascination. But it's Elena's money, if she wanted—"

"Fascination?" Momentarily the subtle color of near-synonyms in the Spanish misled Mendoza.

"No, it wasn't," said Teresa. "It's—it was worth the money, Papa, and that Miss Weir's real nice, you know I seen her once, when I met Elena uptown to shop. It's a charm school"—turning back to Mendoza—"you know, they teach you what's right to wear and so on. Me, I say it was O.K. for Elena to try to improve herself, sure. Even if she had to quit her job like she did, it's a six-week course an' every day—she could get another easy enough after. What *was* silly about it, those Wades aren't all so much that she had to feel nervous about them! Mother of God, you'd think they were millionaires with a butler maybe like in the movies, way she talked. He's just a bookkeeper in some office, but—you know—they're the kind put their noses in the air at *us*, dirty low-class Mexes, they say to each other, *an'* Catholic which they don't like so much either. Me, I don't let people like that bother me, not one little bit. Maybe we do rent a house instead of own-ing one, an' maybe our street isn't so high-class, an' we don't have no car or telephone or electric washing machine—maybe Papa does just drive a delivery truck—what's that got to do with any-thing? We're respectable folks, Papa's worked for Mr. Reyes all the time since he come over, and that's nearly twenty years, and we don't owe nobody no money like I'll bet the Wades do. I got a good job typing for *El Gente Méjico,* 'n' I've saved nearly three hundred dollars toward furniture an' so on for when Carlos and me get married this summer—which I'll bet is more than Mrs. Wade can say she did!" Teresa gestured contemptuously. "People like them, let them talk! But it bothered Elena, see."

"You have much common sense," said Mendoza with a smile. "I think Carlos is lucky. So nothing was said last night about where your sister and Mr. Wade were going?" She shook her

---

*"The People Mexico," evidently a local newspaper. The name was invented by Linington, who admittedly spoke Spanish poorly—the proper name should have been *La Gente Méjico.*

head. "But you would certainly have expected that he'd see her home?"

"Oh, sure. I can't figure out how she came to be alone—she must've been, for whoever—did it—to sneak up on her. You said—the corner at Commerce an' Humboldt? She must've been on her way home then, and from that Palace rink too, coming that way."

"We'll find out. Mr. Ramirez, you'll have to identify the body formally, and there'll be an inquest, of course. I'll send someone to take you down to the morgue."

"Identify—that mean you're not sure it *is* Elena?" asked the girl sharply.

"No, that we know. It's only a formality of the law."

"Yes, I understand," said Ramirez. "You're kind, we thank you."

Mendoza took the girl's arm and led her out to the dining room. She looked up at him alertly, half-suspicious. "Well, what now?"

"No need to upset your father more," he said easily. "Will you give me the address of this school your sister attended, please—how long had she been going there?"

"A—about three weeks it was, yes, just three because today's Saturday an' she began two weeks ago last Monday. I don't know that it was doing her much good at that, she couldn't seem—"

"Miss Ramirez, you're a smart girl. You can look at things straight, and I don't think you'll lie to me just to defend your sister's memory. Tell me, do you think she'd have let a stranger pick her up, as they say?"

Teresa put a hand to her cheek. "That's a hard one to answer, mister. Right off I'd say no, an' not to, like you said, make out Elena was better than she was. When I said we're respectable folks, that wasn't no lie either—us girls've been raised proper, know what's right 'n' wrong, even if maybe we don't know everything like about which forks an' spoons. No, sir, Elena wouldn't ever have gone with a strange fellow, way you mean, somebody whistled at her on the street or offered her a ride. But it might be she *would* think it was O.K. if it was somebody she'd seen around, if you know what I mean, and he acted all right. This rink place, f'r instance, she went there a lot, belonged to some crazy club they got for regular customers, and if some fellow there got talking to her and maybe offered her a ride home, if she was alone, or said he'd walk with her, she might've thought it was O.K., if he seemed polite and all. She— she couldn't size people up very good. I know—I told her time an' again—she made herself look cheap, bleaching her hair and all that make-up, but she wasn't like that really. She was"—her face twisted suddenly—"she was just a kid. Roller-skating…"

"I see, thank you. Someone will come for your father—you'll see he's ready? I'll cease to intrude for the moment then, but as this and that comes up, one of us will be back to ask more questions."

"I s'pose you got to."

"Were you very fond of your sister, Miss Ramirez?" he asked, soft and offhand.

She was silent, and then looked up to meet his eyes. "She was my sister. That don't say I couldn't see her faults—nobody's all good or bad. It don't seem fair—she should die like that before she was even nineteen, hadn't had nothing much. But it's a thing that happens, people dying, age don't seem to have an awful lot to do with it sometimes. Little babies, like a couple of Mama's. You got to figure God must know what He's doing. And think about them that's still alive."

There was in her round brown eyes all the sad, inborn, fatalistic wisdom of the primitive tribe living close with the basic realities of life and death.

At the door, Mendoza met the priest just arriving: round-faced, rich-voiced, middle-aged Irishman, the self-introduction as Father Monaghan unnecessary to guess his ancestry. "You are—? Oh, yes—but what an incredible, tragic thing, I can hardly believe—Before I go in, then, Lieutenant, perhaps you would tell me in more detail—" And when he had heard, steady blue eyes fixed on Mendoza, he said quietly, "God grant you find this poor wicked man soon. If there is any way I can be of help—I know this district well, and most of those living here, you know—"

"Yes, thank you, we'll keep it in mind."

"You said, Lieutenant—Mendoza? At least it must be some comfort to them that one of their own people should be investigating, one of their own faith who—"

"Not for some while of that or any, Father."

"Ah," said the priest, "but not forever, my son, will you say that to God. One day you will return the full circle."

Mendoza smiled, stood back to let him pass, and went out to the porch. Adjusting his hat, he said to himself, "*¡Muy improbable, venga lo que venga—nada de eso!*"*

The man called Tío Tomás was leaning on the porch railing. He showed yellow snags of teeth in a brief grin. "Nothing doing—that's what I say to them kind too. All they're after is money. For a cop maybe you got a little brains." The grin did not change his wary cold eyes. His skin was bad, showing relics of the smallpox.

"You will be a brother to Manuel Ramirez, I think."

"Sure, that's right, but I don't live here, I'm just visiting. Too bad about Elena, she was a nice kid."

Mendoza looked him over thoughtfully. "I'll hear your permanent address."

"I live in Calexico, I got a business there, I didn't have nothing to do with—"

"Indeed?" said Mendoza; small satisfaction warmed him for something, however irrelevant and minor, to take hold of. The most respectable families had black sheep, and this was one

*"Very unlikely, whatever comes—nothing like that!"

of them, that he could see with half an eye. "You're a Mexican national, not a citizen? I'll see your entry permit." The man brought it out promptly; it was in order. "Exporter. What do you export?"

"I got a silversmithy," said Ramirez. "Nothing big, you know, just a man and four girls—jewelry. You know how the tourists go for native stuff, and here too. I make a better profit on it up here even with the duty, you can mark it up higher. I'm just up on a little business trip."

"With success?" asked Mendoza genially.

"Oh—sure, sure. Got to get back, though, the business don't run itself." His eyes shifted. "Say, I won't have to stay, just account this thing about Elena? I didn't have nothing to do with—I mean, it was some crazy fellow killed her, wasn't it—"

"It would be as well if you stay for the inquest," said Mendoza, gave him a last smiling inspection and went unhurriedly down the walk to his car; he felt the man's eyes on him. He drove back to Commerce and caught Higgins and Dwyer comparing notes before leaving for headquarters. No one in the block had heard anything unusual last night.

He had not expected much from that. He sent Dwyer with the headquarters car over to Liggitt Street, to keep an eye on Tomás Ramirez. "Maybe a waste of time. Maybe something for us, but not connected with the murder. He's been in trouble, I think he's been inside, anyway he doesn't like cops—not too close. Exporter, his papers say. He might be just that, indeed."

Dwyer said, "Marijuana—or the big H. Sure, he might. And how about this, Lieutenant—the girl finds it out and either says she'll turn him in or wants a cut, so he—"

"Whatever he is or isn't, he's small time. I don't think so, but of course it's a possibility we'll have to check. Stay on him, I'll send a man to relieve you." He took Higgins back to headquarters to pick up another car and ferry the father down to the morgue.

Himself, instead of returning to his office where he should be attending to other matters, he set off to see the Wades. There should be just time before lunch. It was a very routine errand, something for Hackett or even one of Hackett's underlings, and not until he was halfway there did Mendoza realize clearly why he felt it important to see to it himself, why he had gone to the Ramirez house. The sooner all this personal matter was cleared out of the way, proved to be extraneous, the better. And he must satisfy himself doubly that it was irrelevant, because it was always dangerous to proceed on a preconceived idea. He had been seized by the conviction, looking at the body, that this girl had been killed by the killer of Carol Brooks—but it was little more than a hunch, an irrationality backed by very slender evidence.

Carol Brooks, three miles away over in East L.A.—maybe a bigger loss than this girl had been. A young, earnest, ambitious girl, who had earned her living as a hotel chambermaid and spent her money not on clothes but voice lessons—with an expensive trainer of high repute, too, who thought a good deal of her, was giving her a cut price. He had said she needed constant encouragement, because she didn't believe a black girl could get very far, unless she was really the very best, and she'd never be *that* good. Maybe she would have been; no one would ever know, now.

Nothing very much to support his conviction, on the surface evidence. And he must guard against holding it blind, if other evidence pointed another way. As it would—as it did. Nobody lived long without giving at least a few people reasons for dislike, sometimes reasons for murder. They might turn up several here. And that was the easy way to look for a murderer, among only a few, the immediate surroundings and routines of the girl who'd been killed.

If he was right, they'd need to spread a wider net. For someone quite outside, someone without logical motive. Someone, somewhere among the five million people in this teeming metropolitan place sprawling in all directions—someone who was dangerous a hundred times over because the danger from him was secret, unsuspected.

This time Mendoza would like to get that one. Because he had missed him six months ago, another girl was in a cold-storage tray at the city morgue now.

Four

They met for a not-too-leisured lunch at Federico's, out on North Broadway. Hackett left him to mull over what meager information they had; his own next stop was obviously the skating rink. The waiter whisked away the relics of the meal, apologetically; they never hurried you at Federico's, you could sit as long as you pleased. "More coffee, sir?"

"Please." Mendoza brooded over his refilled cup; he should go back to his office and occupy himself at being a lieutenant; there were other cases on hand than this.

The girl who had found the body, nothing there immediately: nothing known against her, but little emerged of her background either. It was a very long chance that she had anything to do with it, but of course she had to be investigated. As did every aspect of the Ramirez girl's life. And after that, where to look?

He drank black coffee and dwelt for a moment on Mrs. Elvira Wade. In her appallingly cluttered, tasteless, middle-class-and-proud-of-it living room: a God-fearing upright citizen, Mrs. Wade, who had spread a little too much in the waist and hips, not at all in the mind.

"Of *course* we didn't like it, to say the least—a Mexican

girl—and *such* a girl, all that cheap-looking bleached hair and perfectly dreadful clothes, but of course they're always so fond of garish colors, you know. And then of course there was the *religious* question. Really, boys have no sense, but it's *beyond* me how a son of mine could be so taken in, after all you'd think he'd have some finer instincts, the way I've tried to bring him up. Not that I'm not sorry for the poor thing, the girl I mean, and one shouldn't speak ill of the dead. I try to take a Christian view I'm sure and after all people can't help being born what they are, but when it comes to accepting them into one's *family*—"

It was something, however, to have embarrassed such a woman even momentarily: her belated furtive glance at his card, her ugly pink flush, almost ludicrous. "And of *course*," she had added hurriedly, "there's all the difference in the *world* between people like that and the real high-class old Spanish families, everyone knows *that*, I understand the peasant class is actually mostly Indian and the real Spaniards wouldn't have anything to do with *them*. But I'm sure you can see how we, my husband and I, felt—"

Mendoza sighed into the dregs of his coffee. It did not, apparently, cross Mrs. Wade's mind that she had perhaps, in a sense, contributed to the girl's death. The boy had been strictly forbidden to see Elena again ("really such strong measures were *necessary*, though he is nineteen and ordinarily I don't believe in *iron* discipline"), and when it was discovered, through a garrulous acquaintance of Ricky's, that he had *not* borrowed the family car to go to the movies last night but to take Elena to that awful skating place—"Well, I said to Mr. Wade, when it comes to lying to his own parents, *something drastic* must be done! You can see how she corrupted him, he'd never done such a thing before—I said to Mr. Wade, you'll go right down there and—" So Mr. Wade (could one conjecture, breathing fire, or were the men married to such women capable of it?—at least he seemed to have acted effectively) had, by bus, sought out the

Palace rink, publicly reprimanded the erring Ricky, and fetched him ignominiously away. After this soul-searing experience, nineteen-year-old Ricky had probably been in no state to consider how Elena would get home, and if it had occurred to the Wades, presumably they had thought a girl like that would be used to going about alone at night.

As, Mendoza conceded, she had been: she had probably got home alone before. He pushed his coffee cup round in a little circle, aimlessly; and of course the girl would also have been angry, humiliated—quite possibly she might have let a stranger pick her up, a thing she wouldn't ordinarily do. Someone at the rink?

He wondered what Hackett would find out there. He paid the bill, redeemed the Ferrari from the lot attendant, and instead of turning back downtown for headquarters, negotiated his way through the bottleneck round the Union Station and turned up Sunset Boulevard. It had begun to rain steadily, after long threat.

The address Teresa had given him was close into town, along the less glamorous stretches of that street. It proved to be the upper half of a small office building, not new. A narrow door and a steep stair brought him to a landing and a sign: THE SUN-SET SCHOOL OF CHARM. A mousy girl with a flat figure and harlequin glasses was scrabbling among papers at the receptionist's desk.

"Miss Weir?"

"Oh, dear me, no." She moved the glasses up to focus on him better. "No classes on Saturday, sir, and we don't enroll gentlemen anyway."

"Which is not what I am here for," said Mendoza, annoyed at the implication. "I want to see Miss Weir on private business."

"Not here on Saturdays... Of course I have her home address, but I don't know—oh, well, I suppose it's all right."

New directions took him, tediously, several miles into Hollywood, to a street of solidly middle-aged apartment buildings, a little shabby, thirty years away from being fashionable addresses, but neatly kept up. The row of locked mailboxes in the foyer of the Blanchard Arms informed him that Miss Alison Weir lived on the fourth floor. A hand-lettered placard further informed him that the elevator was out of order. Mendoza said mildly, "Damn," toiled up three flights of dark, dusty-carpeted stairs, pressed the bell of 406 and, regaining his breath, hoped his quarry was in.

When the door opened to him, he was gratified for more reasons than one. Miss Alison Weir was worth the drive through traffic, worth a wasted afternoon. A middling tall young woman, with an admirably rounded yet slender figure, less conventionally pretty than charmingly provocative—rather square chin, a nose too small, a mouth too large, alert gray-green-hazel eyes under feathery brows, a magnificent matte-white complexion, and crisply cut and curled hair somewhere between copper and auburn, which was moreover nature's own choice for her. Her tailored dress was exactly the color of her hair, there were discreet gleams of topaz costume jewelry, her lipstick and nail polish were of the same burnt-orange shade. Twenty-nine, thirty, he said to himself: recovered, thank God, from the arch uncertainty of girlhood, and miraculously not bent on maintaining it: one might even suspect that great rarity in a woman, a sense of humor.

"Yes?" And her voice matched the rest of her, a warm contralto.

As he produced his credentials, explained, he swore mentally at the destiny which involved the woman in a case. It was not a good idea to mix personal matters with the job, and he was scrupulous about it. Until this woman was proved definitely to be clear of any connection with the case—he would be extremely surprised if she had, but it had to be checked, of course—strictly business, Luis, he said to himself regretfully.

"Good lord!" she exclaimed. "Well, come in, Lieutenant—you're lucky to catch me, I've just got in myself."

"Then you're excellent advertisement for your business. Any woman who can come in out of a rainstorm looking so charming—" It was the usual apartment of this vintage, but the personal touches were firmly individual: a good many books in cheap low cases against the wall, a row of framed pen sketches above them, a coffee table with Chinese teak underpinning topped with a large Benares brass tray,* in serene indifference to incongruity with the rest of the furniture, and an enormous aerial photograph of a suspension bridge over the simulated hearth. He sat down facing that, at her gesture, on the sofa, and disposed his hat and coat beside him.

"I shouldn't give myself away," she smiled, "but I came in looking like a drowned rat, I'm afraid. I'd be in a hot bath now if Marge hadn't called to warn me that a mysterious sinister-looking stranger—"

"That one's not such a good advertisement," he grinned.

"But I can't keep books. What's all this about the Ramirez girl? Cigarettes in that box, by the way—and don't you usually hunt in couples?"

"I've got no business hunting at all," said Mendoza, lighting her cigarette, then his. "I ought to be in my office doing this and that about a dozen other cases. As it is, I'm tying up loose ends"—he gestured—"you might say, on the perimeter of this business. I don't think it was a personal business, you see—I think it was more or less chance that the Ramirez girl was the one killed—but we have to be sure. I don't know what I expect from you, but you've been seeing the girl five days a week for the last couple of weeks, and anything she said to you—any little problem she mentioned, maybe—?"

"I see." Alison studied her cigarette. "You're always reading about these things in the papers—never think of its happening to anyone you know. The poor kid... I don't know that I can tell you anything."

---

*Brassware from the city of Benares, India (or in the style of such brassware).

"I'm hoping you can't," he said frankly. "We've already run across a couple of things in her personal life that might—just might—have led to murder. They have to be looked into. If you tell me something else, that's got to be investigated too. And I don't believe anything personal is behind it, I don't want to waste time on that."

"I see," she said again. "One of these psychos, blowing off steam every so often, on anyone convenient at the moment."

"They exist. Something like that, anyway. And I don't think this is his first, either. I'd like to find him before he, shall we say, has the impulse again."

"Amen to that," she said seriously. "But how on earth do you even start to look for a man like that? It might be anybody."

"I could give you a superior smile and say, We have our methods." He shrugged. "There are places to start looking. The records of any recently discharged mental patients—our own records of similar assaults—sex offenders who might have graduated to something more serious. We went through all that on the first case."

"And didn't come up with anything? So then what do you do?"

"Then," said Mendoza rather savagely, "you file all the records neatly away marked Case Pending, and you wait for it to happen again. Of course ideas occur to you about other places to look—but to put them into effect, I'd need about three times the number of men I've got." He sighed and put out his cigarette. "Of course, if one like that kills a dozen people a week, and obligingly leaves evidence to show it's all his own unaided work, the upper echelons get excited—and I get the men. But nobody, not even a lunatic killer, reaches the top of his career all at once—there's a build-up."

"Everyone has to start small?" She smiled briefly. "I see what you mean. Well, I don't think I can add anything to what you've probably got from her family and so on, but fire away—what do you want to know?"

"Did you have much to do with the girl personally? You teach classes, or whatever they're called, yourself?"

"Oh, lord, yes, I'm all there is. It may sound like a racket, Lieutenant, and maybe it is in some cases, but I think I offer them something, you know." She leaned to the table to put out her cigarette; her smile was wryly humorous. "The ones like this girl—and some others who might surprise you. Natural good taste and so on isn't standard equipment with the so-called upper classes. I've known girls from the same sort of background as Elena Ramirez who knew how to dress and had better instincts, as we say, than girls from wealthy homes. Mostly I get girls who are serious about improving themselves, but what they want to know, all I try to get over to them, is pretty simple. The very basic things about clothes and make-up and manners. You wouldn't believe what some of them look like when they come—"

"But I would," said Mendoza sadly. "I've seen them in the street, for my sins. Generally in those things mistakenly called toreador pants."*

She threw back her head and laughed, and he admired the clean white line of her throat. "Oh, my lord, I know!"

"I have no moral objection whatever, you understand—in fact it's enough to turn a man celibate for life—it's the aesthetic view I object to."

"And how right you are, with most of them. Well, as you might say yourself, *¿A qué viene eso?* What—"†

"You speak Spanish, Miss Weir?"

"By accident. I was born in Durango—my father was a structural engineer and worked in Mexico a good deal. That"—she nodded at the big photograph—"is his last piece of work. Funny sort of decor for a living room, I suppose I'm sentimental about it—he was very proud of it." She lit another cigarette. "In a sort

---

*These were tight pants, ending above the calf, so called because of the resemblance to the pants worn by bullfighters.

†"What are things coming to?"

of roundabout way, that's how I got into this business. You see, I'm a painter—or shall we say I hope I am—and that doesn't bring in much of a living unless you're really good—or at least known. Dad didn't leave me much, and I have to earn a living some way. What with moving around the way we did for his work, I got a rather sketchy education, and then like a fool I quit high school to get married—which turned out a mistake in more ways than one—and, well, I thought I'd try this, and it's worked out surprisingly well. Leaves me a fair amount of time for my own work, and at the same time I really enjoy it, you know. Not to bore you—"

"But how could you indeed?"

"And this isn't getting to what you want to know, anyway. It's a fairly small group, I never take more than twenty-five in a class and it's usually around twenty girls. I try to keep it on a more or less personal basis, you see. The course is six weeks, five days a week, but some of that time is spent on group reading and some on—private counseling, to give it a fancy name. Generally, I'll see each girl privately, oh, say a total of two hours or so a week. So you see, while I knew the girl, you can't say I knew her intimately."

"But you're no fool at sizing up people," he said placidly, leaning back, arms folded behind his head. "And the girl poured out her problems into your sympathetic ear?"

"That she did. You probably know about that—the superior boy friend and his family's objections. She was rather a pathetic little thing, really—awfully earnest, but—" She paused for a word.

"The first one comes to your mind about her," he prompted softly.

"Stupid," said Alison unhesitatingly. "She was stupid. She had no imagination, subtleties of any sort just didn't penetrate—you know the type. Oddly enough, her older sister is quite intelligent—I met them in town one day—"

"Yes, that girl has brains."

"Elena was honest, and—though she didn't look it—quite a respectable girl, in the old-fashioned sense. Immature for her age. But stupid."

"Immature and honest," he murmured. A little something there. The man Tomás, if there was anything in that, this girl would probably have been too stupid to discover it. If anyone in that household had seen something suspicious about the visiting uncle, it would not have been Elena, but the sharp-eyed Teresa. "That's no surprise," he said, half to himself. "Even dead, she was—unsubtle. I haven't met the boy yet—judging by Mrs. Wade, I'd say that his persistence was less attraction to Elena than rebellion against his mother."

"Like that?" She looked amused, and then sobered. "But that's another thing that happens, Lieutenant—the old, old story. I've never laid eyes on him either, don't know what kind of a boy he is, but—"

"Oh, yes, that's the first thing one thinks of here—if it was a private killing, so to speak. If she was pregnant, if she could make trouble for him, if he lost his head—It's happened. It'll happen again. We'll find out if it happened here."

"And how easy," she said, "to talk about it like a—crossword puzzle. After all, she's dead. Nineteen... She had a private session with me yesterday. She said she'd decided to stop bleaching her hair—" Alison stopped abruptly and looked up at him. "I *have* thought of something, but it doesn't sound like much—"

"I'll tell you whether it does when I've heard it, Miss Weir—or is it Mrs.?"

"I got my own name back after the divorce," she said absently. "It was only a year. And aren't you the autocratic male. Well, for what it's worth, Elena asked me yesterday what to do about 'a guy who annoys you'—that's how she put it—she said he 'sort of' followed her and stared at her."

"¡No me diga!" He sat up. "Don't tell me! That might be it, you know. Tell me every last little word she said about it!"

"But there wasn't anything, really! I'm afraid I didn't take it as very important. You mean it might have been—?"

"It might have been. There aren't any rules for lunatics—or part-time lunatics—but even lunatics don't often kill utter strangers without some reason. Nor what you or I'd call a logical reason, but a reason. I'm not even at the point of guessing about that here, but it's probable that at least he'd seen the girl before—consequently she may have noticed him. Let's have it—all of it!"

Alison looked stricken. "You'll want to murder *me*, Lieutenant—I didn't give her a chance to say much about it. In fact, I used it as an excuse to give her a neat little lecture on Making Oneself Conspicuous. She said—let me think!—'Miss Weir, what should you do about a guy who annoys you?' and I asked, Annoys you how? That was when she said he 'sort of followed' her and stared at her. And as I say, I seized the opportunity to point out that sometimes a girl seems to invite such attentions by making herself look cheap—and so on and so on—" Her voice died; she shut her eyes and pressed both hands to her cheeks, trying to remember. "There *wasn't* anything else—she said she understood about that, and that was when she told me she'd decided to stop bleaching—we talked about different things, you know, one thing leading to another—"

"That you needn't tell me! Women, they never keep to the subject!"

"But there *was* something else, I know it. Yes—" She straightened. "Just as she got up to leave, she said, 'But it's not exactly like that, Miss Weir, like he was trying pick me up or nothing like that. It's just—funny. Awful funny.' And I said something like, Well, just be sure you're not encouraging him, and that was that—she left, her consultation time was up."

"God favor me with patience!" said Mendoza violently. "And they say women are curious and fond of gossip! This girl tells you some strange man is annoying her, and you talk about hair dye and never ask one question? She says there's something 'funny' about him, and you—"

"How should I know it was anything important? If I'd—no, but listen, Lieutenant—*she* didn't say it as if *she* thought it was important, anything to be worried about! You see? If there'd really been anything *very* queer about him, to frighten her—" Her voice dropped.

"Yes, you've remembered that she was a stupid girl," he said sardonically. "And how did she mean that 'funny'?"

"*Extraño,*˙ like that—she said, 'It's just funny' or 'He's just funny,' and then she said it in Spanish, as if the English word didn't quite express what she meant. *Es un muchacho extraño.*"

"I will be damned," said Mendoza. "Something at last, maybe. 'A queer boy.'" He looked at her in cold exasperation. "And you didn't ask so much as where and when she saw him, what he looked like?"

"There's a saying about hindsight," retorted Alison, but meekly. "Would you have?"

"No, but then I'm not a woman. My God, I'd have thought you'd be a *little* curious! Well, it can't be helped." He got up. "I'll ask you to make a formal statement about this, if you will."

"Yes, of course." She went to the door with him. "Where do I go and when?"

"Tomorrow will do." Abruptly in better humor again, he smiled down at her. "I'll take you down to headquarters myself, not to expose any of my sergeants to temptation. I make it a rule not to mix business with pleasure, but if you turn out to be irrelevant to business, I'll be back—*con su permiso.*"

"Permission be damned, you mean! I do like your nerve," said Alison pleasantly, leaning on the open door. "When you're quite satisfied that I didn't murder the girl—maybe because she was so stupid—or egg your lunatic onto her, you'll condescend to find me good enough to be seen with. *Un hombre muy*

---

*Strange, odd.

arbitrario, in fact! And doesn't it occur to you that I might have a possessive six-foot admirer hanging about to raise objections?"

"What, to compete with *me*? I don't let those worry me any day."

"As if I needed telling. What time tomorrow?"

"In a hurry to be rid of me? One o'clock?"

"But *naturally*," she said, widening her eyes at him. "I'm panting for you to get to work and absolve me of guilt, what else, with such a reward offered? One o'clock—I'll be ready." The small amusement faded from her eyes then and she added, "I hope I *have* helped. Good luck with it."

"That I've had my share of for today. Until then." Scarcely a wasted afternoon, no—however you looked at it. He reflected pleasurably and with anticipation on Alison Weir—a sophisticated, shrewd, sensible woman (deliver him from romanticizing and possessive young girls!) and a very lovely one—until he slid behind the wheel and started the engine. He then removed his mind from her firmly and thought about what she had told him.

———

Hackett was waiting for him in his office; Hackett had been busy, and there was quite a list of miscellaneous bits and pieces to think about. Of greatest importance was the Ricky Wade business. That had to be looked into: it was so obvious. Hackett agreed with that: he would call there this evening, to catch both the boy and the father at home: a phone call assured that they would be, Mrs. Wade sounding surprised and uneasy (but what have *we* to do with this sordid matter, her tone implied).

The proprietor of the rink had been out, but some useful information had been obtained from his two employees, and Hackett was to see him at four. Two of Hackett's men were now out chasing down the patrons definitely stated to have been in the place last night. That was a place to be very thorough, the rink and everybody connected with it, for the girl had almost certainly been on her way home from there.

When Hackett left, Mendoza shoved aside everything to do with this case, conscientiously went over all the other pending matters under his authority. The still-unidentified corpse found in the freight yards; Sergeant Clock hadn't come up with anything new. The liquor-store holdup, a clerk shot; Sergeant Brice was on a faint track there, from the usual anonymous Information Received. The woman who'd shot her husband before witnesses: nothing to investigate but much tiresome routine, collecting statements for the District Attorney's office, in that sort of thing. Sergeant Galeano thought he had it about tied up now. A new memo from the captain's office, more routine: particulars of a man New York wanted for parole violation, one Ray Dalton, five-ten, one-eighty, age 42, Caucasian—

Mendoza swore to himself and reached for Hackett's notes again.

The two men at the rink, Hayes and Murphy, described themselves as attendants. They kept the place cleaned up (Hackett's comment: "This is news to anyone who's seen it"), one of them was on the floor at all times during open hours, to hand out skates and generally keep an eye on the patrons, and on occasion they spelled Ehrlich, the owner-proprietor, at the ticket desk. Not often, because Ehrlich didn't trust nobody much but himself with money. Ehrlich's wasn't getting rich, but business was so-so: most nights and Saturday afternoons they had maybe thirty, forty people in. All kids, sure: teenagers; some of those were crazy about it, maybe the ones had been too poor ever to have skates. They were good enough kids, not punks: the kind of kids carried switch knives, roamed round in gangs, all that, got in trouble with the cops—to them kind roller skating was for the birds. Sure, the kids got noisy and rambunctious sometimes like kids do, but there wasn't never anything real bad, knives pulled or an honest-to-God fight. No, neither

of them ever remembered an adult coming in—not to *skate*.
There'd been a kind of fad for it once, like that miniature golf
and ping-pong, that was when Ehrlich had opened this place,
but nowadays anybody grown-up, they'd feel like a damn fool
roller skating. Well, the chairs round the sides were for people
to sit and watch, sure, but this wasn't like an Ice Palace where
there was a show to see, for God's sake—just a bunch of kids
skating—nobody came just for that, the chairs were mostly
used by the kids themselves, resting and talking.

As for the club thing, it wasn't really a club but a kind of
season-ticket deal, see. You got a cut rate if you joined as a "regular patron": there weren't no meetings or nothing, all a card
meant was they'd paid three or six months in advance. All the
kids with cards didn't necessarily know each other: sometimes
yes, sometimes no. A card was an automatic pass good for three
nights a week up to the date on it. What with kids sixteen and
seventeen getting maybe forty a week at some job, a lot of them
had more money than was good for them, to throw away.

Both men knew the Ramirez girl and confirmed that she had
been in last night. What with the row, they could hardly miss
her. Ehrlich had been damned mad about it too, the guy saying the rink was a low dive and all: Ehrlich was death on liquor
in the place. This fellow barged right in, about twenty minutes
to ten it was, and pulled the kid off the floor—one that was
with this girl. Gave him hell, way the kids both looked: but not
shouting, private-like at the side of the rink, see, where it was
kind of dark, account the overhead lights were just in the middle, to light the skating floor. The fellow took the boy out finally,
maybe five minutes later—practically dragged him, hardly give
him time to take his skates off and turn them in. Yes, off the
premises—Ehrlich probably saw them go out to the street or
wherever, he was arguing at the guy and followed them. The girl
was mad too, naturally. And she didn't stay long after; a couple
other kids come up and talked to her, but she probably didn't

feel much like staying to skate alone, thought it made her look silly, have her boy friend dragged away from her like that. She took off her skates when the other kids left her, and turned them in to Hayes who was on duty then, and left the floor. Murphy, who was having a cigarette in the little foyer, had noticed her come out; she'd gone into the rest room—those were opposite sides of the foyer, with the ticket desk in the center. Ehrlich was sitting there again by then, he would have seen her too. She was in the rest room maybe five minutes, and come out, and left. That was maybe ten or five after.

It sure was awful, what had happened to her to think of a guy who'd do that walking around loose. No, neither of them could say offhand if anybody left right after her—the kids came and went all the time, there was a Coke machine in the foyer. And what the hell were the cops getting at with that?—somebody from here the one killed her? If Ehrlich heard that he'd hit the ceiling—besides, they were all *kids* in here last night, like every night, and no kid had done *that*.

Dwyer had called in at one-thirty to report that Tomás Ramirez had left Liggitt Street and was sitting alone in a bar—and that it might be a good idea if the relief man sent to join Dwyer understood Spanish. Sergeant Lake's prim script appended *Sent Smith*, so that had been taken care of.

Mendoza got up restlessly and stood at the window, not really focusing on the panoramic view of the city spread out before him. He wished the Ramirez house had a phone; there was, he had thought, no such great urgency about the matter that it could not wait a couple of hours—he would stop on his way home, or Hackett could see them tomorrow. Now suddenly he felt that it *was* urgent.

It was four o'clock. He told himself he was a single-minded fool, and on his way out told Sergeant Lake he'd be back in half an hour. He drove the few blocks to Liggitt Street, and as he pulled up at the curb before the house Teresa Ramirez came out.

Scarf over her hair for the rain, shabby brown coat, folded string shopping bag—on her way to market, probably for tonight's dinner. ("You got to think about them that's still alive.") He lowered the window and beckoned her.

She ducked in beside him for shelter from the rain, held the door shut but not latched. "You found out anything yet?"

"A little. Something else I want to ask you about."

"Well, O.K., only I got the shopping to do—but it don't matter, I guess, if it'll help you catch this fellow."

"I'll drive you wherever you're going. Did your sister—"

"That's real nice of you, but I don't want to put you out. But maybe you get gas allowance on the job?—excuse me, I don't mean to sound nosy, but I guess you don't get paid much, driving such an old car, and I wouldn't want you should go out of your way for me—"

"No trouble at all," said Mendoza without a smile. "Tell me—and take your time to think about it—did your sister say anything to you recently about being annoyed by a man who followed her and stared at her?"

"They did, sometimes," she said, nodding. "I told her it was account of her looking so—you know—and that Miss Weir at that school said so too. But—you mean special, just lately? I can't remember she mentioned anything like that... Wait a minute though, she did! Only it wasn't a man like that, like you mean, somebody whistling at her or making smart cracks. Way she said it, it was more as if there was something sort of *funny* about it. She didn't say much—just about some guy who stared at her, got on her nerves, you know. She said she was going try find out who he was, and get him to stop."

Mendoza almost dropped his cigarette, suppressing an exclamation. "She said that? It sounds as if he were someone local then, someone who lives or works around here?"

"I don't know anything about that, I don't think she mentioned any particular place she'd seen him—except—she *did* say, and I guess that must've been what she meant, she thought she knew somebody who knew this guy. A kid over on Commerce Street, she said... No, I don't know if this kid lived on Commerce or she'd maybe just seen him there, see. She just said, next time she saw him she was going to ask him who this other guy was, and tell him tell the guy stop bothering her."

"She had seen this boy with him?"

"Maybe. I don't know. She must've, or how would she know the boy knew him? All Elena said she knew about him, was his name's Danny... I didn't pay much notice to it, she didn't sound like it was anything important, just—like it made her kind of mad because it was so silly."

Do we start moving at last? Mendoza asked himself. A little something, a nuance, no more—maybe nothing at all—but a starting place. He was pleased. He asked her where she wanted to go.

"Main an' First, it's nice of you. You mean you think this guy might be the *one*? But it wasn't anything at all, or I'd sure have remembered and told you before! She didn't sound like she was *scared* of him or anything. You might ask that Miss Weir about it, though, if you think it's real important, because Elena did say she was going to tell her all about it—maybe she told her more than she did me."

Five

Martin Lindstrom put on the blue corduroy jacket that was getting too small for him, and buttoned it up slowly. He didn't feel very good.

"Where you going?" she asked sharply.

"Just out awhile." He still had fifteen cents left but that wasn't enough to get into a movie, except the one over on Main that had Mexican pictures, and those were never any good even if you could talk Mexican, nothing interesting in them.

"You be back for supper, mind! I don't want you gallivanting all over the streets alla time like these kids their mothers don't care what they're up to. Why you got to go out, Marty? It's raining something fierce, you better stay home."

"I-I-got to see a guy, 's all," he said. "One o' the guys at school, Ma, I said I'd help him with his homework, see."

"Oh." Her tight mouth relaxed a little; she was proud of his good marks at school.

It was a lie; and he didn't want to go out in the rain, but he didn't want to stay here either; he felt bad, but he wasn't sure about what exactly, just everything. He'd been feeling that way a long while, all wrong but not knowing how or where, seemed like. Of course he knew when everything had sort of started to get on top of him like this, it was after Dad went. He wondered where Dad was now. The funny thing was, and it was part of the bad feeling now, he ought to be feeling better about everything because of what that guy this morning said about finding Dad.

"Ma," he said. "Ma, you think that guy *will*—you know— find him, and—" He looked back at her from the door; right then, he dimly knew himself, he was begging her for the reassurance. Things will get like they used to be.

"I don't care if they do or not," she said, and besides the crossness in her voice there was the quivering fear he sensed from her almost all the time now. "It's not right," she whispered to herself, "asking a person all them questions. Just because you get where you got to ask relief, they think they can go nosing into ever'thing. Not as if I *like* to take charity—didn't ask till I *had* to. Nobody in our family ever been on charity before—comes hard to a respectable woman allus held her head up an' took nothing from nobody. Way they act, you'd think I was doing something wrong, ask for enough to keep a roof over our heads 'n' food in our mouths. Forty dollars a month!" She sat hunched in the rocker, thin arms hugging her flat body. "County's got millions. Come poking around with their *questions* before they let me have forty dollars!"

"He only ast four-five things, Ma—"

"He ast four-five things too much! What business is it of *theirs*? No, acourse, they won't find your dad, they'll *never* find him." She said that with fear, with hope, with insistence. "If your dad was minded go off like that, he'd be real careful make it so's nobody'd ever find him, an'—an' it's seven-eight months back he went too."

The boy was silent. He knew all sorts of things in the dumb, vague way thirteen does know—hardly aware that he knew. She made out she didn't mind Dad going off, except for the money, but she did. She was afraid and making out she wasn't. He knew there were things in her mind that for years she'd shut away somewhere, and now they'd got out, they were shapeless unseen monsters crowding in on her and him both.

"Don't you stay out later than six," she said. "Six is supper like allus."

Then, all of a sudden, he knew why he felt bad—why he'd been feeling like this all the time since. In awful clarity it came to him that things never stayed the same, or even got back to what they'd been before. However bad things were, you were safe, knowing what a day would be like, tomorrow and next week; but it would change so you didn't ever know, and you couldn't stop it any way. *She* wanted to, and she thought she had, and now she'd found nobody ever could. One of the invisible monsters right here with them now was the threat and promise of change to come.

It was knowledge too big for thirteen, and he turned blindly and ran out, and down the dark rickety stair into the rain.

The rain was cold coming down but like mostly in California when it rained it wasn't really cold, not cold like back in Minnesota with the snow and all. The snow was kind of nice, though—Dad said—Dad didn't like California much—maybe he'd gone back east, and—

He stopped, breathless, and leaned on the window of the drugstore on the corner there, as if he was looking at the picture of the pretty girl saying Instant Protection, but he didn't see anything in the window. *Oh, Dad!* he cried in silent agony.

He'd lost Dad too, just then, and forever. It wouldn't matter if Dad came back, things would never be like they were, ever again.

"Hi, kid," said Danny behind him.

Marty turned, eager for companionship, for anybody to talk to. "Hi, Danny, wh-what's new?" It came out kind of squeaky-sounding, like a real little kid, and embarrassed him all the more because of Danny being—well, Danny.

"Nothin' much. Say, Marty—"

Mr. Cummings had already turned on the lights in the drugstore, the rain made it so dark—it was getting dark anyway, fast—and Marty could see their blurred reflections in the glass of the window. They looked funny together, him and Danny Smith, but maybe only to anybody knew them. Because he was so big beside Danny, he'd grown so fast just this last year—Dad said their family always did start to grow awful young—last month when all the kids got measured for gym in school, he'd been sixty-eight inches and some over, and that was only four inches shorter than Dad. In the glass there, sideways, he saw himself looking man-size, looming alongside of Danny—but it was the other way round inside them. Danny was like a grown-up somehow, things he knew and said and did, not having to be in any special time, and always having money, and sometimes he smoked cigarettes. It wasn't just Marty, he guessed most of the guys around here felt the same about Danny, and Danny sort of bossed them around, and they let him.

The figures in the window glass weren't sharp, just shapes like, but just the way the smaller one moved you'd know it was Danny, didn't have to really see his sharp straight nose and the way his forehead went up flat, not bulgy, into black hair that was wavy like a girl's with a permanent, or his eyes that moved a lot and were bluer than most blue eyes.

"Say, Marty, why'd you run off las' night?" Danny was asking. "At the show, alla sudden—we hadden seen it right through yet either. You scareda your ole lady, hafta get home when she says?"

"I didn't so sudden," he said quickly. Danny and a lot of the guys around here, they thought that was funny—both kinds of funny; they sort of needled you if your mother said a certain time and you did what she said. "I just decided to," he said. "It wasn't a very good pitcher anyway."

"You kiddin'? It was—"

"I seen it before," said Marty, desperately.

Danny just looked at him. Then he said, "You been down t' see where the murder was?"

Something moved a little, dark and uneasy, at the very bottom of Marty's mind. "What murder?"

"Jeez, don't you know *anything* happens? Right down at Commerce an' Humboldt, you know where that house burn' down across from the wop store. It was some girl, an' boy, was she a mess, blood all over an' one of her eyes punched right out—whoever did it sure musta been mad at her—I dint get there till after they took her away, but you could still see some o' the blood, oney the rain—"

Marty's stomach gave a little jump. He put his right hand over that place on the left sleeve of the blue corduroy coat, where the mark was. It wasn't a very big spot, but it showed dark against the light blue and it was stiff. It hadn't been there this time last night when he put the jacket on; he'd noticed it this morning.

I got it in the theayter last night, he told himself. Of course it wasn't blood. Something on the seat in there, it was.

Empty lot where a house had burned down. All of a sudden he remembered how it had been, in the dark last night: something tripping him, hard squarish cement something when he felt of it, like what was left when a house was burned. A lot of grass around it.

No, it wasn't, he said in his mind frantically, *it wasn't like that, I must remember wrong.* His mind said back at him, *Like you remembered wrong before?*

Danny was going on talking but he couldn't listen. *Please, oh, please, it can't have happened again.* It never did happen, nothing happened before, you just remembered wrong is all. You can't ever be sure in the dark, and it was night then too, of course it had to be, it was always night when—

—When things happened. A light green shirt that time because it was hot, it was summer, and the mark didn't come out when she washed it, you could still see where it'd been. That wasn't blood either, acourse it wasn't, how could it be?

He said louder than he meant to, "I-I got to go home, I better not be late for supper," and walked away fast as he could. He didn't want to hear any more about it, *or he might remember too much.* There wasn't anything *to* remember, he was just making up stories in his head to try and scare her, because he—

There were long times when he never thought about it, but when he did, it was all right there sharp and clear, more like *it* pounced at him instead of him remembering. That other night. *The first time.* Wet red mark on the green shirt and her scolding—because it was late. The big doll with the pink dress and goldy hair. And next day people talking about—what had happened—to that colored girl.

He was almost running now, trying to run away from the voice in his mind, and he blundered into a man walking the other way. The man said something and put out a hand to steady him on his feet, but Marty pulled away and dodged round the corner into Graham Court. He leaned on the broken-down picket fence of the corner house and he hit it with his fist, the breath sobbing in his throat, tears squeezing out from tight-shut eyes.

"I *tole* her," he said low in his throat. "I *tried* tell her!" It was all he could do, wasn't it? What else could thirteen years old do?

But there wasn't much to tell, that time or this time—he really remembered, knew his own self. She said so. He didn't know, he must've remembered wrong, or he was a wicked boy just trying to scare her. Making up stories that couldn't be so.

And she washed the green shirt but the mark still showed after.

After a while Marty straightened and went on, slowly, down the little cul-de-sac. He didn't want to go home; just two things pulled him that way, drearily, as they had before. Habit, and Dad's voice that time a while back, slow and easy like always, Dad saying, "You want to be nice t' your ma, Marty, an' help her all you can, an' don't do nothing to worry her. I know it ain't easy, times, but things ain't easy for her neither. You got to remember she come of folks had a lot more than the Lindstroms, back home—her pa Ole Larsen was a rich man, eleven hundert acres he had all good land too, an' his girls never wanted for nothing. Maybe them Larsens did give theirselves airs, but maybe they had reason too, an' anyways your ma never had cause to make-shift an' scrimp on nothing, till she married me—an' it ain't exactly been a easy row to hoe for her, not noways. I know she gets cross-tongued once in a while, but you got to remember things is hard for her too."

That had been before—anything happened. If it had.

Marty went up the stairs of the apartment building slow, hanging onto the shaky railing. He felt another thing he'd got to feeling almost all the time lately, and that was as if there were two of him: one was a little kid whose ma was right whatever she said or did, just naturally because she was Ma—and the other was, well, nearest he could come was Marty-separate-from-Ma, who knew Ma might be wrong about some things. He tried to push that Marty away, because he didn't want to *really* know that, but seemed like that Marty was getting stronger and stronger in him. At the same time there were two other Martys, the one that was just a wicked little boy making up stories—and the one that knew different.

That one was scared, deep and cold inside. Because it was all his fault, must be, even if he'd never meant, never known, if he'd just sort of forgot for a while—

And the bad feeling had begun maybe when Dad went away, but what had made it *so* bad ever since was—that first time, back there on Tappan Street on a breathless night in late September.

He'd *had* to tell her. Things happened that were too big for you, frightening and confusing, that you couldn't do anything about yourself—you told your ma or dad, and they knew what to do. Only Dad hadn't been there.

And there was a third place the real bad feeling started, after she wouldn't believe, wouldn't listen—when she did something she'd never done before, ever: when she went out and bought a newspaper, and read about—It. And said like to herself in a funny kind of whisper, "Only some nigger girl, anyways. Prob'ly trash—just trash."

And the next day she'd gone and found this place for them to move, account it was cheaper, she said.

He got to the dark top of the stairs, and he thought frantically, I *got* to tell her. I got to try. Because—

He was sick and shaking with fear, with guilt, with the weight of a thing thirteen couldn't bear alone. The door was locked like always and he knocked and she said sharp, "Who is it?"

"It's me, Ma, let me in." And there wasn't any other way to say it than he did, then: "Ma, it's happened again! Ma—please listen—I didn't *mean* to—I never meant nothing to happen—but it must've, because—"

She just stood and stared at him.

"—Because it *was* blood on my coat, 's morning." He gulped and went on through the lump in his throat, "And—and the place they found—it—it was right where I—"

The fear pulled her face all tight and cross-looking for a minute, but then it changed to being mad at him, and she said quick, "I don't listen to a boy tells lies!"

He looked at her dumbly. He knew what else she'd say, like she had before; but this time he knew something else—that what she said wasn't just at him, it was at that place *she* had way inside her where she knew it was so—it was to shut the door to that place and forget it was there at all. And now she was asking him to help her, seemed like, not mad any more but *asking*.

"You get washed an' eat your supper while it's hot, an' then you set right down to that schoolwork you shoulda done last night—I'm allus tellin' you, don't want to end up like your dad, not enough schoolin' for a decent job—you're a real smart boy,

Marty, you take after my folks, an' last thing I do I see you get educated good, maybe even college. But you got to remember you don't know ever'thing yet, see, an'—an' kids get mixed up in their minds, like, that's all—"

He whispered, "I'm not awful hungry, Ma."

And all the while the secret was there in the room with them, neither of them daring to look at it open: that she wouldn't see for what it really was, that he was getting more and more afraid of—that they had to live with somehow.

———

Danny stood there by the drugstore awhile after Marty left.

On top of his mind he thought, That big lummox of a Lindstrom kid, sure a dumb one. But most of him was occupied with the job he was on, and he felt kind of tensed-up because it was the first time his dad had taken much notice of him, acted like he was a person with any sense, and he wanted to do this right.

It had been a big surprise to him to feel the way he did. Asked him last week, he'd have said it wasn't nothing to him, whatever his dad did or said—been three and a half years since he'd laid eyes on him, anyways—and that went other way round too, they'd always just sort of stayed out of each other's way. Same as with his mother, but she was just a nothing, like a handful of water, and there was at least something *to* his dad. And he'd felt a new, funny feeling when his dad said that: *Kind of a sharp kid, you can maybe be some use to me.*

Besides, this was different from hooking little stuff off store counters or stripping cars at night. This was a big job.

When the man came, he spotted him right off from what his dad had said he looked like; but he waited awhile, just went on looking in the drugstore window. The guy stopped and stood there too, waiting, under the store canopy. Nobody came past after him, and when Danny walked down the block there weren't any cops watching from alleys, nobody at all. It was all going just like his dad had planned, but of course you had to play it smart. Danny walked back to the drugstore; he didn't stop by the guy waiting there, just slowed down, and he said, "He's changed his mind, mister, he says meet him at the Paradise Bar on Second, right now."

The man said, "What?" sort of dumb and surprised, and then he made as if to grab for him, but Danny slid away in the dark, into the alley round the corner, and waited. After a minute the man started to walk up toward Second Street, not very fast; he looked back a couple of times, but once away from the corner lights it was dark and Danny stayed close up against the buildings.

On Second Street there were more lights, but people on the sidewalk, too, to hide him; he stayed farther behind, but he could still see the guy when he turned in under the pink neon sign that said PARADISE. So that was O.K. And no cops.

Danny turned and sauntered back to the corner; another man stood there, looking in the window of the liquor store. "O.K.," said Danny. "He's in, and no cops."

"You sure?"

"You think I can't smell a cop?"

The man relaxed a little, grinned. "Maybe you ain't so smart as you think, but I guess you're not so dumb neither. Chip off the ole block like they say, huh? O.K., you go along. Now I just let the guy stew awhile an' get real worried." He went back to looking in the window.

———

Inside the bar a jukebox was pounding, and the blood-hammer in Morgan's head began to keep time with it. He went all the way in to the last of the little booths opposite the bar, and sat down; the waiter who came up gave him a sour look for taking a booth instead of going to the bar, but he didn't say anything and he'd come over promptly because Morgan was a lot better dressed than the usual customer in here and might be drinking something besides beer or wine.

Morgan asked for whiskey, but when it came he just left it there on the table; he'd never been much of a drinker and not at all the last eight years, since—Which was a useless gesture, maybe: morbid.

He sat there and waited. The place wasn't crowded on a rainy night, only ten or a dozen men at the bar. It was stuffy, too hot after the street, and he realized he still had his coat on, slid out of the booth to take it off, fold it beside him. The clock on one side of the bar said half-past six, but Morgan knew he'd better keep his eye off the clock—the man wanted him to sweat, and might not show up for hours. In his mind he knew that, while all the rest of him was tense and agonizing to get *to* it, have it done, the ultimate doom arranged.

He lit a cigarette and set himself to wait, and wait, and wait some more; and his intellect told him further (methodical, plodding Morgan) that if he let himself go over and over this thing emotionally, he'd be in just the softened-up state the bastard wanted, at the end. So he made himself think about anything, everything else than Sue and Janny.

The first thing he seized on to think about was that boy. Using a youngster, for this. That was a conventional thought out of the small neat circle of life he'd always lived in up to now: correction, up to being on the job he held now, for that (even before his own private nightmare) should certainly have taught him about lives lived elsewhere and otherwise, where children weren't automatically screened from the uglier realities because they were children. It didn't occur to him that the boy was just relaying a message, didn't know what he was mixed into: he'd seen his expression. And there were two things about that, that turned this into something like a real nightmare where ordinary sights and sounds made no sense or a new monstrous kind of sense. That boy hadn't realized, maybe, that there on the rain-swept empty corner, as he swaggered past Morgan, the lights from the store fell unshadowed on him. Oh, yes, the boy had known just what he was doing.

Morgan looked down at his hands on the wet, scarred table, and as he looked they began to shake violently, so he put them in his lap.

Quite a handsome boy. Even in that deceiving light, he had seen the regular features, fair skin with the black hair and blue eyes all the more emphasized for it, the thick brows going up in little wings at the end. He knew that curve by heart, the very angle, *Janny's brows winging up at the corners off Janny's blue eyes*—

Not to think about Janny, or Sue. Janny, just about now, being tucked into bed with that ridiculous stuffed tiger Mrs. Gunn had got her, that she was so crazy about. Warm and powdery from her bath, buttoned into the woolly blue pajamas.

That boy had just had on jeans and a leather jacket. That boy who was, who must be—

For God's sake! said his mind to him savagely.

He glanced sideways at the clock. It was twenty-five minutes to seven.

He remembered a while ago, couldn't remember where, reading an article on juvenile delinquents that had interested him. It was funny, there was a clear picture in his mind of himself saying to Sue, "The man's got something there, you know," but he couldn't recall now who the author was, some official or a senator or whatever. Anyway. Often the most intelligent children, it said, those with imagination and ability, the nonconforming minds any society needs—but for this and that reason turned in the wrong direction.

All right, yes; up to a point; some of them, the leaders. Most, well—

Hell, maybe the man was right.

The boy—*led to Janny and he mustn't think about Janny.* Quick, something else.

Another boy. Barging into him in the street there, dodging past. Didn't know it was a boy—big as a man, as tall as Morgan himself—until he heard the sobbing light breath, had a glimpse of him close in the reflected street light. That was the Lindstrom boy, that one; they lived around here, of course. Clumsy big ox of a kid, one of those got all his growth at once, early, and wouldn't quite learn how to handle his size for a while; and still so baby-faced, any roundish, smooth, freckle-nosed thirteen-year-old face, that you expected to see half a foot below where this one was. Lindstrom was what, Danish, they grew big men mostly.

Generalizing again, he thought; you couldn't, of course. The archetype Scandinavian wasn't a wife-deserter, but this one was. That report wasn't made up yet either, and he had to have it ready Monday morning for Gunn. Something queer there about the Lindstroms, something that smelled wrong, hard to say what. It could be another case of collusion to get money out of the county, but Morgan didn't think so; he didn't think that, whatever was behind the indefinable tension he'd sensed in that place, it came from dishonesty. Anything so— uncomplicated—as dishonesty. The woman was a type he knew: transplanted countrywoman, sometimes ignorant, frequently stubborn at clinging to obsolete ways and beliefs, always with a curious rigid pride. That type might be dishonest about anything else, but not about money.

Invariably the first thing that kind said to him was, "I've never asked nor took charity before." Marion Lindstrom had said that. She hadn't told him much else.

But the report had to be made out, and the hunt started for Eric John Lindstrom.

It was a quarter to seven. Morgan kept himself from watching the door; his mind scrabbled about desperately for something else irrelevant to occupy it. He heard the door open, couldn't stop himself looking up to see: outside he was still uncomfortably warm, but there was an ice-cold weight in his stomach, and it moved a little when he saw the man who'd come in—a stranger, not the one.

And right there something odd happened to him. Suddenly he knew what was behind the queerness he'd sensed in that Lindstrom woman, this morning. The few minutes he'd been there, talked to the woman and the boy. It was fear: secret fear. He knew it now because it was his own feeling: the sure recognition was emotional.

He thought without much interest, I wonder what *they're* afraid of.

At seven o'clock, because of the looks he was getting from the barman, he drank the whiskey and ordered another. It was cheap bar whiskey, raw. At a quarter past seven he ordered a third; he decided the whiskey was just what he'd needed, because his mind had started to work again to some purpose, and suddenly too he was no longer afraid. That was a hell of a note, come to think, getting in a cold sweat the way he had without ever even considering whether there were ways and means to deal with this, come out safe. What had got into him, anyway? There must be a way, and what he'd told himself this morning still went: to hell with any moral standards. If—

When at half-past seven someone slid into the booth opposite him, he'd almost finished a fourth whiskey. He looked up almost casually to meet the eyes of the man across the table, and he wondered with self-contempt that didn't show on his face why he'd ever been afraid of this man.

"You been doin' some thinkin', Morgan?" The man grinned at him insolently. "Ready to talk business?"

"Yes," said Morgan, cold and even. "I've been doing some thinking, but not about the money. I told you before, I haven't got that kind of money."

The man who called himself Smith laughed, as the barman came up, and he said, "You'll buy me a drink anyways. Whiskey."

The barman looked at Morgan, who shook his head; he'd had just the right amount now to balance him where he was. "Don't give me that," said Smith when the man was gone. "You're doin' all right. You got money to throw away once, you got it to throw away twice."

Money to throw away... But that was perfectly logical reasoning, thought Morgan, if you happened to look at things that way. He looked at Smith there, a couple of feet across the table, and he thought that in any dimension that mattered they were so far away from each other that communication was impossible. He found, surprisingly, that he was intellectually interested in Smith, in what made him tick. He wondered what Smith's real name was: he did not think the name the woman had used two years ago, Robertson, was the real name any more than Smith. Smith's eyes were gray: though his skin was scarred with the marks of old acne and darkened from lack of soap and water, it was more fair than dark. And his eyebrows curved up in little wings toward the temples. Morgan stared at them, fascinated: Smith had worn a hat pulled low when he'd seen him before, and the eyebrows had been hidden. The eyebrows were, of course, more confirmation of Smith's identity. With detached interest Morgan thought, Might be Irish, that coloring.

"You know," he said, "you might not be in such a strong position as you think. Your story wouldn't sound so good to a judge—not along with mine."

"Then what're you doin' here?" asked Smith softly.

And that of course was the point. Because it was a no man's land in law, this particular thing. Anyone might look at Smith, listen to what that upright citizen Richard Morgan had to say, and find it incredible that any intelligent human agency could hesitate at making a choice between. But it wasn't a matter of men—it was the way the law read. And in curious juxtaposition to the impersonal letter of the law, there was also the imbecilic sentimentality, the mindless lip service to convention—the convention that there was in the physical facts of parturition some magic to supersede individual human qualities. He could not take the chance, gamble Janny's whole future, Sue's sanity maybe, on the hope that some unknown judge might possess a little common sense. Because there was also the fact that, as the law took a dim view of buying and selling human beings, it didn't confine the guilt to just one end of the transaction.

Smith knew that, without understanding it or needing to understand it; but the one really vital fact Smith knew was that there had never been a legal adoption. They had hesitated, procrastinated, fearing the inevitable questions...

"—A business proposition, that's all," Smith was saying. "Strickly legal." His tone developed a little resentment, he was saying he had a legitimate grievance. "You made a Goddamn sharp deal with my wife, a hundred lousy bucks, an' you got away with it, she didn't have no choice, on account she was up against it with me away like I was, flat on my back in the hospital I was, an' the bills runnin' up alla time—you took advantage of her not knowin' much about business, all right! I figure it same way like a bank would, Morgan—innerest, they call it, see?"

There was an appalling mixture of naïve satisfaction and greed in his eyes; Morgan looked away. (Interest, just how did you figure that kind of interest? Twenty-six months of a squirming warm armful that weighed fourteen pounds, eighteen, twenty-two, and a triumphant twenty-nine-and-a-half?—he forgot what the latest figure was, only remembered Sue's warm chuckle, reporting it. Twenty-six months of sticky curious baby-fat fingers poking into yours, into the paper you were trying to read, into what was almost a dimple at the corner of Sue's mouth: of the funny solemn look in the blue eyes: of ten pink toes splashing in a sudsy tub. That would be quite a thing to figure in percentages.)

"You can raise the dough if you got to," said Smith.

"Not ten thousand," said Morgan flatly. "I might manage five." And that was a deliberate lie; he couldn't raise five hundred.

"I don't go for no time-payments, Morgan." The gray eyes were bleak. "You heard me the first time. I give you a couple days' think about it, but don't give me no more stall now. Put up or shut up."

Poker, thought Morgan. Bluff?—that he'd bring it open, go to law? You couldn't take the chance; and in this last five minutes it had come to him that he didn't have to. There was only one way to deal with Smith, and Morgan knew how it could be done, now: he saw the way. He could take care of Smith once for all time, and then they would be safe: if necessary later, he could handle the woman easier, he remembered her as an indecisive nonentity. There was, when you came to think of it, something to be said for being an upright citizen with a clean record. And it would not trouble his conscience at all. In the days he'd worn Uncle's uniform,* he had probably killed better men, and for less reason.

There was hard suspicion now in the gray eyes; Morgan looked away, down to his empty glass, quickly. He'd been acting too calm, too controlled; he must make Smith believe in his capitulation. He made his tone angry and afraid when he said, low, "All right, all right—I heard you the first time! I—I guess if I cash in those bonds—I might—but I'll get something for my money! You'll sign a legal agreement before you touch—"

"O.K., I don't mind that."

"You've got to give me time, I can't raise it over Sunday—"

"Monday night."

"No, that's not long enough—"

"Monday," said Smith. "That's the time you got—use it. Make it that same corner, seven o'clock, with the cash—an' I don't take nothing bigger than fives, see?" He slid out of the booth, stood up.

---

*"Uncle Sam," that is—the American armed forces.

"Yes, damn you," said Morgan wearily. Without another word Smith turned and walked toward the door.

Morgan took out his wallet below the level of the table, got out the one five in it, held it ready. When Smith looked back, going out, Morgan was still sitting there motionless; but the second Smith turned out of sight to the left, Morgan was up, quick and quiet. He laid the five on the table and got into his coat between there and the door; outside, he turned sharp left and hugged the building, spotting the back he wanted half a block ahead.

Because Kenneth Gunn, who had been a police officer for forty years and sure to God ought to know, had once said to him, "They're a stupid bunch. Once in a long while you get a really smart one, but they're few and far between. The majority are just plain stupid—they can't or won't think far enough ahead."

Maybe this was Smith's first venture into crookedness, but it should qualify him for inclusion in that; Morgan hoped so. There was a chance that the boy was posted to watch, of course; but he had to risk that. The precautions about the meeting place, beforehand, were to assure Smith that Morgan came alone: and satisfied of that, Smith's mind might have gone no further.

Smith had made another mistake too, one frequently made by men like him. They always underestimated the honest men.

It had stopped raining and turned very cold. This was the slack hour when not many people were out, and it was easy to keep Smith spotted, from pool to pool of reflected neon lights on the sidewalk. If he had looked back, he'd have found it as easy to spot Morgan; but he didn't look back. He walked fast, shoulders hunched against the cold, round the next corner to a dark side street.

When the trail ended twenty minutes later Morgan told himself, almost incredulously, that his luck had turned; he was due for a few breaks... He'd had a job to keep Smith in sight and still stay far enough back, down these dark streets, and he'd lost all sense of direction after they got off Second. But at that last corner, stopping in shadow, watching Smith cross the narrow street ahead, Morgan realized suddenly where they were. He was at the junction of Humboldt and Foster, a block down from Commerce; it looked as if Humboldt ended here, where Foster ran straight across it like the top bar on a T, but it only took a jog, started again half a block to the left. What made the jog necessary was Graham Court, a dreary little cul-de-sac whose mouth gaped narrowly at him directly opposite. He'd been here before, just this morning. And Smith was going into Graham Court.

Morgan jaywalked across Foster Street and under the lamp-post whose bulb had been smashed by kids, and into Graham Court. It was only wide enough for foot traffic: there were three dark, dank, big frame houses on each side, cheap rooming places, and right across the end of the court, a four-story apartment building of dirty yellow stucco. A dim light from one of the ground-floor windows there showed Smith as he climbed the steps and went in.

"I will be damned," said Morgan half-aloud. Luck turning his way?—with a vengeance! The building where the Lindstrom woman lived: where on his legitimate comings and goings Richard Morgan, that upright and law-abiding citizen, had every reason to be, a real solid beautiful excuse, good as gold.

And that was just fine, better than he could have hoped for: he saw clear and confident how it would go, now.

Six

Mendoza realized they'd have to let the Danny go: it might not be impossible to find the Danny Elena Ramirez had known, if it would be difficult; but more to the point, there was no way of identifying the right Danny. What was interesting about this matter was that by implication it narrowed the locale.

He had formed some very nebulous ideas—mere ghosts of hypotheses—overnight, out of the evidence a second murder inevitably added to the evidence from a first one; and he thought that a restricted locale was natural, if you looked at it a certain way. At least, it was a fifty-fifty chance, depending on just what kind of lunatic they were hunting. If he was the kind (disregarding the psychiatrists' hairsplitting solemn terms) whose impulse to kill was triggered suddenly and at random, the odds were that his victim would be someone in the area where he lived or worked: and considering the hour, probably the former. If he was the kind capable of planning ahead, then the place of the crime meant nothing, or very little, for he might have been cunning enough to choose a place unconnected with him. But to balance that there was the fact that madmen capable of sustained cunning generally chose victims by some private logic: they were the ones appointed by God to rid the world of prostitutes, or Russian spies, or masquerading Martians. Like that. And to do so, they had to be aware of the victims as individuals.

So there was a chance that this one, whatever kind he was, lived somewhere fairly near the place he had killed. And that might be of enormous help, for it suggested that he had lived (or worked) somewhere near the place Carol Brooks had been killed last September. If he was the man who had killed her, and Mendoza thought he was.

Sunday was only another day to Mendoza; he lay in bed awhile thinking about all this, and also about Alison Weir, until the sleek brown Abyssinian personage who condescended to share the apartment with him, the green-eyed Bast, leapt onto his stomach and began to knead the blanket, fixing him with an accusing stare. He apologized to her for inattention; he got up and laid before her the morning tribute of fresh liver; he made coffee. Eight o'clock found him, shaven and spruce, poring over a small-scale map of the city in his office.

When Hackett came in at nine o'clock, he listened in silence to Alison Weir's contribution of the *muchacho extraño* who stared, and grunted over the neat penciled circles on the map. In the center of one was the twenty-two-hundred block of Tappan Street, and in the center of the other the junction of Commerce and Humboldt. Each covered approximately a mile in diameter, to the map scale: call it a hundred and fifty square blocks.

"Now isn't that pretty!" said Hackett. "And where would you get the army to check all that territory—and for what? The idea, that I go along with, and if your pretty circles happened to have prettier centers, say like Los Feliz and Western, I'd say we might come up with something, just on a check to see who'd moved where recently. But you know what you got here!" He stabbed a blunt forefinger at the first circle. "About half of this area is colored, and none of it, white or black, is very fancy. Which also goes with bells on for the other area. Out on the Strip, or along

Wilshire, a lot of places, you've got people in settled lives, and they leave records behind. City directory, phone book, gas company, rent receipts, forwarding addresses. Here—" he shrugged.

"You needn't tell me," said Mendoza ruefully. "This is just a little exercise in academic theory." In these networks of streets, some of the most thickly populated in the city, drifted the anonymous ones: people who wandered from one casual job to another, who for various reasons (not always venal) were sometimes known by different names to different people, and who owned no property. Landlords were not always concerned with keeping records, and most rent was paid in cash. There were also, of course, settled householders, responsible people. For economic reasons or racial reasons, or both, they lived cheek-by-jowl, crowded thick; they came and went, and because they were of little concern to anyone as individuals, their comings and goings went largely unnoticed.

"If we had a name—but we'd get nothing for half a year's hunt, not knowing what to look for. ¡*Qué se le ha de hacer!*'—it can't be helped! But if the general theory's right, there's a link somewhere."

"I'll go along with you," said Hackett, "but I'll tell you, I think we'll get it as corroborative evidence after we've caught up with him by another route. Somebody'll see a newspaper cut, and come in to tell us that our John Smith is also Henry Brown who used to live on Tappan Street. We can't get at it from this end, there's damn-all to go on."

"I agree with you—though there's such a thing as luck. However!" Mendoza shoved the map aside. "What did you get out of the Wades?"

"Something to please you." Circumstantially, the Wades were counted out. Ehrlich and his two attendants at the rink had seen father and son leave, and agreed on the time as "around ten to ten." The girl had been a good ten or twelve minutes after them.

---

*"What is there to do!"

By the narrowest reckoning it was a twenty-minute drive to the Wades' home, probably nearer thirty, and a neighbor had happened to be present in the house on their arrival, an outside witness who was positive of the time as ten twenty-five. There hadn't been time, even if you granted they'd done it together, which was absurd... The Wades, *pater* and *mater familias*, might be snobs, with the usual false and confused values of snobs (though much of their social objection to the Ramirez girl was understandable: Mendoza, supposing he were ever sufficiently rash or unwary to acquire a wife and family, would probably feel much the same himself). But it could not be seriously conjectured that a respectable middle-aged bookkeeper had done murder (and such a murder) to avoid acquiring a daughter-in-law addicted to double negatives and peroxide. And if he had, it would hardly be in collusion with the boy.

"The boy," said Hackett, "hasn't got the blood in him to kill a mouse in a trap anyway—all you got to do is look at him."

"I'll take your word for it," said Mendoza absently. He wasn't interested in the boy, never had been much; the Wades were irrelevant, but he was just as pleased that by chance there was evidence to show that. And the Wades ought to be very damned thankful for it too: they'd probably never realize it, but without that evidence the boy could have found himself in bad trouble. From Mendoza's viewpoint that would have been regrettable chiefly because it would have diverted the investigation into a blind alley. They had wasted enough official time as it was.

He looked again at his map, and sighed. The lunatic—of this or that sort—was his own postulation, and he could be wrong: that had sometimes happened. Ideally an investigator should be above personal bias, which—admitted or unconscious— inevitably slanted the interpretation of evidence.* And yet

*Compare Mendoza's view to that of Sherlock Holmes: "We approached the case, you remember, with an absolutely blank mind, which is always an advantage. We had formed no theories. We were simply there to observe and to draw inferences from our observations." Arthur Conan Doyle, "The Cardboard Box," *Strand Magazine* 5, no. 1 (January 1893): 61–73.

evidence almost always had to be interpreted—full circle back to personal opinion. There was always the human element, and also what Dr. Rhine* might call the X factor, which Mendoza, essentially a fatalist as well as a gambler, thought of as a kind of cosmic card-stacking. Much of the time plodding routine and teamwork led you somewhere eventually; but it was surprising how often the sudden hunch, the inspired guess, the random coincidence, took you round by a shorter way. And sometimes the extra aces in the deck fell to the opponent's hand, and there was nothing you could do about that. The law of averages had nothing to do with it.

"I dropped in to see if the autopsy report's come through… oh, well, suppose we couldn't expect it over Sunday. Nothing much in it anyway. Back to the treadmill—" Hackett got up. "I've still got some of the kids to see, ones at the rink that night."

"The rink," said Mendoza, still staring at his map. "Yes. We'll probably get the autopsy report by tonight—the inquest's been set for Tuesday. *Yes—Vaya…todo es posible.* Yes, you get on with the routine, as becomes your rank—me, I'm taking the day off from everything else, to shuffle through this deck again, *por decirlo así*†—maybe there's a marked card to spot."

He brooded over the map another minute when Hackett had gone, and penciled in a line connecting the two circles. He shrugged and said to himself, Maybe, maybe—folded the map away, got his hat and coat and went out.

Downstairs, as he paused to adjust the gray Homburg, a couple of reporters cornered him; they asked a few desultory questions about the Ramirez girl, but their real interest was in Sergeant Galeano's husband-killer, who was of a socially prominent clan. The more sensational of the evening papers

---

*Joseph Banks (J. B.) Rhine (1895–1980) was the father of parapsychology, establishing the *Journal of Parapsychology* and forming the Parapsychological Association and also the Foundation for Research on the Nature of Man (FRNM), a precursor to the Rhine Research Center. His experiments "proving" the existence of extrasensory perception and psychokinesis have never been replicated and hence are largely discredited.

---

†"So to speak."

had put Elena Ramirez on the front page, but it wasn't a good
carry-over story—they couldn't make much out of a Hartners'
stock-room girl, and the boy friend wasn't very colorful either.
The conservative papers had played it down, an ordinary back-
street mugging, and by tomorrow the others would relegate
it to the middle pages. They had the socialite, and the freight
yard corpse, besides a couple of visiting dignitaries and the
Russians; and a two-bit mugging in the Commerce Street area,
that just happened to turn into a murder, was nothing very new
or remarkable.

Maneuvering the Ferrari out into Main Street, Mendoza
thought that was a point of view, all right: almost any way
you looked at it, it was an unimportant, uninteresting kill. No
glamor, no complexity, nothing to attract either the sensation-
alists or the detective-fiction fans. In fact, the kind of murder
that happened most frequently... The press had made no connection between Elena Ramirez and Carol Brooks. No, they
weren't interested; but if the cosmic powers had stacked the
deck this time, and that one stayed free to kill again, and again,
eventually some day he would achieve the scare headlines, and
then—*de veras, es lo de siempre,** Mendoza reflected sardonically,
the mixture as before: our stupid, blundering police!

———

Once off the main streets here, away from the blinding gleam of
the used-car lots, the screamer ads plastered along store-fronts,
these were quiet residential streets, middle-class, unremarkable.
Most of the houses neatly maintained, if shabby: most with carefully kept flower plots in front. Along the quiet Sunday sidewalks, dressed-up children on the way to Sunday school, others
not so dressed up running and shouting at play—householders
working in front gardens this clear morning after the rain. This

*"It is really the same as always."

was all Oriental along here, largely Japanese. When he stopped at an intersection a pair of high-school-age girls crossed in front of him—"But honestly it isn't fair, ten whole pages of English Lit, even if it is on the weekend! She's a real fiend for homework—" One had a ponytail, one an Italian cut; their basic uniform of flat shell pumps, billowy cotton skirts and cardigans, differed only in color. At the next corner he turned into Tappan Street; this wasn't the start of it, but the relevant length for him, this side of Washington Boulevard.* He drove slow and idle, as if he'd all the time in the world to waste, wasn't exactly sure where he was heading: and of course he wasn't, essentially. It was a long street and it took him through a variety of backgrounds.

Past rows of frame and stucco houses, lower-middle-class-respectable houses, where the people on the street were Oriental, and then brown and black; there, late-model cars sat in most driveways and the people were mostly dressed up for Sunday. Past bigger, older, shabbier houses with Board-and-Room signs, rank brown grass in patches, and broken sidewalks: dreary courts of semidetached single-story rental units, stucco boxes scabrous for need of paint: black and brown kids in shabbier, even ragged clothes, more raucous in street play. A lot of all that, block after block. Past an intersection where a main street crossed and a Catholic church, a liquor store, a chiropractor's office and a gas station shared the corners. Past the same kind of old, shoddy houses and courts, for many more blocks, but here the people on the street white. Then a corner which marked some long-ago termination of the street: where it continued, across, there were no longer tall old camphorwoods lining it; the parking was bare. The houses were a little newer, a little cleaner: they gave way to solid blocks of smallish apartment buildings, and all this again was settled middle-class, and again the faces in the street black and brown.

---

*Washington Boulevard is a major arterial road in Los Angeles, running east-west for more than twenty-seven miles. Much of South-Central Los Angeles, historically home to the black community, is south of Washington Boulevard.

At the next intersection, he caught the light and sat waiting for it, staring absently at the wooden bench beside the bus-stop sign on the near left corner. Its back bore a faded admonition to Rely on J. Atwood and Son, Morticians, for a Dignified Funeral. There, that night, Carol Brooks had got off the bus on her way home from work, and some time later started down Tappan Street. She had had only three blocks to walk, but she had met—something—on the way, and so she hadn't got home… The car behind honked at him angrily; the light had changed.

Across the intersection, he idled along another block and a half, slid gently into the curb and took his time over lighting a cigarette. Three single-family houses from the corner, there sat two duplexes, frame bungalows just alike, one white and one yellow. They were, or had been, owned by the widowed Mrs. Shadwell who lived in one side of the yellow one. On that September night the left-hand side of the white one had been empty of tenants, the tenants in the other side had been out at a wedding reception, the tenants in the left side of the yellow duplex had been giving a barbecue supper in their back yard, and Mrs. Shadwell, who was deaf, had taken off her hearing aid. So just what had happened along here, as Carol Brooks came by, wasn't very clear; if she'd been accosted, exchanged any talk or argument with her killer, had warning of attack and called for help, there'd been no one to hear. She'd been found just about halfway between the walks leading to the two front doors of the white duplex, at twenty minutes past nine, by a dog-walker from the next block: she had then been dead for between thirty minutes and an hour.

It occurred to Mendoza that he was simply wasting time in the vague superstitious hope that the cosmic powers would tap his shoulder and drop that extra ace into his lap. He tossed his cigarette out the window, which was now by law a misdemeanor carrying a fifty-dollar fine, and drove on a block and a half: glanced at the neat white frame bungalow where Carol

Brooks had lived, and turned left at the next corner. This was a secondary business street, and it marked one of the boundaries: that side Negro, this side white. The streets deteriorated sharply on the white side, he knew, lined with old apartment buildings only just not describable as tenements. He turned left again and wandered back parallel to Tappan, turned again and then again and came to the corner where the bus stopped, past the two duplexes, and drew into the curb in front of the bungalow numbered 2214.

A woman came up the sidewalk from the opposite direction, turned in at the white house, hesitated and glanced at the car, and turned back toward it. Mendoza got out and took off his hat. "Mrs. Demarest. I wondered if you still lived here."

"Why, where else would I be?" She was a tall, slim, straight-backed woman, and had once perhaps been beautiful: the bones of beauty were still there, in her smooth high forehead, delicate regular features, small mouth. Her skin was the color of well-creamed coffee. She was neat, even almost smart, in tailored navy-blue dress and coat, small gold earrings. She might be seventy, she might be older, but age had touched her lightly; her voice was firm, her eyes intelligent. "It's Mr. Mendoza," she said. "Or I should say 'Lieutenant.' You know, if I was a superstitious woman, Lieutenant, I'd say there's more in it than meets the eye, you turning up. Did you want to see me about something?"

"I don't know. There's been another," he said abruptly. "I think the same one."

"Another colored girl?" she asked calmly.

"No. And miles away, over on Commerce Street."

"That one," she said, nodding. "I think you'd best come in, and I'll tell you. It's nothing much, though it's queer—but it's something you didn't hear about before, you see. At first I thought I might write you a letter about it, and then I said to myself"—they were halfway up the walk to the house, and he'd taken the brown-paper bag of groceries from her—"I thought, it's not important, I'd best not trouble you. But as you're here, you might as well hear about it." She had been away from Bermuda half her life, but her tongue still carried the flavor, the broad A's, the interchange of V's and W's, the clipped British vowels. She unlocked the front door and they went into the living-room he remembered, furniture old but originally good and well cared for. "If you'll just fetch that right back to the kitchen, Lieutenant—you'll have a cup of coffee with me, we might as well be comfortable and it's always hot on the back of the stove. Sit down, I'll just tend to the Duke here and then be with you."

The cat surveying him with cold curiosity from the hallway door was a large black neutered tom; he established himself on the kitchen chair opposite Mendoza and continued to stare. "I didn't remember he was the Duke," said Mendoza.

"The Duke of Wellington really, because he always thought so almighty high of himself, you know. We got him Carol's second year in high, and she was doing history about it then. Cats, they're like olives, seem like—either you're crazy about them or you just can't abide them. I remembered you like them. It's why I was out, after his evaporated milk. Fresh he won't look at, and the evaporated he lets set just so long till it's thick the way he fancies it. You see now, he knows I've just poured it, he won't go near. You take milk or sugar?—well, I always take it black too, you get the flavor."

She set the filled cups on the table and sat in the chair across from him. "You'll have missed your granddaughter," he said. It was another absurd superstitious feeling, that if he asked, brought her to the point, it would indeed be nothing at all.

"Well, I do, of course. Sometimes it doesn't seem right that there the Duke should be sitting alive, and her gone. It'd be something to believe in some kind of religion, think there was a God Who'd some reason, some plan. I never came to it somehow, but maybe there is. I've had two husbands and raised six children, and luckier than most in all of them—and you could say I've worked hard. It was a grief to lose my youngest son, that was Carol's dad, but I had to figure I'd five left, and the other grandchildren too. Take it all in all, there's been more good than bad—and what you can't change, you'd best learn to live with content. I enjoy life still, and I don't want to die while I've still my health and my mind, but you know, Lieutenant, I won't be too sorry in a way when the time comes, because I must say I *am* that curious about the afterward part."

"It's a point of view," he agreed amusedly. "So am I now and then, but I'd rather be curious than dead."

She laughed, with a fine gleam of even white teeth. "Ah, you're lucky, you're half my age! But I said I'd something to tell you. It's just a queer sort of thing, maybe doesn't mean much." She sipped and put down her cup. "Maybe you'll remember that that night when Carol was killed, I told you I hadn't been too worried about her being late home, because she'd said something about shopping along Hawke Street, that'd be when she got off the bus. It was a Monday night, and all the stores along there, they stay open till nine Mondays and Fridays. There's a few nice little stores, and it's handy—not so crowded as downtown, and most everything you'd want, drugstore and Woolworth's, besides a Hartners', and a shoe store and a couple of nice independent dress shops, and Mr. Grant at the stationery-and-card place even keeps a little circulating library—and then there's Mrs. Breen's."

He remembered the name vaguely; after a moment he said, "The woman who had a stroke."

"That's right. She's had that little shop a long while, and sometimes you find things there that're, you know, unusual, different from the big stores. You mightn't remember, no reason you should, but on the one side she's got giftware as they call it—china figures and fancy ash trays and vases and such—and on the other she's got babies' and children's things. Real nice things, with handwork on them, the clothes, and reasonable too. You'll remember that your men asked around in all the shops if Carol had been in that night, to get some idea of the time and all. And that was the very night Mrs. Breen had a stroke, so you couldn't ask her if Carol'd been in there, and it didn't seem important because you found out that she'd been in the drugstore and a couple of other places."

"Yes—nothing unusual anywhere, no one speaking to her, and she didn't mention anything out of the way to the clerks who waited on her."

"That's so. It didn't seem as if Mrs. Breen could've told any more. She was alone in her place, you know, and all right as could be when her daughter come at nine or a bit before, to help her close up and drive her home. It was while they were locking up she had her stroke, poor thing, and they took her off to hospital and she's been a long while getting back on her feet. Well, Lieutenant—let me hot up your coffee—what I'm getting to is this. It went out of my mind at the time, and when I thought of it, I hadn't the heart to bother about it, didn't seem important somehow—and Mrs. Breen was still in the hospital and her daughter'd closed up the shop. It'd have meant asking her, Mrs. Robbins I mean, to go all through the accounts and so on, and with her so worried and living clear the other side of town too, I just let it go."

"You thought Carol had been in and bought something there?"

"It was for Linda Sue," she said, and the troubled look in her eyes faded momentarily. "My first great-grandchild, see, my granddaughter May—that's Carol's cousin, May White—Linda Sue's her little girl. May and Carol were much of an age, and chummed together, and Carol was just crazy about Linda Sue. It was along in June, I remember, Carol saw this in Mrs. Breen's, and she wanted to get it for Linda Sue's birthday in October. She told me about it then, and if I thought it was foolish, that much money, I kept still on it—she wanted to get it, and it was her money. Twenty dollars it was, and she asked Mrs. Breen if she could pay a bit on it every week or so. Mrs. Breen's obliging like that, and she said it was all right, but she left it in the window for people to see, case anybody wanted one like it she could order another."

The Duke, who had been drowsing between them, suddenly woke up and began to wash himself vigorously. Mrs. Demarest finished her coffee and sighed. "It was a doll, Lieutenant—and while that seems like an awful price for a doll, I must say it was a special one. It'd be nearly as big as Linda Sue herself, and it was made of some stuff, you know, that looked like real flesh—and it had real hair, gold hair it was, that you could curl different ways, and it had on a pink silk dress with hand smocking, and silk underwear with lace, and there was a little velvet cape and velvet slippers, rose color. Well, Carol was buying it like that. I wasn't sure to a penny how much she still owed on it, up to that night. And of course Monday wasn't a payday for her, I didn't think it was likely she'd stopped in at Mrs. Breen's that night, because she'd do that the day she got paid, you see. It was just that she *had* paid on it, but as I say, way things were, I didn't bother about going ahead with it. There was time to sort it out, Mrs. Breen and Mrs. Robbins are both honest. I got other things for Linda Sue's birthday, and once in a while I just said to myself, some day I'd best ask about it, straighten it out with Mrs. Breen.

"Well, just last week Mrs. Breen came into her shop again. She was sick quite awhile, and then up-and-down like at her daughter's, and now she's better, but not to be alone any more, and she's selling off what stock she has and going out of business. So I went round, last Thursday it was, to ask about Carol's doll.

"And Mrs. Breen says that Carol came in that night and paid all the rest she owed, and took the doll away with her. She remembers it clear—the stroke didn't affect her mind, she's a bit slower but all *there*. She didn't hear about Carol for quite awhile, naturally, being sick and all, and of course when she did, she naturally thought everyone knew about the doll. Because, you remember—"

"Yes," he said. He remembered: in the glare of the spotlights, the stiffening disfigured corpse and the several small parcels scattered on the sidewalk. A card of bobby pins, two spools of thread from the dime store: a magazine, a bottle of aspirin, a candy bar from the drugstore: an anniversary card from the stationery store. He looked at Mrs. Demarest blankly. "That's very odd," he said. "She *had* it—the woman's sure?"

She nodded vigorously. "She showed me the accounts book, Lieutenant. There's the date, and while there's no time put down, it's the next-to-last entry that night, and she says the last customer came in was a woman she knows, a Mrs. Ratchett, and it was just before nine. She thinks Carol came in about eight-thirty, a few minutes before maybe. Probably it was the last place Carol stopped, you see—nobody else remembers her with a big parcel. She paid Mrs. Breen seven dollars and forty-six cents, all she still owed, and she didn't have the doll gift-wrapped because she wanted to show it to May and me first. And she took it with her." Mrs. Demarest held out her hands, measuring. "Like that it'd have been—a big stout cardboard box, white, a good yard or more long, and maybe eighteen inches wide and a foot deep. Heavy, too. And inside, along with the doll, three yards of pink silk ribbon and the tissue paper for wrapping it, and a birthday card. The whole thing was wrapped up in white paper and string, and Mrs. Breen made a little loop on top for her to carry it by."

They looked at each other. "But that's *very* damned odd indeed," he said softly. "Not much time there, you know. She was dead by nine, at the latest. It's possible that someone else came by and found her first, didn't want to get involved, but picked up the biggest parcel, maybe the only one he noticed in the dark, on the chance that it was worth something. But you'd think, in that case, he—or she, of course—might have taken time to snatch up the handbag too, after cash... and that hadn't been touched, the strap was still on her arm."

"I guess you'd better hear how she came to get the money, not that it matters. One of the girls worked at the hotel with her came to see me, two-three days afterward—a nice girl she was, Nella Foss—to say how sorry they all were, and give me a little collection the hotel people'd taken up. They thought maybe I'd rather have the money, you know, instead of flowers for the funeral—it was real thoughtful of them. Well, Nella said that very afternoon there'd been a lady just checked out of the hotel came back after a valuable ring she'd left, and Carol'd already found it, doing out the room you know, and turned it in. And the lady gave her five dollars as a present. I expect Carol decided right off she'd finish paying for the doll with it. At the time, I thought of course what was in her purse, three-eighty-four it was, was what she'd had left out of the five."

"Yes... but so little time! Do we say it was the murderer took it away? Just that?—not a finger on her handbag after cash? And why?"

"Now, that I couldn't say," said Mrs. Demarest, placidly. "It's queer, certainly. I'd say the same as you—well, I guess detecting things is just a matter of using common sense and reasoning things out. I suppose somebody might think there was something valuable in a big parcel like that, and steal it just on the chance—but a thief who'd do that, it's just not logical he wouldn't take the handbag too, at least rummage through it." She cocked her head at him, and her brown eyes were bright as a sparrow's. "Lieutenant, would you think I'm a woolgathering silly old woman—you're too polite ever *say* it, if you did—if I said, Maybe whoever took it knew right well what was in that parcel?"

"You'd say whoever killed her? For a doll—"

"I don't know that. Maybe somebody else, first—or afterward. But I can tell you something else. I've studied about it, and I went back to ask Mrs. Breen a couple other things. I said she'd left the doll in the window, didn't I? Well, I go past there three-four times a week, up to the market, and I do think I'd've noticed if that doll had been gone out of the window right *after* Carol was killed, and put two and two together, and asked then. But Mrs. Breen took it out of the window about a week before, so I didn't expect it there, if you see what I mean. And she says now, reason she did is that she had notice from the factory or whatever that made them, that they weren't making this particular doll anymore—so she didn't want to show it, and have to disappoint anybody wanted one. And, this is what I'm getting at, the morning of that day Carol was killed, there was a woman came into the store and wanted to buy that doll. She wanted it real bad, Mrs. Breen said she was almost crying that she couldn't have that one or get Mrs. Breen to order another, and she stayed a long while trying to argue Mrs. Breen into selling her the one Carol was buying."

An extra ace to pad his hand, Mendoza had hoped: but could it be? Such a small thing—such a meaningless thing! "Did she know this woman?"

"She'd seen her before. It was a white woman, Lieutenant, from over across Hunter Avenue. She couldn't call the name to mind, but she thinks she's got it written down somewhere because the woman made her copy down her name and address and promise to find out couldn't she get a doll like that *somewhere*. You'd best see Mrs. Breen and ask, if you think it means anything at all... She thinks she remembers it was a middling-long sort of name, and started with an L."

Seven

Mendoza felt rather irritated at the cosmic powers; if they intended to direct a little luck his way, they might have been more explicit. Still, one never knew: it might lead to something.

The gift shop was closed, of course; he would come back tomorrow. And it was possible that this Breen woman had simply told a lie to avoid having to pay back twelve or thirteen dollars; but such a relatively small amount—and Mrs. Demarest was emphatic on assurance of her honesty. Judge for himself...

He drove tedious miles across the city, cursing the Sunday traffic, to Alison Weir's apartment, and was late by some minutes. She opened the door promptly and told him so, taking up her bag, joining him in the hall. She was in green and tan today, plain dark-green wool dress, high-necked: coat, shoes, bag all warm beige, and copper earrings, a big copper brooch.

He settled her in the car and sliding under the wheel said, "Unsubtle, that dress. Every woman with red hair automatically fills her wardrobe with green."

"It's only fair to tell you," said Alison amiably, "that like practically all women I *detest* men who know anything about women's clothes."

"As intelligent people we should always try to overcome

these illogical prejudices." He had not moved to start the engine; he smiled at her. "You know, it would be regrettable if you were lying to me, Miss Weir."

The little amusement died from her green-hazel eyes meeting his. "Do you think I've lied to you? Why? I—"

"No, I don't think so. But Teresa Ramirez says her sister meant to tell you about this 'queer boy,' and yet you don't know quite as much as she told Teresa."

"I told you about that. She probably did mean to tell me a lot more, but I took up her consultation time with lecturing her. You can't regret it any more than I do, Lieutenant! If I'd listened to her—"

"Yes," said Mendoza. He'd turned sideways to look at her, his right arm along the seat-back; he laughed abruptly and slid his hand down to brush her shoulder gently, reaching to the ignition. "I'll tell you why I'm not just a hundred percent sure—I mustn't be. Because I'm working this on a preconceived idea, and that's dangerous. I find something that doesn't fit, I'm tempted to think, let it go, it's not important—because I don't want to prove my beautiful theory wrong. Just now and then I *am* wrong, and it's not an experience I enjoy."

"I see. I also dislike egotistical men."

"*Mi gatita roja,*⃰ what you mean is that you dislike the ones honest enough to admit to vanity—nobody walking on two legs isn't an egotist. And you should have more common sense than to talk so rudely to a rich man."

"*Are* you?"

"I am. None of my doing—in case you were thinking of bribes from gangsters—my grandfather was shrewd enough to buy up quite a lot of land which turned out to be just where the city was expanding—office buildings, you know, and hotels, and department stores—all crazy for land to build on. And fortunately I was his only grandson. It was a great shock

⃰"My red kitten."

to everybody, there he was for years in a thirty-dollar-a-month apartment, saying we couldn't afford this and that, damning the gas company as robbers if the bill was over two dollars, and buying secondhand clothes—my God, he once got a hundred dollars out of me on the grounds of family duty, to pay a hospital bill—and me still in the rookie training school and in debt for my uniforms! And then when he died it all came out. My grandmother hasn't recovered from the shock yet—she's still furious at him, and that was nearly fifteen years ago."

"Oh. Why?"

"For fifty-eight years she'd been nagging at him to stop his gambling—she'd been telling him for fifty-eight years that gamblers are all wastrels, stealing the food out of their families' mouths to throw away, and they always die without a penny to bless themselves. And that's where he got his capital—his winnings. And to add insult to injury—because if she'd known about it, she'd have found some way to save face and also, being a woman, something else to nag him about—he managed to get the last word by dying before she found it out. Frankly, I think myself it wasn't all luck, the old boy wasn't above keeping a few high cards up his sleeve, but you know the one about the gift horse. And unfortunately," added Mendoza, sliding neatly ahead of an indignant bus to get in the right-turn lane, "by then I'd got into the habit of earning an honest living, and I've never cured myself."

"Well, it's an *original* approach to a girl," said Alison thoughtfully. "Such a fascinating subject too—I've always been so interested in money, if only I'd had the chance to study it oftener I might have developed real talent for it. But I must say, I should think you'd bolster up your ego more by doing the King Cophetua business,* instead of practically offering a bribe. Not at *all* subtle."

---

*King Cophetua was a legendary African king who spied a beggar woman out his window, fell in love at first sight, and married her. The tale was preserved in poetry and art and merged into the Pygmalion myth of the transformation of a statue into a woman, ultimately emerging as *Pygmalion* by George Bernard Shaw (and, of course, the musical *My Fair Lady*).

"I'm always loved for myself alone. And why? *Es claro*—a woman of high principle like you, she's afraid to be taken for a gold digger, so she starts out being very standoffish. She's so busy convincing me she's not interested in my money, *vaya*, she's never on guard against my charm."

"Ah, the double play. I keep forgetting you're an egotist. But what about the stupid ones?—the ones like Elena, all bleached curls and giggles and gold ankle chains? The ones those tired middle-aged businessmen—"

"*¡Vaya por Dios!* I never go near such females, except in the way of work. There's no credit to the marksman in an easy target."

"Or to the wolf who catches the smallest lamb? I see what you mean."

"So I'll let you have the last word. You'll do me a favor tomorrow—"

"What?" She regarded him warily.

Mendoza grinned at her. "Don't sound so suspicious, I don't operate so crude and sudden as that! Look, I want you to ask all your girls if Elena said anything at all to them about this staring man. Don't tell them much, don't lead them—a couple of them might make up this or that to be important—but you'll be more apt to get something helpful out of them if anything's there to be got. Official questioning might encourage them to romanticize."

"Oh, well, certainly I'll do that, I meant to anyway. Yes, I think you're right about that."

At headquarters he piloted her upstairs to his office. She looked around curiously. "What exactly is the procedure? I've never done this before."

"I've made a rough draft, here, of the substance of what you told me. Just look it over and see if you want to change or add anything, and then we'll get it typed for you to sign. And what do *you* want?" he added as Hackett wandered in after them. "I thought you were safely occupied for the afternoon."

---

*Literally, "Go for God!" meaning something like, "For God's sake!"

"*Una expectativa vana,*"* said Hackett, spreading his hands. "Kids! It's the damnedest thing, they'll be budding Einsteins at twelve, but the minute they hit their teens I swear to God they all turn into morons. You'd think they were blind and deaf." His eyes were busy on Alison.

"It's a phenomenon known as puberty," said Mendoza. "Nothing?"

"*Nada.* You goin' to remember your manners, or do I count as the hired help around here?"

"Miss Weir—the cross I am given to bear, Sergeant Hackett."

"The brawn," said Alison wisely, nodding at him. "I knew you must have somebody to do the real work."

"And she has brains too," said Hackett admiringly. "You got a visitor, Luis, before I forget. That Ramirez girl." He jerked a thumb.

"Oh?" Mendoza got up. "You'll excuse me, Miss Weir—if this cave-man type gets obstreperous, you've only to scream."

Standing there by the clerk's empty desk in the anteroom, before she spoke, she wasn't this century at all. Black cotton dress too long, the shabby brown coat over her arm, and a black woolen shawl held around her, both hands clasping it at her breast. No make-up: she'd come straight from church, from late mass, probably. This large official place had somewhat subdued her.

"You wanted to see me, Miss Ramirez? Sit down here, won't you?"

"Oh, thanks, but it won't take long, what I come for. I wasn't sure you'd be here, Sunday an' all, I thought I'd ask could I leave a note for you—" She took a breath. "There was some of your guys come with a warrant, to look all through Elena's things— Mama, she just had a 'fit, she don't understand about these things so good—"

"I'm sorry it troubled her. We have to do that, you know."

---

*"A vain expectation," meaning "a lost cause."

"Sure, I know, it don't matter, we haven't nothing to hide."

He wondered: the visiting uncle? The faint defiance over the honesty in her round brown eyes looked convincing. He thought, whether they caught the shifty Tío Tomás at anything or not, that was a wrong one; but he also thought the Ramirez family hadn't an inkling of that. He waited; she had something else to say. She fidgeted with the shawl, burst out a little nervously, "I—I thought of something else, Lieutenant, that's why I come."

"Yes?"

"I don't want to sound like I'm telling you your own business, see, but—well, you *are* sort of looking into that Palace skating place, aren't you? I mean—"

"We are. Why?"

"I don't know nothing about it," she said. "I never been there myself, and anyway I guess this don't have anything to do with it, I mean whoever runs it, you know. But I got to thinking, after you asked me yesterday about any guy bothering Elena, I tried to remember just what she did say, if there was anything I hadn't told you. And I remembered one more thing she said. It was when she was talking about this fellow watching her, she said, 'He gets on my nerves, honest, I nearly fell down a couple times.'"

"Now that's very interesting," said Mendoza.

"See, she must've meant it was at the rink she saw him. Once, anyways. Because where else would being nervous make her almost fall down? I—"

"Yes, of course." And there were a number of possibilities there; a little imagination would produce a dozen different ideas. He thought about some of them (Ehrlich, the attendants, the other kids) as he thanked the girl for coming in. Alison came out of his office with Hackett and was sympathetic, friendly with Teresa, asking conventionally about the funeral. The girl was a little stiff, responding, using more care with her manners and grammar.

"Well, I—I guess that's all I wanted tell you, Lieutenant, I better get home—"

Alison sent Mendoza a glance he missed and another at Hackett which connected; he said he was going that way, be glad to drive her home, and gave Alison a mock-reproachful backward look, shepherding Teresa off.

"Your draft's quite all right. Hey, wake up, I said—"

"Yes," said Mendoza. "Is it? Good." He summoned one of the stenos on duty, took Alison back to his office to wait, gave her a chair and cigarette but no conversation. She sat quietly, watching him with a slight smile, looking round the room; when the typed pages were brought in she signed obediently where she was told and announced meekly that she *could* get home by herself.

Mendoza said, "Don't be foolish." But he was mostly silent on the drive across town. When he drew into the curb at the apartment building, he cut the motor, didn't move immediately. "Tell me something. Did you like dolls when you were a little girl?"

"Against my better judgment you do intrigue me. Most little girls do."

He grunted. "Ever know any little boys who did?"

"When they're very young, otherwise not. Though I believe there are some, but they can't be very normal little boys. The psychiatrists—"

"I beg you, *not* the doubletalk about Id and Ego and Superego. Especially not about infantile sexuality and the traumatic formation of the homosexual personality. *Esto queda entre los dos.* Just between the two of us, I find a most suggestive resemblance between the Freudians and those puritanical old maids who put the worst interpretation on everything—and with such damned smug self-satisfaction into the bargain."

She laughed. "Oh, I'm with you every time! But what's all this about dolls?"

He got out a cigarette, looked at it without flicking his lighter. "Suppose you're taking one of those word-associations tests, what do you say to that?—*doll.*"

"Why, I guess—*little girls.* Why?"

"And me too," he said. "Which is what makes it difficult. Well, never mind—inquisition over for today." He lit the cigarette and turned to her with a smile. "You'll have dinner with me tomorrow night, tell me what you get out of your girls, if anything."

Alison cocked her auburn head at him. "I seem to remember you said you didn't mix business and pleasure. Do I infer I'm absolved already?"

"I'm always making these impossible resolutions." He got out, went round and opened the door for her. "Black," he said, gesturing, "something elegant, and *decolleté.* Maybe pearls. Seven o'clock."

She got out of the car, leisurely and graceful, and tucked her bag under her arm; she said, "Charm isn't the word. But I have heard—speaking of the Freudians—that there are some women who really enjoy being dominated. Seven o'clock it is, and I'll wear what I damned well please, Lieutenant Luis Mendoza!"

"*Mi gatita roja,*" he said, smiling.

"And," said Alison, "I am *not* your little red kitten, you—you—*¡tú, macho insolente!*"

"What language for a lady. Until tomorrow." He grinned at her straight back; there was—he was aware—a certain promise in being called an insolent male animal, by a female like Alison.

———

It sat on the corner of Matson and San Rafael, a block up and a block over from Commerce and Humboldt. Not really much of a walk home for Elena, a quarter of an hour by daylight: down San Rafael to Commerce, to Humboldt, across the empty lot and down a block to Foster where Humboldt made a jog to bypass a gloomy little cul-de-sac misleadingly called a court: another block to Main, another to Liggitt and half a block more to home. Little more than half a mile, but that could be a long way at night. Main was neon lights and crowds up to midnight anyway, but these other streets were dark and lonely.

It was a big barn of a building. Matson Street wasn't residential, but strung with small warehouses, small businesses that must permanently balance on the edge of insolvency—rug cleaning, said the faded signs, tools sharpened, speedy shoe repair, cleaning & dyeing—and in between, the secretive warehouses unlabeled or reticent with WHOLESALE PARTS, INC.—MASTERSON BROS.—ASSOCIATED INDUSTRIES. At Matson and San Rafael, there was a graveyard for old cars on one corner, with a high iron fence around it (SECONDHAND PARTS CHEAP), and warehouses on two other corners, and on the fourth the Palace Roller Rink. The building wasn't flush to the sidewalk like the warehouses, but set back fifteen or twenty feet, to provide off-street parking on two sides.

Mendoza parked there, among six or eight other cars: mostly old family sedans, a couple of worked-over hot-rods. It was ten past four, a good time for the experiment he had in mind. He fished up a handful of change from his pocket, picked out a quarter, a dime, and a nickel, and walked up to the entrance.

There were big double doors fastened back, but at this time of year, the place facing north, not much light fell into the foyer. That was perhaps ten feet wide, three times as long up to the restroom doors at either end. There was a Coke-dispensing freezer and a big trash basket under a wall dispenser for paper cups. In the middle of the foyer was a three-sided plywood enclosure with a narrow counter bearing an ancient cash register; and inside, on a high stool with a back, sat Ehrlich the proprietor, a grossly fat man in the late sixties, bald bullet-shaped head descending to several rolls of fat front and rear, pudgy hands clasped over a remarkable paunch: wrinkled khaki shirt and pants, no tie. Ehrlich, peacefully drowsing— still, very likely, digesting a solid noon dinner which had ended with several glasses of beer. Mendoza surveyed him with satisfaction, walked quietly up and laid the silver on the counter. The fat man roused with a little grunt, scooped it up and punched the register, and produced from a box under the counter a sleazy paper ticket, slid it across. Mendoza picked it up and passed by.

At the narrower door into the main part of the building, he glanced back: Ehrlich's head was again bowed over his clasped hands. So there we are, thought Mendoza. The man had raised his eyes just far enough to check the money: if the exact change was laid out, a gorilla in pink tights could walk by him without notice.

The second door led Mendoza into more than semidarkness. It was a rectangle within a rectangle: a fifteen-foot-wide strip of dark around all four sides of the skating floor. That was a good hundred and fifty feet long, a little more than half as wide, of well-laid hardwood like a dance floor. There was an iron pipe railing enclosing it, with two or three gaps in each side for access to the occasional hard wooden benches, scattered groups of folding wooden chairs, along the four dark borders. A big square skylight, several unshaded electric bulbs around it, poured light directly down on the skating floor, but not enough to reach beyond: anywhere off the edge of that floor it was dark. The effect was that of a theater, about that quality of light, looking from the borders to the big floor.

Straight ahead from the single entrance, at the gap in the rail there, sat one of the attendants, sidewise in a chair to catch the light on his magazine. Beside him was a card table, a cardboard carton on it and another on the floor; those would hold the skates. Not just the skates, Mendoza remembered from the statements taken: flat shoes with skates already fastened on—something to do with the insurance, because as Hayes (or was it Murphy) had put it, otherwise some of these dumb girls would come in with four-inch heels on. As Elena had, he remembered.

It was shoddy, it was dirty, a place of garish light and dense shadow, of drafts and queer echoes from its very size. No attempt was evident to make it attractive or comfortable: the sole amenities, if you could so call them, appeared to be the Coke machine and, at the opposite side of the floor, an old nickel jukebox which was presently emitting a tired rendition of "The Beautiful Blue Danube." And yet the fifteen or twenty teenagers on the floor seemed to be enjoying themselves, mostly skating in couples round and round—one pair in the center showing off, with complicated breakaways and dance steps—half a dozen in single file daring the hazards lined down the far side, a little artificial hill, a low bar-jump. Those girls shrieked simulated terror, speeding down the sharp drop; the boys jeered, affected nonchalance. It was all very innocent and juvenile—depressingly so, Mendoza reflected sadly from the vantage point of his nearly forty years.

But he hadn't come here to philosophize on the vagaries of adolescence... If you went straight down to the attendant, to give up your ticket and acquire your skates, you would be noticed; otherwise, he could easily miss seeing you. Mendoza had wandered a little way to the side from the door, and stood with his back to the wall; he was in deep shadow and he'd made no noise. He stood there until his eyes had adjusted to the darkness, to avoid colliding with anything, and moved on slowly. He knew now that it was possible to come in here without being noticed, but could anyone count on it five times out of five? There would be times Ehrlich was wider awake, for one thing.

He sat down in a chair midway from the railing, twenty feet from the attendant. In five minutes neither the man nor any of the skaters took the slightest notice of him. He got up, drifted back to the wall, and began a tour of the borders.

When he got round to the opposite side of the floor, he made an interesting discovery. In the corner there a small square closet was partitioned off, with a door fitted to it. He tried the door and it gave to his hand with a little squeak. He risked a brief beam from his pencil-flash: rude shelving, cleaning materials, an ancient can of floor wax, mops and pails. Hackett was quite right; nobody had disturbed the dust in here for a long time. He shut the door gently and went on down the rear width of the building.

The jukebox was never silent long; it seemed to have a repertoire only of waltzes, and now for the third time was rendering, in all senses of the word, "Let Me Call You Sweetheart."

He came to the far corner and with mild gratification found another closet and another door. "At a guess, the fuse boxes," he murmured, and eased the door open. A quick look with the flash interested him so much that he stepped inside, pulled the door shut after him, and swept the flash around for a good look.

Fuse boxes, yes: also, of course, the meter: and a narrow outside door. For the meter reader, obviously: very convenient. He tried it and found himself looking out to a narrow unpaved alley between this building and the warehouse next to it.

And does it mean anything at all? he wondered to himself. He retreated, and now he did not care if he was seen or not; he kept the flash on, the beam pointed downward... How very right Hackett had been: this place had not been so much as swept for years. But full of eddying drafts as it was, you couldn't expect footprints to stay in the dust, however thick. He worked back and forth between the rail and the wall, dodging the chairs. He had no idea at all what he was looking for, and also was aware that anything he might find would either be completely irrelevant or impossible to prove relevant to the case.

Now, of course, he had been noticed; he heard the attendant's chair scrape back, and a few of the skaters had drifted over to the rail this side, curious. He didn't look up from the little spotlight of the flash: he followed it absorbedly back and forth.

"Hey, what the hell you up to, anyway?" The attendant came heavy-footed, shoving chairs out of his path. "Who—"

"Stop where you are, for God's sake!" exclaimed Mendoza suddenly. "I'm police—you'll have my credentials in a minute, but don't come any closer."

"Police—oh, well—"

And Mendoza said aloud to himself, "So here it is. But I don't believe it, it's impossible." And to that he added a rueful, "And what in the name of all the devils in hell does it mean?"

In the steady beam of the flash, it lay there mute and perhaps meaningless: a scrap of a thing, three inches long, a quarter-inch wide: a little strip of dainty pink lace, so fine that it might once have been the trimming on the lingerie of a very special doll.

———

Ehrlich went on saying doggedly, "My place didn't have nothing to do with it." That door, well, sure, the inside one oughta be kept locked, it usually was—but neither he nor the attendants would swear to having checked it for months, all three maintaining it was the other fellow's responsibility. Mendoza found them tiresome. Hackett and Dwyer, summoned by phone, if they didn't altogether agree with Ehrlich were less than enthusiastic over Mendoza's find; Hackett said frankly it didn't mean a damned thing. He listened to the story of Carol Brooks' doll and said it still didn't mean a damned thing.

"I don't want to disillusion you, but I've heard rumors that real live dolls sometimes wear underwear with pink lace on— and just like you say, it *is* nice and dark along here. Not havin' such a pure mind as you, I can think of a couple of dandy reasons—"

"And such elegant amenities for it!" said Mendoza sarcastically. "A wooden bench a foot wide, or a pair of folding chairs! I may be overfastidious, but I ask you!"

"There's a classic tag line you oughta remember: It's wonderful anywhere."*

"So maybe it doesn't mean anything. Nevertheless, we'll hang onto it, and I want a sketch of this place, showing that door and the exact spot this was found."

"O.K., will do." There was always a lot of labor expended on such jobs, in a thing like this, that turned out to have been unnecessary; but it couldn't be helped. And in case something turned out to be relevant, they had to keep the D.A.'s office in mind, document the evidence.

"And what happened to you?" added Mendoza, turning on Dwyer, who was sporting a patch bandage taped across one eye.

Dwyer said aggrievedly he ought to've run the guy in for obstructing an officer. All he'd been doing was try to find out more about that Browne girl who'd found the body—as per orders. First he'd got the rough side of her landlady's tongue— the girl wasn't home—for asking a few ordinary little questions, like did the girl ever bring men home, or get behind in the rent, and so on—you'd have thought she was the girl's ma, the way she jumped on him—if the police didn't have anything better to do than come round insulting decent women—! She's still yakking at him about that when this guy shows up, who turns out to be some friend of the girl's, and before Dwyer can show his badge, the guy damns him up and down for a snooper and hauls off and—"Me, Lieutenant! It was a fluke punch, he caught me off balance—"

---

*There is a story, perhaps apocryphal, about Captain "Pete" Olmsted of the USS *Arizona*. Sometime in the late 1930s, Olmsted granted ten days' leave to a sailor to get married and enjoy a honeymoon. When the sailor cabled the ship to ask for an extension of the leave, he wrote: "Request five days extension of leave. It's wonderful here." Olmsted reportedly replied, "It's wonderful anywhere. Request refused. Rejoin the ship." Ken Jones and Hubert Kelly Jr., *Admiral Arleigh (31-Knot) Burke: The Story of a Fighting Sailor* (Philadelphia: Chilton Books, 1965), 69.

"That's your story," said Hackett.

"I swear to—Me, walking into one off a guy I could give four inches and thirty pounds—and his name turns out to be Joe Carpaccio at that!"

"So now you've provided the comic relief, what did you get?"

"Not a damn thing but the shiner. Except she's only lived there three months or so. But how could she be anything to do with it, Lieutenant?"

"I don't think she is, but no harm getting her last address."

"Well, that was why—"

"Let me give him all the news," said Hackett. "You take the car and go on back, send Clawson over to do a sketch. And then go home and nurse that eye, you've had enough excitement for one day." Dwyer said gratefully he'd do that, he had the hell of a headache and he must be getting old, let anything like that happen. Hackett said, "Let's sit down. I've got a couple of little things for you. First, Browne. I was bright enough to ask for her last address when we took her formal statement—let her think it was a regulation of some kind—thought it might be useful. And you might say it was. She gave one, but it turned out to be nonexistent. Which is why I sent Bert to sniff around some more."

"That's a queer one," said Mendoza. "You think it's anything for us?"

Hackett considered. "It doesn't smell that way to me, no. She struck me as an honest girl, and sensible too, which means it's not likely she's mixed into anything illegal. But they say everybody's got something to hide. We might trace her back, sure, but I think all we'd find would be the kind of thing innocent people get all hot and bothered about hiding—an illegitimate baby or a relative in the nut house, or maybe she's run away from an alcoholic husband. I think it'd be a waste of time myself, but you're the boss."

"It might be just as well to find out," said Mendoza slowly.

"In a thing like this, any loose end sticking out of the tangle, take hold and pull—maybe it isn't connected to the main knot, or maybe it is—you can't know until you follow it in."

"O.K., I got more for you." The brief flare of the match as he lit a new cigarette brought some looks his way again. The kids on the floor were more interested in them than skating, now gathering in little groups, slow-moving, to whisper excitedly about it; some of them would have known Elena.

Mendoza stared out at them absently, listening to Hackett. It was now just about thirty-three hours since the body had been found; a lot of routine spadework had kept a lot of men busy in that time. A dozen formal statements had been taken, from the Ramirez family, from three or four of the kids present here on Friday night, from Ehrlich and the two attendants, from the Wades and their visiting neighbor. A great many other people had been questioned, and of course written reports had been turned in on most of this and a new case-file started by the office staff. Again, as six months before, routine enquiry was being made into all recently released or escaped mental patients, and the present whereabouts of persons with records of similar violent assaults. The official machinery had ground elsewhere, arranging for the coroner's inquest... As inevitably happened, crime had touched the lives of many innocent people, had grouped together an incongruous assortment of individuals whose private lives had in some part been invaded, you could say—if incidentally and with benevolent motive.

And—he finally stopped fingering the cigarette he'd got out five minutes ago, and lit it—he would offer odds that if, as, and when they caught up with this one, it would turn out to be one of the many homicides any police officer had seen, which need never have happened if someone had used a little common sense, or more self-control, or hadn't been a little too greedy or vain or possessive or impatient.

Like Mrs. Demarest, he sometimes felt it would be nice to

believe there was a master plan, that some reason for all this existed. He disapproved on principle of anything so disorderly as blind fate.

"After telling you you're chasin' rainbows," Hackett was saying, "I'll give you a little more confirmation. I saw the Wade boy again, and he says maybe there was such a guy, Elena mentioned it to him. Twice. He thinks the first time was about a week ago, but they were out together two nights running and he won't swear which it was—they came here both nights. Anyway, she asked him did he see the guy sitting there at the side staring at her all the time—"

"Here," said Mendoza, sitting up. "Right here? So—"

"Don't run to get a warrant. The boy says he looked, and there was somebody sitting where she said, but he couldn't see what he looked like in the dark, just that there was somebody there. He didn't pay much attention, because he thought it was just one of the other kids, and Elena was imagining things—'like girls do,' he said—when she said it was the same guy she'd seen in here before, and that he never took his eyes off her. You'll be happy to know that Ricky also came to this conclusion because he didn't see how she could recognize a face that far off, in this light—he couldn't. He wears glasses for driving and movies, and he didn't have them on, never wears them in here on account of the danger of breakage."

"*¡Fuegos del infierno!*"* exclaimed Mendoza violently. "Of course, of course!"

"Go on listening, it gets better. He says Elena told him she'd seen the guy here five or six times, always in about the same spot, but Ricky thought then she'd maybe seen a couple of different kids, different times, and imagined the rest. O.K. On Friday night, when they first got here, she looked, and he wasn't there. But later on, all of a sudden she spotted him, and made Ricky look, and there he was—or there somebody was. Now,

---

*An unusual expression—"fires of hell!"—idiosyncratic to Mendoza (or Linington)!

mind you, just like her sister, Ricky didn't think she was afraid of this fellow, that there was anything like that to it. If he had, if she'd acted that way, all the people she mentioned it to would've thought of it right off, and I read it myself that she started out being kind of flattered and annoyed at once, which would be natural, and then just annoyed. Because there was something 'funny' about him. So, when she spotted him again Friday night, she acted so worried about it that Ricky decided to get a closer look, to watch for the guy again, if you follow me. Elena said he'd showed up so sudden it was like magic, one time she looked and no guy, and about three seconds later she happened to look again and there he was—"

"Yes, of course. So?"

"So then, finish. Before Ricky gets over to take a close look, Papa comes in breathing righteous wrath and yanks him out."

This time Mendoza didn't swear, merely shut his eyes.

"And if you're still interested, Smith has tagged the Ramirez uncle visiting what is probably a cat-house* on Third—at least the address rang a bell, and I checked with Prince in Vice—he pricked up his ears and said we'd closed it twice, and he was glad to know somebody had opened up again, they'll look into it. After that Ramirez took a bus way across town to treat himself to a couple of drinks at a place called the Maison du Chat, on Wilshire. Which Smith thought was sort of funny because it's a very fancy layout where you get nicked a dollar and a half for a Scotch highball, and six dollars for a steak because it's in French on the menu."

"I don't give one damn about Ramirez's taste in women, let Prince look into that. The other, yes, we'll follow it up—find out what you can about it, it may be a drop for a wholesaler. If anything definite shows up, throw it at Narcotics then and let them take over."

"I'm ahead of you. I got Higgins and Farnsworth on it. All

---

*A brothel. The term "cat," meaning a prostitute, can be traced to the fifteenth century.

they got so far is the owner's name, which is Nicholas Dimitrios." Hackett dropped his cigarette and put a careful heel on it. "Just what's your idea about all this, anyway?—dolls, yet! I don't see you've got much to get hold of."

"¡*Me lo cuenta a mí!*—you're telling me! But I'll tell you how I see it happening. Somewhere around here is our lunatic—and don't ask me what kind he is—nor I won't even guess why he finds a back way into this hellhole and gets a kick out of watching these kids on skates. It makes a better story if you say he was following Elena. Anyway, here he is, and nobody else seems to have noticed him particularly. Neither of the attendants has much occasion to come down to this end of the floor, and if any of the kids noticed him, they took him for one of themselves. And about that, *de paso,*ˍ I think we can deduce that he's a fairly young man. Elena called him a boy, and the odds are an older man would have been noticed by others in here, would have stood out—as it is, I think he was seen, casually, by some of the kids, and accepted as one of them. On the other hand, he seems to have taken some care not to be noticed much, sitting back against the wall—" Mendoza shrugged. "It's pretty even, maybe, but I think the balance goes to show he's fairly young. All right. She had seen him at least once elsewhere, with another boy or several others, one of whom is named Danny—"

"All of which is very secondhand evidence."

"Don't push me. He was here on Friday night, he saw her leave alone. Evidently he hadn't made any attempt before to approach her, speak to her, and I think he did then because he saw her boy friend taken out and thought this was his chance. He followed her, using his private door, so Ehrlich and the attendants didn't notice him leave. So he had to walk round the building, which put him just far enough behind her that he didn't catch up for a block or so. Finish. And I don't know why he killed her, if that was in his mind from the start or a sudden impulse. I'm inclined

---

*"On the way," meaning "in passing."

to say impulse, because you couldn't find two girls more differ-ent than Brooks and this one—so he doesn't pick victims by any apparent system, though there's holes in that reasoning, I grant you—he may have some peculiar logic of his own, of course."

"I'll buy all that, but there's no evidence at all, a lot of hearsay and a lot of ifs. And how do you tie in Brooks and the doll?"

"Oh, damn the doll," said Mendoza. "I can't figure the odds on that, if it ties in or not—it's just as possible that somebody stum-bled on Brooks after the killer left her, and stole the thing—or that she was robbed of it before she ran into the killer. And I can say—*¡claro está!*—it's a lunatic, and the same lunatic—and when we find him, we'll find that last September he had some reason to frequent Tappan Street. There's even less evidence on all that." He stood and took up his hat from the bench, flicked dust off it automatically. "Here's Clawson. I'm going home."

"I might've expected that—walk off and leave me enough work so I can't try to beat your time with that redhead."

"That," said Mendoza, "to quote another classic tag line, would be sending a boy to do a man's work. But you have my permission to try, Arturo—I never worry about competition."

Eight

All the same, that doll intrigued him; it was such an incongruous thing.

When he unlocked the door of his apartment, automatically reaching to the light switch as he came in, the first thing that met his eyes was the elegant length of the Abyssinian cat draped along the top of the traverse-rod housing across the front windows, a foot below the ceiling.

Which meant that Bertha was here. Bast intensely resented Bertha and her vigorous maneuvers with mop, dustcloths, and vacuum cleaner, and took steps to keep out of her way. He was unsurprised to find her there on a late Sunday afternoon; the seven or eight people who shared Bertha's excellent services were used to her ways. If she felt like doing a thorough job on the Carters' Venetian blinds when she ought to be at the Elgins', or got behind because she'd decided to turn out all the Brysons' kitchen cupboards, she was apt to turn up almost anywhere at any time, and no one ever complained because, miraculously, Bertha really did the work she was paid for, and had even been known to dust the backs of pictures and the tops of doors.

She appeared now from the kitchen, jamming an ancient felt hat over her tight sausage curls. "I was just leavin'. There you go, switchin' on lights allovera place—your bill must be somethin' sinful! You found out yet who that dead man in the yards was?"

He admitted they had not; and yes, the forces of law were so unreasonable as to have arraigned the society beauty for murder, even after hearing all the excellent reasons she had for shooting her husband. He looked at Bertha thoughtfully (the average mind?) and said, "Do me a favor, and pretend you're taking one of those word-association tests, you know, I throw a word at you and you say the first thing that comes into your head—"

"I know, it's psychological." She looked interested.

"So, I say *doll* to you—what do you think of?"

"Witches," said Bertha. "I just saw a movie about it last night. The witch takes and makes this doll and names it and all, and sticks this big pin right through—"

"I get the general idea," said Mendoza sadly. "Thanks very much, that'll do." Witches: that was all they needed! When Bertha had slammed the door cheerfully after herself, he took off his coat, brought in the kitchen step-stool, and spent five minutes persuading Bast that it was safe to trust her descent to him. That was one puzzle he would never, probably, solve: she had no trouble getting up there, but hadn't yet found out how to get down. As usual, she emitted terrified yells as he backed down the steps, and, released, instantly assumed the haughty *sang-froid* of the never-out-of-countenance sophisticate. She turned her back on him and studied one black paw admiringly before beginning to wash it.

There were times Mendoza thought he liked cats because, like himself, they were all great egotists.

"Witches," he said again to himself, and laughed.

———

"And you put that coat away tidy where it belongs! On a hanger, not just anyhow. Clothes cost money, how many times I got to tell you, take care of what we got, no tellin' when we can get new."

"All right," said Marty. He got out of bed and picked up the corduroy jacket. He couldn't take down a hanger and put the jacket on it and hang it over the rod, all with his eyes shut, but he did it fast and he tried not to look down at the floor. She was fussing round the room behind him.

But he couldn't help seeing it, even if he didn't look right *at* it, and anyway, he thought miserably, even if he never opened the closet door, never had to see it, it didn't change anything— the thing was still there, he'd still know about it.

So did she, and for another reason he only half-understood himself. That was partly why he got the door shut again quick. She might know, all right, but she was different—if she didn't see it, she could keep from thinking about it. He felt like he was in two separate parts, about that, the way he felt about a lot of things lately—twin Martys, like looking in a mirror. He didn't see how she could, but in a funny kind of way he didn't want to make her *have* to see it—long as she could do like that.

He got back in bed and pulled the covers up. It was just like something was pulling him right in half, like two big black monster-shapes were using him for tug of war. And he had to just lie there, he couldn't do anything, because *she* wouldn't. And even if she was wrong, she was his Ma, and—and—

She said from the door, "You be real good now, no horsing round, you go right to sleep." She sounded just like always.

A funny idea slid into his mind then, the first minute of lying there in the dark—alone with the secret. He wondered if she'd forgot all about it, if maybe now she could look right *at* it and never really see it at all. Like it was invisible—because she wanted it to be.

But even in the dark with the door shut, he could still see it.

The box had gone a long while ago, got stepped on, and the big piece of thin white fancy paper and the pink shiny ribbon

had got all crumpled and spoiled pretty soon, from handling...
The doll wasn't new any more either. It sat in there on the closet
floor, leaning up against the wall, even when he shut his eyes
tight he could see it.

It had been awful pretty when it was new, even if it was just
a silly girl's thing. It wasn't pretty any more. The spangly pink
dress was all stained and torn, and most of the lace was torn off
the underwear, and one of the arms was pulled loose. The gold
curls had got all tangled and some pulled right off, and one of
the blue eyes with real lashes had been poked right in so there
was just a black hole there and you could hear the eye sort of
rattle around inside when you—The other eye still shut when
the doll was laid down.

Marty always had a funny hollow feeling when he heard that
eye rattling round inside. You'd think sometime it'd fall out, but
it never did.

He'd been lying here, felt like hours, still as he could, in the
dark. This was the worst time of all, and lately it had been getting
harder and harder to let go, and pretty soon be asleep. Because
in the dark, it seemed like the secret was somehow as big as the
whole room, so he couldn't breathe, so he felt he had to get *out*
and run and run and tell everybody—yell it as loud as he could.

He lay flat, very still, but he could hear his heart going *thud-
thud-thud*, very fast. You were supposed to say a prayer when
you went to bed, she'd made him learn it when he was just a little
kid and when they lived over on Tappan and he'd gone to the
Methodist Sunday school, it'd been up on the wall there in the
Sunday-school room, the words sewed onto cloth some fancy
old-fashioned way and flowers around them, in a gold frame.
He could see that now sort of in his mind, red and blue flowers
and the words in four lines. It was the only real prayer he knew
by heart and he was afraid to say it any more, because if you said
any of it you had to say it all and it might be worse than bad luck
to say the end of it. *If I should die before I—*

Most of the time, like at school, anyway in daylight, he could stand it. But this was the bad time, alone with it. A lot of feelings were churning around inside him, and they didn't exactly go away other times, they were still there but outside things helped to push them deeper inside, sort of—school and baseball practice and being with other kids and all. But like this in the dark, they got on top of him—a lot of bad feelings, but the biggest and worst of all was being just plain scared.

There were times, like yesterday, when he thought she was too; and then again, seemed like, she made up her mind so hard that nothing so awful like that could be so, for her it just wasn't. Maybe grownups could do that. He sure wished he could. Like looking right at that doll and never remembering, never thinking—

Marty felt shameful tears pricking behind his eyes, but the fear receded a little in him for the upsurge of resentment at her unfairness... She'd told a lie, a lie, he knew it was a lie, he wasn't crazy, was he?—if Dad had been there she'd never have dared say he was the one telling lies, but—what could you do when a grownup, your own Ma—

"I *bought* it," she'd said, and he thought he remembered it was one of the times she sounded afraid too... "I did so buy it, Marty, you're just pretendin' not to remember!—you got to remember, all that money—I saved it up, and I bought it *yesterday*—" About the money wasn't a lie; she had, but the rest wasn't so, he remembered—

What he remembered made terrible pictures in his mind, now he put it all together.

The fear that was never very far away now, even at school—outside—came creeping over him again like a cold hand feeling.

The doll. It had been awful pretty—then.

He wished he could forget that picture, all it said under it, in the newspaper. She hadn't got it this time, she wouldn't talk or listen about anything to do with it now—seemed like something just made him get that paper, and it had cost ten cents too. Elena. It was a pretty name. But he wished he could stop seeing the picture because it was the same girl, he'd known it would be but it was worse knowing for real sure—the picture—and the very worst about it was something silly, but somehow terrible too. *The picture that looked like that doll when it'd been new.* Before the eye had—

He thought he heard a noise over by the closet door. It wasn't really, he told himself. It wasn't.

In California they didn't hang people for murder, they had a gas chamber instead. It sounded even worse, a thing maybe like a big iron safe and with pipes that—

But other people, they shouldn't get killed like that—even if he didn't know, didn't mean—even if Ma—It wasn't right. Dad would say so too, whatever it meant, even something awful like the gas.

Somebody'd ought to know, and right off too, before it ever happened again. But Ma—

And that was a noise by the closet door.

Primitive physical fear took him in what seemed like one leap across the room and out to where it was light, in the parlor.

She had an old shirt in her lap she'd been mending, the needle still stuck in it, but she was just sitting there not doing anything. "What's the matter with you now?" she asked dully.

He tried to stop shaking, stop his teeth chattering. "P-please, Ma, can I—can I sleep out here on the sofa, I—I—I don't like the dark, it—"

She looked at him awhile and then said, "You're a big boy, be scared of the dark."

"Please, Ma—"

"I guess, if you want," she said in almost a whisper. She went in and got the blanket off his bed.

He lay on the sofa, the blanket tucked around him and face turned to the arm but still thankfully aware of the comforting light. And after a while a kind of idea started to come to him—about a way he might do...

Because somebody ought to—and she'd never let—she'd made him promise on the Bible, something awful would happen if you broke that kind of promise, but if he didn't *say* anything, just—

It was a frightening, tempting, awful idea. He didn't see how he could, he didn't know if he'd dare. And *where?*—it had to be a place where—

Danny said cops were all dumb. But Marty didn't think that could be right, because his dad must know more than Danny, and Dad had always said, Policemen, they're your friends, you go to them for help, you're ever in trouble.

Trouble... he felt the slow hot tears sliding down into the sofa cushion, fumbled blind and furtive for the handkerchief in his pajama pocket. The gas chamber. *I never meant nothing bad—*

But you had to do what was right, no matter what. Dad always said, and anyway it was a thing you just knew inside.

———

Morgan had got used to the oddly schizophrenic sensation—that was the word for it, wouldn't it be, for feeling split in halves?—more or less. He wondered if everybody who'd ever planned or done something criminal had the feeling: probably not. The visible Morgan, acting much as usual (at least he hoped so), going about his job—and the inside one, the one with the secret.

That one was still, in a detached way, feeling slightly surprised at this Morgan who was showing such unexpected capacity for cool planning. (The Morgan who'd been kicked around just once too often and this time was fighting back.) The original Morgan was still uneasy about the whole thing, but quite frankly, he realized, not from any moral viewpoint: just about Morgan's personal safety, the danger of being found out.

He wrote down the address as the man read it out to him. "How's that spelled?—it's a new one to me."

"T-A-P-P-A-N. Over past Washington some'eres, I think."

"Well, thanks very much," said Morgan, putting his notebook away.

"I still can't hardly believe it," said the clerk worriedly. "Lindstrom, doing a thing like that! Last man in the world, I'd've said—why, he thought the world of his wife and the boy. Never missed a lodge meeting, you know, and I don't ever remember talkin' with him he didn't brag on what good grades his boy got at school, all like that. One of the *steady* kind, that was Lindstrom—no world-beater, but, you know, *steady.*"

"That so?" said Morgan. He lit a cigarette. He felt a kind of remote interest in this Lindstrom thing, no more, but it constituted his main lifeline, and it must appear that he'd been working hard on it, been thinking of nothing else all today.

"Never any complaints on him, he always did an honest day's work, I heard that from a dozen fellows been on the job with him. He was working for Staines Contracting, like I said. He was a member here for three years, always paid his dues regular. We did figure it was sort of funny, way he quit his job and quit coming to meetings all of a sudden. When his dues didn't come in, we sent a letter, but it come back. But things come up in a hurry sometimes, sickness or something. You know. Last thing in the world I'd've expected a guy like Lindstrom to do—walk out on his family." He shook his head.

"You haven't heard anything from him since, no inquiries from other lodges of your union?"

"No, not since last August when he stopped showing up."

"Well, thanks." The man was still shaking his head sadly when Morgan came out to his car.

If it hadn't been for this other thing, he'd have been

interested in the Lindstroms more than he was. Funny setup: something behind it, but hard to figure what. Had the hell of a time getting a definite answer out of the woman about where they'd been living when the husband walked out. Sometimes they let out something to one of the neighbors, a local bartender: it was a place to start. Then, when he did, she gave what turned out to be a false address. He hadn't tackled her about that yet; it wasn't the first time such a thing had happened, and there were other ways to check. He'd found Lindstrom, got this last address for him, through his affiliation with the Carpenters' Union.

The thing was, concentrate on Lindstrom today, keep the nose to the grindstone. Forget about tonight, what was going to happen tonight. It would all work out fine, just as the inside, secret Morgan had planned it.

There was only one thing both Morgans were really worried about, and that was, *whether* and *when*, about telling Sue. Not, of course, before; she mustn't guess, or she'd be too nervous with the police. Not easy to put over the story on her, Sue knew him too well, but he thought he'd got away with it—that he was still stalling Smith, trying to bring him to compromise. It was going to be very tricky, too, afterward, when he had given the police one story and had to meet Sue before them. There was also the woman and the boy, but you had to take a chance somewhere. It was very likely that the woman (if indeed she was still living with Smith at all, and knew about this) would be too afraid of getting in trouble herself to speak up. And Sue was very far from being a fool; Sue he could count on.

It would go all right, always provided that the man was *there*. Otherwise it could be awkward, but Morgan figured that as Smith was renting a three-room flat instead of just a room, the chances were that his wife, or some woman, was with him, and he'd be home sometime around the dinner hour. So that was the first way it might go: the upright citizen Morgan, visiting one of his cases on his lawful occasions—if it was after hours, well, it was a case he'd got interested in, there was no law against zeal at one's job. The Lindstroms' flat was on the second floor; Smith's was on the third, so the mail slots told him. Those landings would be damn dark at night, not lighted anyway. Wait for him to come down on his way to collect—*the ransom*, only word—wait on the second-floor landing. And get up close, to be sure—but no talk. The first story, then: this man put the gun on me at the top of the stairs, before I got to the Lindstroms' door—I never saw him before, no, sir—he was after my wallet, when he reached for it I tackled him, tried to get the gun—we struggled, and it went off—

Remember (and not much time to see to it, after the shot) to get his prints on the gun. They were so very damned careful and clever these days, about details.

And if he missed Smith there, it would have to be in the street. If he was at that corner: or, if again he redirected Morgan to a bar, stall him off in there, and follow. A chance again, that the bartender would be honest, would remember them together: but in most of these places down here, hole-in-the-wall joints, the chance probably on Morgan's side. The second story: I was on my way back to my car, when this man tried to hold me up—

They would never trace the gun, never prove it didn't belong to Smith. Nobody could. Morgan had taken it off a dead German in 1944, the sort of ghoulish souvenir young soldiers brought home, and he'd nearly forgotten he had it; he had, being a careful man, taken the remaining three cartridges out of the clip, but they'd been put with the Luger in the old cash box his father had kept for odds and ends, locked away in a trunk in the basement. Morgan had gone down there at three this morning, when he was sure Sue was asleep, and got the gun and the cartridges. It was an unaccustomed weight in his breast pocket right now.

He ought to be somewhere around where this street came in;

he began to watch the signs. The third was Tappan. He turned into it and began to look for street numbers.

———

At that precise moment, Mendoza was having an odd and irritating experience. He was discovering the first thing remotely resembling a link between these two cases (if you discounted that gouged-out eye) and it offered him no help whatsoever. If it wasn't merely his vivid and erratic imagination.

"I'm real glad I clean forgot to th'ow that ol' thing out," said Mrs. Breen, soft and southern, "if it's any help to you findin' that bad man, suh. Ev'body knew Carol thought the world an' all of her, nice a gal as ever was. Terrible thing, jus' terrible."

Mendoza went on looking at the thing, fascinated. It was a good sharp commercial cut, three by five inches or so, one of a dozen in this dog-eared brochure, three years old, from a local toy factory. Mrs. Breen, maddeningly slow, determinedly helpful, had insisted on hunting it up for him, and as he hadn't yet penetrated her constant trickle of inconsequential talk to ask any questions, he'd been forced to let her find it first.

"You can see 'twas a real extra-special doll. Tell the truth, I was two minds about puttin' it in stock, not many folks'd spend that much money."

Was it imagination? That this thing had looked—a little—like Elena Ramirez? After all, he told himself, the conventional doll would. The gold curls, the eyelashes, the neatly rouged cheeks, the rosebud pout, the magenta fingernails. The irrational thought occurred to him that even the costume was exactly the kind of thing Elena would have admired.

He said to himself, I'm seeing ghosts—or catching at straws. What the hell, if the thing did look like her, or the other way around? *Dolls*. The whole thing was a mare's nest. Overnight he had begun to suspect uneasily that he was wrong, dead wrong about this thing; he hadn't taken a good long look at all the dissimilarities—he'd wanted to think this was the Brooks killer again, without any real solid evidence for it. Wasting time. Look at the rest of the facts!

Brooks: the handbag not touched. Ramirez: bag found several blocks away. True, apparently nothing taken, for Teresa said she wouldn't have been carrying more than a little silver, to the rink where she'd leave her bag and coat on a chair at the side.

Brooks: colored, not pretty, not noticeable. Ramirez: very much the opposite.

Brooks: attacked on a fairly well-frequented street, in a fairly good neighborhood—just luck that there hadn't been a number of people within earshot. Ramirez: attacked in that lot away from houses and in a street and neighborhood where a scream wouldn't necessarily bring help.

The chances were, just on the facts, that there were two different killers: say irrational ones, all right, because there didn't seem to be any good logical reason for anyone in either of the private lives wanting those girls dead. But two: and the first could be in Timbuctoo by now.

He was annoyed at himself. He said, "May I have this? Thank you." Let Hackett laugh at him for an imaginative fool! "Now, about this woman, the one who came in and wanted to buy the doll—"

"Shorely, Lieutenant, I had a good rummage firs' thing this mornin' when Mis' Demarest call me 'bout it, and I found that bitty piece o' paper with the name and address—"

Nine

Because afterward, thought Morgan (both Morgans), there would be a time when Sue would look at him, that steady look of hers, and want the truth. And he had better know what he was going to say.

He wondered if he could tell her half the truth convincingly (my God, no, I never *meant*—but when he got mad and pulled a gun, I—and afterward, I knew I couldn't tell the police the whole story, you know—) and go on forever after keeping the rest a secret. He'd never been very good at keeping secrets from Sue. But a big thing like this—and there was also the consideration, wouldn't it be kinder, fairer, not to put this on her conscience as it would be on his? Let her go on thinking it was— accident. Because he guessed it would be on his conscience to some extent. You couldn't be brought up and live half your life by certain basic ethics and forget about them overnight.

All the while he was thinking round and about that, at the back of his mind, he was talking to this woman, this Mrs. Cotter, quite normally—must have been, or she'd have been eying him oddly by this time. He saw that he had also been taking notes in his casebook of a few things she'd told him, and his writing looked quite normal too.

As usual now, he was having some trouble getting away: people liked to talk about these things. You had to be polite and sometimes they remembered something useful. He managed it at last, backing down the steps while he thanked her for the third time.

His car was around the corner, the only parking space there'd been half an hour ago; now, of course, there were two or three empty spaces almost in front of the building. As he came by, a long low black car was sliding quiet and neat into the curb there. The car registered dimly with him, because you didn't see many like it, but he was past when the driver got out. It was the car, a vague memory of it, pulled Morgan's head round six steps farther on. The driver was standing at the curb lighting a cigarette, in profile to him.

Morgan stopped. Absurdly, his mouth went dry and his heart missed a few beats, hurried to catch up. *You damn fool,* he said to himself. *They're not mind readers, for God's sake!*

But, he thought confusedly, but—An omen? Today of all days, just run into one—like this. Casual.

That was a man from Homicide, a headquarters man from Kenneth Gunn's old department. Lieutenant Luis Mendoza of Homicide. Morgan had met him, twice—three times—at the Gunns', and again when their jobs had coincided, that Hurst business, when one of the deserted wives had shot herself and two kids.

Luis Mendoza. Besides the childish panic, resentment he had felt before rose hot in Morgan's throat: unreasonable resentment at the blind fate which handed one man rewards he hadn't earned, didn't particularly deserve—and also more personal resentment for the man.

Mendoza, with all that money, and not a soul in the world but himself to spend it on: no responsibilities, no obligations! Gunn had talked about Mendoza: ordinary back-street family, probably not much different from some of these in neighborhoods like this—nothing of what you'd call background...and the wily grandfather, and all the money. What the hell right had he to pretend such to-the-manner-born—if indefinable—insolence? Just the money; all that money. Do anything, have anything he damned pleased, or almost. And by all accounts, didn't he! Clothes—and it wasn't that Morgan wanted to look like a damned fop, the way Mendoza did, but once in a while it would be nice to get a new suit more than once in five years, and not off the rack at a cheap store when there was a sale on. That silver-gray herringbone Mendoza was wearing hadn't cost a dime less than two hundred dollars. An apartment some-where, not in one of the new smart buildings out west where you paid three hundred a month for the street name and three closet-sized rooms, but the real thing—a big quiet place, spa-cious, and all for himself, everything just so, custom furniture probably, air-conditioning in summer, maid service, the works. It was the kind of ostentation that was like an iceberg, most of it invisible: that was Mendoza, everything about him. Nothing remotely flashy, all underplayed, the ultraconservative clothes, that damned custom-built car you had to look at twice to know it for what it was, even the manner, the man himself—that precise hairline mustache, the way he lit a cigarette, the—

A womanizer, too: he would be. And easy to think they were only after the money: not, for some reason, altogether true. God knew what women found so fascinating in such men. But he remembered Gunn saying that, a little rueful as became a solid family man, a little indulgent because he liked Mendoza, a lit-tle envious the way any man would be—*Poker and women, after hours, that's Luis, his two hobbies you might say, and I understand he's damn good at both...* A lot of women would be fools for such a man, not that he was so handsome, but he—knew the script, like an actor playing a polished scene. And all for casual amuse-ment, all for Mendoza, and when he was bored, the equally polished exit, and forget it.

Gunn had said other things about Mendoza. That he was a brilliant man—that he never let go once he had his teeth into something.

All that, while the lighter-flame touched the cigarette, and was flicked out, the lighter thrust back into the pocket. Mendoza raised his head, took the cigarette out of his mouth, and saw Morgan there looking at him. And so Morgan had to smile, say his name, the conventional things you did say, meeting an acquaintance.

"How's Gunn these days? He's missed downtown, you know—a good man. I understand that's quite an organization he's set up."

Morgan agreed; he said you ran into some interesting cases sometimes, he had one now, but one thing for sure, you certainly had a chance to see how the other half lived—but that'd be an old story to Mendoza.

"That you do," said the man from Homicide, and smoke trickled thin through his nostrils; if he took in the *double-entendre* he gave no sign of it.

"Well, nice to run into you—I'll give Gunn your regards." Morgan seemed to be under a compulsion to sound hearty, make inane little jokes: "I hope, by the way, we're not concerned with the same clients again, like that Hurst business—nasty."

"I want 2416."

It was the building Morgan had just left; he said, "That's it. Be careful of the third step—it's loose. I nearly broke my neck."

"Thanks very much." And more conventionalities of leave-taking, and he was free. He started again for his car. The gun was suddenly very heavy there against his chest. When he got out his keys, he saw his hand shaking a little. *Damn fool*, he thought angrily.

It's going to be all right. Just the way I want it to go. No matter who, no matter what. And, by God, if it isn't, if the very worst happens—whatever that might be—this was one time anyway he wouldn't stand still to be knocked out of the ring. He'd have tried, anyway.

———

Mrs. Irene Cotter was rather thrilled and wildly curious. *Two* men, *detectives* of all things, calling in one morning, and both about those Lindstroms. If you'd asked her, she'd have said—in fact, she was saying it now to Mendoza—that most any other tenants she'd ever had while she was manageress here, and that'd been eleven years, were more likely to bring *detectives* around. That blonde hussy in 307, for instance, or Mr. Jessup who was, not to beat round the bush, just a nasty old man—and there'd been that couple in 419 that got drunk most nights and threw things.

She told him about them all, at some length and, when she remembered, taking pains with her grammar, because this one was a lot more interesting-looking, and seemed more interested in her, than the first one. She always thought there was *something* about a man with a mustache. This one looked a little bit like that fellow in the movies, the one that was usually the villain but personally she thought about a lot of the movies she'd seen with him in that the girl was an awful fool to prefer some sheep-eyed collar-ad instead, but there was no accounting for tastes. And a real gentleman too, beautiful manners; of course that was one thing about these Mexes, people said things about them, but of course there was classes of them just like anywhere, only when they were high-class like this one, you said Spanish.

"—And I tell you, when he up and left, and everybody knew it, nobody couldn't hardly believe it! You'd never have thought they was that kind at all, fly-by-nights I mean that don't go on steady, you know what I mean, all their lives. But I tell you, Lieutenant, I like to sort of study people, and G—goodness knows I get the chance in my job, and I said to myself at the time, There's something behind it."

"There usually is. The man left in August, you said, early."

"I couldn't swear to the date, but it was after the rent was due—*and* paid. They was never a day late. Good tenants. Maybe the first week."

"And how long did the woman and boy stay on?"

"Oh, I can tell you that to the day. It was the twenty-second of September they left, she told me in the morning, late, round noon maybe, and they went that night. I remember because she was paid to the end of the month, but they went before, and I *did* think that was funny, because it must've meant she'd paid extra wherever they were moving, you know, to move in before the first. And already bein' paid up to the first here, you'd think—Of course, all *I* know, *she* didn't say, they might've been going back east or somewheres. I did ask, account of mail, not that they ever had much of that, mostly ads—but she never said, just looked at me as if I was being nosy. And I'll tell you something else, Lieutenant, you can believe it or not, but that was just exactly the fourth time I'd spoke to Mis' Lindstrom, all two years they'd been here. That was the kind they was—her, anyways. Why, they'd moved in a week or more before I ever laid eyes on *her*—it was *him* rented the place, and paid, and like people mostly do they moved in at night, after work, you know—not that they had much to bring, a few sticks o' furniture. But I was telling you about when *he* went. It was Mis' Spinner in 319 told me, right next to them, they had 320, you can see that I wouldn't notice right off, especially with them, sometimes I'd see him going off in the morning or coming home, but not every day. And Mis' Spinner thought I ought to know he'd left, at least hadn't been there she didn't *think* four-five days, time she told me. Well, they was paid up to the end of August, I didn't go asking questions till then, none o' my business, but when September first come round, it was *her* come down to pay the rent and then I did figure, better know where we stood, if you see what I mean. Without wanting to be *nosy*," added Mrs. Cotter virtuously. "She wouldn't admit he'd gone and left her, froze right up and said I needn't worry about the rent, and some rigmarole about he was called back east sudden. But alla same, it wasn't a week before she had to get herself a job, so I knew all right. And if you ask me—"

"Where did she work, do you know?"

"Sure, it was a night job cleaning offices downtown—the Curtis Building. And that's what I was goin' to say, Lieutenant— that kind of job, it shows you what she was *like*, and you ask me, it all ties in, it was prob'ly all her fault, whole thing. She was one of them old maids married like they say, for *sure*. Went around with a sour look alla time, never a smile or a friendly word in passing—and as for looks! Well, I don't s'pose she was more than forty, and I tell you, she looked like her own gran'mother! Hair screwed up in a little bun behind, and skin like a piece o' sand-paper, you could tell she never took any care of herself, prob'ly used laundry soap and that's that—never a scrap of make-up, and cheap old cotton house dresses was all I ever seen her in. You know's well as me there's no call for a woman to let herself *go* like that, these days! And if she acted to *him* the way she did to everybody else, even the youngster, well, between you 'n' me 'n' the gatepost, I don't blame him for walkin' out. A man can take just so much. She'd've been the kind wouldn't let him sleep with her either, a regular prunes-an'-prison old maid like they say, if you know what I mean. Why, if she'd taken a little trouble, fix herself up and act nice, she coulda got a better job, waiting in a store or something, you know, daytimes. There's just no *call* for a woman to look like that, if she's got any self-respect! But she wasn't one you could talk to friendly, you know, give any advice, like—she was downright rude to everybody tried to make friends, so after a while nobody tried no more, just left them be. And I do think *he'd* have been different. Times he came by to pay the rent, or if you met him goin' out or like that, he always acted friendly and polite. I figure he just got good and fed up with the whole way she was—it musta been like livin' with a set bear trap."

The detective grinned at that and she permitted herself a ladylike titter, smoothing her defiantly brown pompadour. "I gather you didn't exchange much casual talk with the woman at any time."

"Nobody did, she wouldn't let 'em... Ever hear her mention goin' to buy a *doll*? That I did not. It wasn't a girl she had, it was a boy, I thought I said. Marty, his name was. He favored his dad, I must say he was a nice-raised boy. Always took off his cap to you, and he was real quiet—for a boy, you know. He'd be about eleven or a bit past when they come, and that last year they was here, he all of a sudden'd started to shoot up, early like some do—going to be as big as his dad, you could see. A real nice boy, he was, not like his Ma at all... Well, I'm sure I don't know why she'd be buying a *doll*, unless it was for some of their fambly back east, might be she had a niece or something. But *for goodness' sake*, Lieutenant, won't you tell me what this is all about—what's she *done*?—or is it *him*? I mean—"

"I don't know that either of them's done anything. It's a matter of getting evidence, that's all, not very important." He was standing up.

"Oh. I must say, I can't help being *curious*—two of you coming, same day, ask about *them*! You can't blame me for that, couldn't you just—"

"So Mr. Morgan was asking about the Lindstroms too?" He looked thoughtful, and then smiled and began to thank her. She saw she wouldn't get any more out of him, but that didn't stop her from speculating. The Lindstroms, of all people!

Mrs. Cotter watched him down the walk to his car, heaved an excited sigh after him, and hurried upstairs to tell Mrs. Spinner all about it.

———

The clock over the row of phone booths, in the first drugstore he came to, said ten past twelve. Mendoza spent an annoying five minutes looking up the number in a tattered book, finally got the office, and just caught Gunn on his way out to lunch.

"Oh, Luis—how's the boy?—good to hear from you. Say, I'm afraid Andrews' idea didn't pay off, you know, about that hood New York wants for jumping parole. It was a long chance, find him through the wife, and of course it may be she's collecting from some other county agency. If he wants—What's that? Sure thing, anything I can tell you... Morgan, well, he's probably having lunch somewhere right now."

"It's one of his cases, that's all. And all I want from you is the present address. The name is Mrs. Marion Lindstrom. Apparently she's only recently applied for relief."

"If we're working on it, that's so, within a few months anyway—it'll be right here in the current file, hang on and I'll look."

Mendoza opened the door for air while he waited. He was rapidly developing a guilty conscience: wasting time over this meaningless thing. He didn't get paid—or shouldn't—for listening to inconsequential gossip. A dozen things he should have been doing this morning besides—

"—Graham Court," said Gunn's voice in his ear.

"Oh? Any idea approximately where that is?"

"Somewhere down the wrong side of Main, that area— below First or Second. We've got—"

"*¡No puede ser!*"* said Mendoza very softly to himself. "It can't be, not so easy, I don't believe it... When Morgan comes in, tell him to wait, I want to see him. Call me at my office *inmediata-mente*—or even quicker! I want everything you've got on these people. Let me have that address again."

———

*"It can't be!"

It was Gunn, of course, and not Hackett, who said all the things Hackett might say later; before outsiders, like this, Hackett paid lip service to rank. Gunn had once been Mendoza's superior; he spoke up. By the same token, of course, Mendoza wouldn't have talked so freely if Gunn hadn't been a retired Homicide man.

"You've got your wires crossed, Luis. What you've got here is just damn-all, it doesn't mean a thing. First off, how many people d'you suppose moved out of that section of town last September? There's no narrowing it down to a couple of blocks, you have to take in at least a square mile—call it even half a mile—at a guess, seven-eight thousand families, because you're taking in apartments, not just single houses. In that kind of neighborhood people aren't settled, they move around more. And—"

"I know, I know," said Mendoza. "And that's the least of all the arguments against this meaning anything at all. But say it— it's not even very significant that the move should be from the twenty-four-hundred block on Tappan to within two blocks of Commerce and Humboldt, because those are the same sort of neighborhoods, same rent levels, same class and color of people. All right. Evidence—!" He hunched his shoulders angrily, turning from staring at the view out Gunn's office window. "Say it. Even if it *is* the same killer, no guarantee he lived anywhere near either of the girls. So all this is *cuentos de hadas*, just fairy tales."

Hackett made a small doleful sound at his cigarette. "I guess you're saying it for yourself, Lieutenant."

"You've got no evidence," Gunn said flatly. "You'd just like to think so, which isn't like you, Luis. What the hell *have* you got? I—"

"I've got two dead girls," said Mendoza, abrupt and harsh. "And they don't matter one damn, you know. The kind of murders that happen in any big town, this week, next week, next year. No glamour, no excitement, no big names. Nothing to go in the books, the clever whimsy on Classic Cases* or the clever fiction, ten wisecracks guaranteed to the page, a surprise ending to every chapter, where fifteen people had fifteen motives for the murder and fifteen faked alibis for the crucial minute, conveniently fixed by a prearranged long-distance phone call. They weren't very important or interesting females, these two, and anybody at all might have killed them. *You* know," he swung on Gunn, "this kind of thing, it doesn't go like the books, the clues laid out neat like a paper trail in a game! You start where you can and you take a look everywhere, at everything—*¿Qué más?*[†]—and then you start all over again."

"*I* know," said Gunn heavily. "What I'm saying is, you've got nothing at all to link these two cases. The doll, that's really out of bounds, boy, that one I don't figure any way. The odds are that somebody found the girl, didn't report it, but picked up the package—"

"You're so right," said Mendoza. "It was dark, and her handbag was half under her, almost hidden."

"Well, there you are. They were killed the same general way, but it's not a very unusual method—brute violence."

"That eye," said Hackett to his cigarette.

Gunn looked at him, back to Mendoza. "If it's a real hunch, Luis, all I've got to say is, keep throwing cold water at it—if it just naturally drowns, let it go."

"What else am I doing?" For they both knew that it wasn't ever all pure cold logic, all on the facts: nothing that had to do with people ever could be wholly like that. You had a feeling, you had a hunch, and you couldn't drop every other line to follow it up, but a real fourteen-karat hunch turned out to be worth something—sometimes. Say it was subconscious reasoning, out of experience and knowledge; it wasn't, always. Just a feeling.

---

*Mendoza may be referring here to the television show *Lock Up* (marketed later as *Cops: Lock Up*) starring Macdonald Carey as Herbert L. Maris, an attorney who devoted his life to *pro bono* criminal defense cases; the stories were referred to as "Classic Cases" and aired from 1959 to 1961.

†"What else?"

"All right," said Hackett amiably, "cold water. I don't like the doll much myself. I said I'd buy all that about the guy at the skating rink, but there's nothing there to show it's the same one. In fact, the little we *have* got on that one, it suggests he admired the girl, wanted to pick her up—like that, whether for murder or sex."

"So it does," said Mendoza. "And no hint of anything like that for Carol Brooks."

Gunn opened his mouth, shut it, looked at Hackett's bland expression, and said, "You saw both bodies, of course—you're a better judge of what the similarity there is worth."

"Oh, let's be psychological," said Mendoza. "Not even that. Art says to me before I looked at Ramirez, 'It's another Brooks'—maybe he put it in my mind."

"Sure, lay it on me."

There was a short silence, and then Mendoza said as if continuing the argument, "Nobody's interested in this kind of killing, no, except those of us who're paid to be interested. But it's the kind everybody ought to take passionate interest in—the most dangerous kind there is—just because it's without motive. Or having the motive only of sudden, impulsive violence. The lunatic kill. So it might happen to anybody. *Claro que sí,*[*] let one like that kill a dozen, twenty, leave his mark to show it's the same killer, then he's one for the books—the Classic Case. And don't tell me I've got no evidence these were lunatic kills. It's negative evidence, I grant you, but there it is—we looked, you know. Nobody above ground had any reason to murder the Brooks girl, and she wasn't killed for what cash she had on her. The couple of little things we've got on Ramirez, nothing to lead to murder—and she wasn't robbed either. Not to that murder. I don't have to tell you that brute violence of that sort, it's either very personal hate or lunacy."

Morgan cleared his throat; he'd been waiting in silence, a

---

[*]"Of course."

little apart, his case book out ready, if and when they remembered him. "I don't want to butt in, you know more about all this, but I can't help feeling you're on the wrong track here, just for that reason. These people—well, after all—I don't suppose you're thinking the woman did it, and a thirteen-year-old kid—"

Again a short silence. Hackett leaned back in his chair and said conversationally, "I picked up a thirteen-year-old kid a couple of months ago who'd shot his mother in the back while she was watching T.V. She'd told him he couldn't go to the movies that night. You remember that Breckfield business last year?— three kids, the oldest one thirteen, tied up two little girls and set fire to them. One died, the other's still in the hospital. I could take you places in this town where a lot of thirteen-year-old kids carry switch-knives and pull off organized gang raids on each other—and the neighborhood stores. And some of 'em aren't little innocents any other way, either. Juvenile had a couple in last week—and not the first—with secondary stage V.D., and both on heroin."

Morgan said helplessly, "But—this kid—he's not like that! He's just a *kid,* like any kid that age. You can tell, you know."

"Something was said," cut in Mendoza, "about his size, that he'd started to get his growth early. How big is he?—how strong?"

"Almost as tall as I am—five-eight-and-a-half, around there. Still—childish-looking, in the face. But he's going to be a big man, he's built that way—big bone structure."

"Weight?"

"Hell, I can't guess about all this," said Morgan angrily. "As far as I can see you've got no reason at all to suspect the Lindstroms of anything. I don't know what's in your mind about this boy— you talk about lunatics and juvenile hoods, so O.K., which is he? You can't have it both ways. The whole thing's crazy."

Mendoza came a few steps toward him, stood there hands in pockets looking down at him, a little cold, a little annoyed.

"I've got nothing in my mind about him right now. I don't know. This is the hell of a low card, but I've got the hell of a bad hand and it's the best play I've got at the moment. Carol Brooks was killed on September twenty-first, and these people left that neighborhood—unexpectedly, and in a hurry—within twenty-four hours. The woman was working at night, so the boy was free to come and go as he pleased. Shortly before Brooks was killed, the woman showed interest in an article Brooks was buying on time, and it now appears that the girl had this with her before she was killed and it subsequently disappeared. I'm no psychiatrist and I don't know how much what any psychiatrist'd say might be worth, here—the boy just into adolescence, probably suffering some shock when his father abandoned them. Let that go. But he's big enough and strong enough to have done—the damage that was done. If. And I may take a jaundiced view of the psychological doubletalk, the fact remains that sex can play some funny tricks with young adolescents sometimes. All right. These people are now living in the neighborhood where Elena Ramirez was killed. I don't say they had anything to do with either death, or even the theft. I'd just like to know a little more about them."

Morgan shrugged and flipped open his notebook. "You're welcome to what I've got. Mrs. Lindstrom applied for county relief six weeks ago, and was interviewed by a case worker from that agency. She says her husband deserted her and the boy last August, she has no idea where he is now, hasn't heard from him since. She took a job between then and a week or so before she applied, says she can't go on working on account of her health. She was referred to a clinic, and there's a medical report here—various troubles adding up to slight malnutrition and a general run-down condition. Approved for county relief, and the case shoved on to us to see if we can find Lindstrom, make him contribute support. He's a carpenter, good record, age forty-four, description—and so on and so on—they both came from a place called Fayetteville in Minnesota, so she said," and he glanced at Gunn.

"Yes," said Gunn thoughtfully, "and what does that mean, either? Sometimes these husbands head for home and mother, we usually query the home town first—and I have here a reply from the vital records office in Fayetteville saying that no such family has ever resided there."

"You don't tell me," said Mendoza.

"This I'll tell you," said Morgan, "because we run into it a lot. Some of these women are ashamed to have the folks at home know about it, and they don't realize we're going to check on it—the same with former addresses here, and she gave me a false one on that too, sure. It doesn't necessarily mean—"

"No. But it's another little something. What have you got on the boy?"

"Nothing, why should I have? He exists, that's all we have to know. He's normal, thirteen years old, name Martin Eric Lindstrom, attends seventh grade at John C. Calhoun Junior High." Morgan shut the book.

"That's all? I'd like to know more about the boy. We'll have a look round. No trace of the father yet?"

"It's early, we've only been on this a few days. Routine enquiries out to every place in the area hiring carpenters—to vital records and so on in other counties—and so on."

"Yes. Will you let me have a copy of all that you've got, please—to my office. We'll keep an eye on them, see what shows up, if anything. Thanks very much."

When the two men from Homicide had gone, Gunn said, "Get one of the girls to type up that report, send it over by hand."

"O.K.," said Morgan. "I suppose—" He was half-turned to the door, not looking at Gunn. "I suppose that means he'll have men watching that apartment."

"It's one of the basic moves. What's the matter, Dick?"

"Nothing," said Morgan violently. "Nothing at all. Oh, hell, it's just that—I guess Mendoza always rubs me the wrong way, that's all. Always so damned sure of himself—and I think he's way off the beam here."

"It doesn't look like much of anything," agreed Gunn. "But on the other hand, well, you never can be sure until you check."

Ten

"I have the feeling," said Mendoza—discreetly in Spanish, for the waiter who had seated them was still within earshot—"that I'd better apologize for the meal we're about to have."

"But why? Everything looks horribly impressive. Including the prices. In fact, after that automatic glance at the right-hand column," said Alison, putting down the immense menu card, "*I* have the feeling I've been in the wrong business all my life."

"I never can remember quite how it goes, about fooling some of the people, etcetera." Mendoza glanced thoughtfully around the main dining room of the Maison du Chat, which was mostly magenta, underlighted, and decorated with would-be funny murals of lascivious felines. "It's curious how many people are ready to believe that the highest prices guarantee the best value." The waiter came back and insinuated under their noses liquor lists only slightly smaller than the menus. "What would you like to drink?"

"Sherry," said Alison faintly, her eyes wandering down the right column.

"And straight rye," he said to the waiter, who looked shaken and took back the cards with a disappointed murmur.

"*Not* in character. I'd expected to find you something of a gourmet."

"My God, I thought I'd made a better impression. The less one thinks about one's stomach, the less trouble it's apt to cause. And I know just enough about wine to call your attention to those anonymous offerings you just looked at—port, muscatel, tokay, and so on. At three dollars the half-bottle, and they'll be the domestic product available at the nearest supermarket for what—about one-eighty-nine the gallon."

"They're not losing money on the imported ones either."

"About a one hundred percent markup." He looked around again casually, focused on something past her shoulder, and began to smile slowly to himself. "Now isn't that interesting…"

"I couldn't agree more—I said I've always found the subject fascinating. You're pleased about something, and it can't be the prices."

"I just noticed an old friend. And what's more, he noticed me. He isn't nearly so pleased about it." The waiter, doing his best with pseudo-Gallic murmurs and deft gestures with paper mats to invest these plebeian potions with glamour, served them. Mendoza picked up his rye and sniffed it cautiously. "*¡Salud y pesetas!*" And if this costs them more than a dollar a fifth whole-sale, they're being cheated, which I doubt."

"Why did we come here? I gather it's new to you too."

"We came because I'm interested in this place, not as a restaurant—professionally. Of course I also wanted to impress you."

"You have."

"And I'm gratified to find you see through these spurious trappings of the merely expensive. Next time I'll take you to a hamburger stand."

"You will not. I like an excuse to get really dressed up occasionally." She had, after all, compromised with his dictation: pearls, and a very modest *décolleté*, but for the rest an oyster-silk sheath.

---

*"Health and fortune!"

"I complimented you once, don't fish for more so early," said Mendoza placidly. "And what I expected to get by coming—besides rooked out of a little money—I don't know. Mr. Torres-Domingo is an unexpected bonus. You see, the uncle of your late pupil went out of his way to visit this place last night, which seemed a little odd."

"Oh! I should think so. Who is the other gentleman you mentioned?"

"I wouldn't say gentleman. He just barely avoided an indictment for homicide about eighteen months ago—he was then the proprietor of a bar on Third Avenue. Another gentleman who later turned out to have been a small-time wholesaler of heroin got himself shot full of holes by a third gentleman who subsequently said that Mr.—the first gentleman—had offered him a substantial sum of money to do the job. We didn't doubt his word—after what showed up—but unfortunately there just wasn't enough evidence. The first gentleman retired modestly across the Mexican border, though he is an American citizen, and it's interesting to know he's back home. I don't want him for anything myself, but Lieutenant Patrick Callaghan will be very interested to hear that he's now the headwaiter at a fashionable restaurant."

"I deduce that the lieutenant is on the narcotics team, or whatever you call it."

"And as you and I are not the only people in the world who speak Spanish, we will now cease to talk shop. What are we offered? All the standard Parisian concoctions. Women living alone subsist mostly on casseroles anyway, no treat to you—I suggest the one concession to Americanism, a steak."

"Medium well," she agreed meekly. And when the waiter had gone, "May I ask just one question? People make a lot of money in that—er—business you mentioned. Wholesaling you-know-what. Why should they go to all the trouble of holding down regular jobs too? I always thought of them as—as coming out at night, slinking furtively down alleys, you know—like that—not punching time clocks."

"Oh, God!" he said. "Now you've taken my appetite away. Well, there's a den of crafty bloodsucking robbers in Washington—you'll have heard of them—"

"Which ones?"

"It says Bureau of Internal Revenue on the door. Now, the L.A.P.D. couldn't get one useful piece of evidence against the gentleman I mentioned—as we can't always against a lot of others in a lot of businesses, and I do mean big businesses, on the wrong side of the law. But we can't poke our noses into some things those fellows can. A hundred-thousand-dollar apartment house—a new Cadillac—a mink coat for the girl friend—you *are* doing well, Mr. Smith, how come you never told your uncle about it? And if Mr. Smith can't explain just where it all came from, he's got a lot more grief than a mere city cop could ever hand him."

"Oh, I *see*. I do indeed. Cover."

"And then," added Mendoza, not altogether humorously, "when uncle has stowed Mr. Smith away in jail for tax evasion, the indignant public points an accusing finger at us and says, Corrupt cops!—they must have known about him! Stupid cops!—if they didn't find out! Why wasn't he arrested for his *real* crimes? You try to tell them, just try, that it's because we have to operate within laws about evidence designed to protect the public... I wonder whether I ought to call in and tell Pat's office about this." Mr. Torres-Domingo, who had made a precipitate exit on first catching sight of him, reappeared round the screen at the service doors, polishing his bald head with a handkerchief. He shot one furtive glance in Mendoza's direction, pasted on a professional happy smile, and began to circulate among the tables, pausing for a bow, a word here and there with a favored patron. "Oh, well, there's no hurry—he won't run away, and for all I know he's reformed and hasn't any reason to anyway."

The steaks could have been less tough; the service might with advantage have been less ostentatious. Mendoza asked her presently whether she'd got anything useful from any of the girls.

"I wondered when you'd ask. Nothing at all, I'm sorry to say—she hadn't said anything to any of them about that. But she didn't know any of them well, after all."

"No. I didn't expect much of that. I've got a queer sort of— can I call it a lead?—from another angle, but I don't know that that means much either… What do you think of the murals? I've never asked you what kind of thing you paint."

Alison said the murals constituted a libel on the feline race and that she was herself unfashionably pre-Impressionistic. "This and that—I'm not wedded to any one particular type of subject. Now and then I actually sell something." They talked about painting; they talked about cats. "—But when you're away all day, you can't keep pets, it's not fair."

"Nobody keeps a cat. They condescend to live with you is all. And as for the rest of it, *I* moved. It's miles farther for me to drive, and the rent's higher, but it's on the ground floor and they let me put in one of those little swinging doors in the back door, out to the yard. You've seen the ads—*let your pet come and go freely.* Yes, a fine idea, but she won't use it—she knows how it works, but she doesn't like the way it slaps her behind, and she got her tail pinched once. Fortunately all the other seven apartments are inhabited by cat people. Four of them have keys to mine and run in and out all day waiting on her, which of course is what she schemes for. I believe Mrs. Carter and Mrs. Bryson," he added, looking around for the waiter, "alternate their shopping tours and visits to the beauty salon—coffee, please—"

"And pairhaps some of our special brandy, sair?"

"That I need," said Alison, "after listening to this barefaced confession. Battening on the charity of your neighbors like that—"

"One of the reasons I picked the apartment. The Elgins keep her supplied with catnip mice, they buy them in wholesale lots, having three Siamese of their own. Of course there *is* a man two doors down who has a spaniel, but one must expect some undesirables in these unrestricted neighborhoods." The waiter came back with the coffee, the brandy, and the bill on a salver, contriving to slide that in front of Mendoza by a kind of legerdemain suggesting that it appeared out of thin air, not through any offices of this obsequious and excellent servant. Mendoza looked at it, laid two tens on the salver and said now he needed the brandy too.

"I have no sympathy for you," said Alison.

When they came out into the foyer, Mendoza hesitated, glancing at the discreet row of phone booths in an alcove. "I wonder if I *had*—" There had appeared no bowing, smiling headwaiter as they left the dining room, to make the last honors to new patrons, urge a return. "Oh, well," and he put a hand automatically to his pocket for more largesse as one of the several liveried lackeys approached with Alison's coat.

"So 'appy to 'ave 'ad you wiz us, sair and madame—I 'ope you enjoyed your dinnair? You mus' come back soon—*Holy Mother o' God*, what the hell was that?" Between them they dropped the coat; the lackey took one look over Alison's shoulder, said, "Jesus, let me out of here!" and dived blindly for the door, staggering Mendoza aside. The second volley of shots was a medley of several calibers, including what sounded like a couple of regulation .38's. From the dark end of the corridor off the foyer plunged a large, shapeless man waving a revolver, and close after him the tuxedo-clad rotundity of Mr. Torres-Domingo, similarly equipped. The checkroom attendant prudently dropped flat behind his counter as the large man paused to fire twice more behind him and charged into the foyer.

"Wait for me, Neddy!" Mr. Torres-Domingo sent one wild shot behind him and another inadvertently into the nearest phone booth as he continued flight.

The first man swept the gun in an arc round the foyer. "Don't nobody move—I'm comin' through—"

Mendoza recovered his balance, shoved Alison hard to sprawl full length on the floor, and in one leap covered the ten feet to the gun as it swung back in his direction. He got a good left-handed grip on the gun-hand as they collided, his momentum lending force to the considerable impact, and as they went down landed one right that connected satisfactorily. Neddy went over backward and Mendoza went with him; the gun emptied itself into the ceiling as they hit the floor with Mendoza's knee in the paunch under him; Neddy uttered a strangled *whoof* and lost all interest in the proceedings.

Mr. Torres-Domingo yelped, fired once more and hit the plate-glass door, turned and ran into the embrace of an enormous red-haired man in the vanguard of the pursuit, which had just erupted down the corridor. The red-haired man adjusted him to a convenient position and hit him once in the jaw, and he flew backward six feet and collapsed on top of Mendoza, who was just sitting up. One of the three men behind the red-haired man dropped his gun and sank onto the divan beside the checkroom, clutching his shoulder.

There was a very short silence before several women in the crowd collecting at the dining-room door went off like air-raid sirens. Mendoza heaved off Mr. Torres-Domingo, sat up and began to swear in Spanish. The red-haired man bellowed the crowd to quiet, and turned to the man nearest him: "Find a phone and call the wagon and an ambulance—and"—flinging round to the man on the divan—"just what in the name of Jesus, Mary, and Joseph did you think *you* were doing, you almighty bastard? You—"

"¡*Hijo de perra!*"—take your hands off that man, you son of a Dublin whore!" Mendoza shoved him away and bent over Higgins, who was fumbling a handkerchief under his coat. "Easy, boy—"

---

*"Son of a bitch!"

"It's not bad, Lieutenant—I just—"

"Before God!—Luis Mendoza!—does *this* belong to you? Just what the holy hell are *you* doing in this?—you tellin' me *you* put this blundering bastard out back there—to bitch up two months' work and the first chance I've had to lay hands on—I ought to bust you right in the—I ought to—"

Mendoza twitched the handkerchief from the red-haired man's breast pocket, wadded it up with his own, shoved Higgins flat on the divan and pulled aside the coat to slap on the temporary bandage. "Temper, Patrick, temper! We're in public—you'll be giving people the idea there's no loyalty, no unity in the police force. And listen, you red bastard, next time you have to knock a man out to arrest him, for the love of God don't aim him at me—you've damn near fractured my spine! There's the squad car. For God's sake, let's clear this crowd back—who's this?"

The little round man who had popped out like a cork from the dining-room crowd was sounding off in falsetto. "I am the manager—I am the owner—what do you do here in my place, shooting and yelling? I call the police!—what is all this about?—shootings—gangsters—I will not have gangsters in my nice quiet place—"

"Then you shouldn't hire one as a headwaiter," said Mendoza. "And you should also change your butcher, your steaks are tough." He pushed past him and went over to Alison, who was just somewhat shakily regaining her feet. "I don't usually knock them down the *first* date, *mi vida*—apologies! Are you all right? Here, sit down."

"*I'm* all right," said Alison, "but you owe me a pair of stockings."

———

Morgan had read somewhere that marijuana did this to you, played tricks with time, so first it seemed to slow down, almost grind to a full stop, and then sent everything past you at the speed of light. His watch told him he'd been standing here on this corner just an hour and twelve minutes, no more and no less; for a while it had felt like half eternity, and then, a while after that, time began to go too fast. Where he'd been tense with impatience, wound up tight for action—*God, God, make him come*—suddenly, now, he could have prayed for time to stop. Not now, he said to Smith frantically in his mind, you can't come now, until I've thought about this, figured it out, got hold of another plan.

Oh, Christ damn Luis Mendoza and his little slum-street mugging!—what the hell did that matter, some damn-fool chippy knocked off, probably she'd asked for it, and that crazy idea about those Lindstroms who couldn't by any fantastic stretch of the imagination have had anything to do... Because, yes, this upright citizen Morgan had a good innocent reason to visit that apartment house, he wouldn't care if the whole L.A. police force stood by in squads to watch him go in—but after he was clocked in by men watching, he couldn't lie in wait maybe an hour, and do what he'd come to do, and then say *Just as I got to the top of the stairs*—Nor could he call at the Lindstroms' first, thinking to say, *Just as I was leaving*—That woman might not be very smart but she could tell time, and suppose he'd left her half an hour before, as might well happen? Also, of course, there was no telling about the cops: where and how and how many. It might be a desultory thing, one man outside up to midnight, something like that; it might be a couple of men round the clock; it could be a couple of men inside somewhere.

So he hadn't dared go near Graham Court at all. It had had to be the street corner; and on his way here, and up to a while ago, he'd been telling himself that after all the street was safer. Once you were off Main, off Second, along here, the streets were underlighted and there weren't many people; in all this while he'd stood and strolled up and down outside the corner drugstore here, only four people had come by, at long intervals.

Safer, and also more plausible that Smith would try a holdup on a darkish side street, instead of in the very building where he lived.

Morgan had been feeling pretty good then: ready for it, coldly wound up (the way it had been before action, when you knew action was coming) but—in control. He'd known just how it would go, Smith coming along (he'd been wary before, sent the boy to check that Morgan had come alone, but this time he wouldn't bother, he thought he had Morgan and—*the ransom*—tied up); and Morgan pretending nervousness, saying he had the money locked in the glove compartment, his car was just round the corner. Round the corner, an even narrower, darker street. Sure to God Smith would walk a dozen steps with him...

Safe and easy. Sure. Before a while ago, when the scraggly bald old fellow had peered out the drugstore door at him.

Morgan knew this window by heart now. Everything in it a little dusty, a little second-hand-looking: out-of-date ad placards, the platinum blonde with a toothy smile, INSTANT PROTECTION, the giant tube of shaving cream, the giant bottle of antiseptic, the cigarette ad, GET SATISFACTION, the face-cream ad, YOU CAN LOOK YOUNGER. In a vague way he'd known the drugstore was open, but the door was shut on this coolish evening, he hadn't glanced inside. When people came by, he'd strolled away the opposite direction: nobody had seemed to take much notice of him—why should they? And then that old fellow came to the door, peered out: Morgan met his glance through the dirty glass panel, by chance, and that was when time began to race.

God, don't let Smith come now, not until I've had time to think.

The druggist, alone there, pottering around his store in the hopeful expectation of a few customers before nine o'clock, or maybe just because he hadn't anything to go home to. Time on his hands. Looking out the window, the door, every so often, for customers at first—and then to see, only out of idle curiosity, if that fellow was still there on the corner, waiting... All that clutter in the window, Morgan hadn't noticed him; not much light, no, but enough—and without thought, when he was standing still he'd hugged the building for shelter from the chill wind. Most of the time he'd have been in the perimeter of light from the window, from the door. God alone knew how often the old man had looked out, spotted him.

The expression in the rheumy eyes meeting his briefly through the dirty pane—focused, curious, a little defensive— told Morgan the man had marked him individually.

And hell, hell, it didn't matter whether the druggist thought he'd been stood up by a date, or was planning to hold up the drugstore, or was just lonely or worried or crazy, hanging around this corner an hour and twelve minutes. The druggist would remember him... That was a basic principle, and only common sense, in planning anything underhand and secret—from robbing Junior's piggy bank to murder: *Keep it simple.* Don't have too many lies to remember, don't dream up the complicated routine, the fancy alibi. The way he'd designed it was like that— short, straight, and sweet. Now, if he went on with it that way, there'd be the plausible lie to figure out and remember and stick to: just why the hell had Morgan been hanging around here, obviously a man waiting for someone?

Half-formed ideas, wild, ridiculous, skittered along the top of his mind. You know how it is, Officer, I met this blonde, didn't mean any harm but a fellow likes a night out once in a while; sure I felt guilty, sure I love my wife, but, well, the blonde said she'd meet me—I tell you how it was, I'd lent this guy a five-spot, felt sorry for him you know, guess I was a sucker, anyway he said he'd meet me and pay—Well, I met this fellow who said he'd give me an inside tip on a horse, only he wouldn't know for sure until tonight, if I'd meet him—

All right, he thought furiously, all *right*; of all the damn-fool ideas... So, produce the blonde, the debtor, the tipster! It couldn't be done that way.

He stood now right at the building corner, close, out of the druggist's view. Think: if, when Smith comes, what are you going to do now? What can you do?

The little panic passed and he saw the only possible answer: it wasn't a very good one, it put more complication into this than was really safe, but that couldn't be helped. Obviously, get Smith away from this place. The farther away the better. In the car. Stall him and get him into the car, and Christ, the possibilities, the dangers *that* opened up—couldn't drive far, maybe not at all, without getting him suspicious. Sure, knock him out with a wrench or something as soon as they got in, fine, and have it show up at the autopsy later on. Great, shoot him in the car under cover of the revving motor, and get blood all over the seat covers. All right: think.

Yes. It could be managed, it had to be: the only way. In the car, then, right away, and in the body, so the clothes would get the blood. Have to take a chance. Then quick around to Humboldt or Foster, only a few blocks, both dark streets too, thank God; park the car, get him out to the sidewalk, get his prints on the gun, make a little disturbance, fire another shot, and yell for the cops. *I was on my way to visit this case I'm on, when*—And the druggist no danger then, no reason to connect a holdup there with his corner.

Not as safe, but it could work: maybe, with luck, it would work fine.

Now let Smith come. Morgan was ready for him, as ready as he'd ever be.

He looked at his watch. It was seventeen minutes past eight.

And suddenly he began to get in a sweat about something else. Smith had made him wait on Saturday night, deliberately, to soften him up: but why the hell should Smith delay coming to collect the ransom he thought was waiting?

Cops, thought Morgan—cold, resentful, sullen, helpless—cops! Maybe so obvious there outside, inside, that Smith spotted them—and thought, of course, Morgan had roped them in? God, the whole thing blown open—

Eleven

Cops, Marty thought. Cops, he'd said. Funny, the words meant the same, but seemed like people who didn't like them, maybe were afraid of them, said "cops," and other people said "policemen."

He sat up in bed in the dark; it was the bad time again, the time alone with the secret. And a lot of what made it bad was, usually, not having outside things to keep him from thinking about it, remembering; but right now he had, and that somehow made it worse.

He sat up straight against the headboard; he tried to sit still as still, but couldn't help shivering even in his flannel pajamas, with the top of him outside the blanket. If he laid right down like usual he was afraid he'd go to sleep after a while, even the long while it'd got to taking him lately; and he mustn't, if he was going to do what he planned safe. He had to stay awake until everybody else was asleep, maybe two, three o'clock in the morning, and then be awful quiet and careful… Like a lesson he was memorizing, he said it all over again to himself in his mind, all he'd got to remember about: don't make any noise, get up when it's time and put on his pants and jacket over his pajamas and get—it—and remember about the key to the door, take it with him so's he could get back in. He knew where the place was, where he was going; it was only three blocks over there, on Main Street.

Wouldn't take long, if nobody saw—or if—

This was the only way to do it if he was going to, and the worst of that was it didn't seem like such a good idea now, a kind of silly idea really but he couldn't think of anything else at all, without breaking the promise, doing the one unforgivable thing. He'd tried this morning, he'd waited until she was busy in the kitchen, thought he could pick—it—up and call out good-bye and go off quick, before—

But it'd gone wrong, he wasn't quick enough; and she'd come in, looked awful queer at him—funny, a bit frightened—and said sharp, "What you up to, still fooling round here?—you'll be late for school, you go 'long now," and he'd had to go, with her watching. So now he was waiting until there'd be nobody awake to see.

And maybe it was silly, it wouldn't make anything happen. Cops, he thought confusedly: but he did remember Dad saying, all new scientific things and like that, they were a lot smarter and some real high-educated now, from college. It might—

Cops. He didn't like loud voices and people getting so mad they hit each other. It made him feel hollow and bad inside—in the movies you knew it was just put on, and when you were interested in the story you didn't mind so much, but even there sometimes it made you feel kind of upset. That was the first time, tonight, he'd seen Danny's dad—since he'd come with them. Danny didn't seem to be ashamed at all, tell his dad had been in jail back east, said it like it was something to brag about, but that was how Danny was. Marty sure didn't think he could be much of a dad to brag on, jail or no jail.

He shut his eyes and just like a movie saw it over again— himself going up the stairs to Danny's apartment, ask if he wanted go to the movies with him, Ma'd given him thirty cents,

said he could go—and the loud voice swearing inside, "*Cops!*
You think I can't smell a cop?—yeah, yeah, you say that to me
before, so you walk right past a couple the bastards outside an'
never see 'em more'n if they was—listen, what the hell you been
up to, bringin' *cops* down on the place—"

And Danny, shrill, "I never done nothing, I—"

"Don't talk back t' me, you little bastard—I ain't fool enough
to think, *him*—I got him too damn scared! If I hadn't spotted
them damned—might've walked right into—What the hell else
could they be after, watching the house? Couldn't've traced *me*
here—you been up to some o' your piddling kid stuff, heisting
hubcaps or somethin', an' they—"

"I never—Listen, I—"

And the noise of fists hitting, Danny yelling, and something
falling hard against the door—Danny, he guessed, because then
it opened and Danny sort of fell out and banged it after him and
kicked it. It was dark in the hall, Marty had backed off a ways,
and Danny didn't see him. Danny leaned on the wall a minute
there, one hand up to the side of his face, maybe where his dad
had hit him—it looked like his nose was bleeding too—and
Marty thought he was crying, only Danny never did, he wasn't
that kind. And then the door opened again and Mr. Smith came
out.

A tough-looking man he was like crooks in the movies, and
there in the room behind that was just like the living room in
the place Marty lived a floor down, was Danny's ma, he'd seen
her before, of course, a little soft-looking lady with a lot of black
hair, and she looked scared and kept saying, "Oh, please, Ray, it's
not his fault, please don't, Ray."

"Oh, for God's sake, I ain't goin' do nothing! So all right,
kid, maybe I got my wires crossed an' it's somethin' else—hope
to God it is—but listen, come here, you gotta go and do that
phone call for me, see, I can't—"

Danny yelled at him, "Be damned if I will, bastard yourself!"

and kicked at his shins and bolted for the stairs as the man snarled at him. Marty had crept back even farther toward the dark end of the hall; Mr. Smith didn't see him either. He made as if to go after Danny, stopped, said, "Oh, hell!" and went back into the apartment.

And Marty slid past the shut door and downstairs, but he didn't see Danny anywhere on the block. He wondered if Danny was hurt bad, his dad looked pretty strong. And if he'd ever hit Danny like that before—probably so, if he got mad that way a lot. For a minute, thinking about it, Marty felt some better himself, because maybe his own dad had gone away and left them, but he'd sure never, ever, hit him or said bad things to him—or anybody. Marty's dad, he always said it beat all how some fellows were all the time getting mad, you always sure as fate did something dumb or wrong when you was mad because you couldn't think straight. There was only a couple of times Marty could remember his whole life when Dad had got real mad, and then he didn't swear or yell, why, he'd never heard Dad say a *damn*, he was right strict about swearing. He didn't talk an awful lot any time, but when he was mad he didn't say anything at *all*.

He'd been awful mad, that last time—that night before he went away. Just didn't come home.

And on that thought, everything it made him remember, Marty stopped feeling better, and stopped wondering why Mr. Smith was so mad at Danny, what he'd been talking about.

He hadn't gone to the movies after all. It was a kind of crook picture and he didn't much want to see it really, though if he'd been with some other fellows he'd've had to pretend he did because it was the kind of thing everybody was supposed to like.

And now he was sitting here in the dark, alone with the secret, waiting for it to be time. And remembering, now, what Mr. Smith had said about cops. Cops outside, watching the house. Something funny happened inside Marty's stomach, like he'd gone hollow, and his heart gave an extra thud. Were they?—was it, was it because—

You had to do what was right, no matter what. Even if it meant you'd die, like in the gas thing they had in California. He knew, and he didn't see how his Ma *could* think a different way, it wasn't right people should get killed—like that—even if he hadn't ever meant, ever known even—Somebody ought to know, and stop it happening again. That was why he was sitting here cold and scared, waiting. Somebody. He hadn't exactly thought, *the cops*—but of course that was what he'd meant. And all of a sudden now, thinking about them maybe outside, *cops* meant something different, terrible, to be more scared of than anything—anything he knew more about...

Sometimes in the movies yelling at guys and hitting them and a thing called the third degree—the gas chamber in California—but once Dad had said, about one of those movies Marty'd told about, that was bad to show, it was wrong because policemen weren't like that at all any more, that was other times. A bright light they had shining right in your eyes and they—But Dad said—

Marty shut his eyes tight and tried to get back to that place, couldn't remember how long ago or if it was Tappan Street or Macy Avenue, where there'd been Dad just like always, sitting at the kitchen table, digging out his pipe with his knife and looking over the top of his glasses and saying—and saying—something about policemen being your friends, to help you.

He couldn't get there, to Dad that time. Where he got to instead was that night before Dad—didn't come home. He was right there again, he saw Dad plain, awful mad he'd been for sure, his face all stiff and white and a look in his eyes said how hard he was holding himself in. Dad saying slow and terrible quiet, "I can't stand no more, Marion—I just can't stand no more."

And Marty knew right this minute just how Dad had felt when he said that. Because he felt the same way, not all of a sudden but like as if he'd only this minute come to know how he felt, plain.

I just can't stand no more.

He relaxed, limp, against the headboard, and a queer vague peace filled him. Like coming to the end of a long, long walk, like getting there—some place—at last, and he could stop trying any more.

It didn't matter what place, or what happened there. It was finished. *I just can't stand no more.*

The gas, and the cops whatever kind and whatever they did or didn't do, and even—more immediate and terrible—his Ma, and what would happen afterward, when she found out. Anything, everything, nothing, it wasn't anyways important any more.

Something had to happen, and what did it matter what or how? May be there were those cops down there, even two or three o'clock in the morning, and they'd see him when he came out with—it—and take him to the police station. Maybe not; some other way, the way he'd thought or—maybe they already *knew*, he couldn't see how but they might. And in the end maybe they'd make him break the promise. It didn't matter how it came: he knew it would come, and it was time, he didn't care.

Time for the secret to be shown open, the terrible secret.

———

When Morgan finally moved, he was stiff with cold and the sense of failure, a resignation too apathetic now to rouse anger in him. He had known half an hour ago that Smith wasn't coming. Why he'd gone on standing here he didn't know.

He turned and went into the drugstore; hot stuffiness struck him in the face after the cold outside. The druggist was rearranging bottles on a shelf along the wall; he turned quickly, to watch Morgan—didn't come up to ask what he wanted. Maybe he thought he was going to get held up. Morgan scraped up all the change in his pocket, picked out a quarter, went up to the man.

"May I have change for the phone, please?"

"Oh, sure thing." The cash register gave brisk tongue; a kind of apologetic relief was in the druggist's eyes as he handed over two dimes and a nickel.

As soon as he was inside the phone booth, Morgan began to sweat, in his heavy coat in that airless, fetid box. He sat on the inadequate little stool and dialed carefully. After two rings the receiver was lifted at the other end.

"Sue—"

"Dick!"—their voices cutting in on each other, hers on a little gasp. "I thought you'd call—been waiting—"

"Has he called?" asked Morgan tautly. "He didn't show, he won't now, and I'm afraid—darling, I'm afraid he's spotted those damn cops and thinks—"

"I don't think so." Her voice steadied. "*She* called, Dick. About ten minutes to eight. She said to tell you he'd got 'hung up' and couldn't make it, it'd have to be tomorrow night—and you'd get a phone call some time tomorrow, to tell you where and when."

Morgan leaned his forehead on the phone box for a second; a wave of tingling heat passed over him and he felt weak. "*He* got—delayed? He didn't—that's damn funny, I don't—Sue, you sure it was the woman, the same—?"

"I'm sure, darling. You remember what a soft, ladylike little voice she had, and she spoke quite well too, not glaringly bad grammar—she's had some education—but awfully timid and meek, as if she was *cowed*. I recognized it right away—and she sounded like a child reciting a lesson, as if she was reading the message off—"

"The woman," he said, "the woman. So she's still with him. Yes, we didn't think she was lying then, about being married.

Yes, a cut above him all right, probably one of those natural doormats—husband's just being the superior male when he knocks her around. *He*—God, I was afraid—so it's just another breathing space, until tomorrow night. I wonder why."

"I don't *like* it—can't stall with him forever, Dick—and in the end we can't pay, he'll—What can you *say* to him any more, to make him—"

"Listen," said Morgan, trying to sound authoritative, confident (don't let her suspect how you're planning to deal with it, convince her), "it's the money he wants, he's not in any rush to get this thing open in court, that's the *last* thing he wants. It's his only hold on us, he's not so anxious to let go of it."

"I—suppose not. But—Dick, I—I've got to where I just want it *over* and *decided*, whichever way. This hanging on—"

"I know, darling, I know. Maybe tomorrow. I'll be right home—half an hour."

———

Lieutenant Callaghan was a good deal less than mollified to be presented with such small fry as Tomás Ramirez; he had been lying hopefully in ambush for a certain big-time eastern wholesaler, and had—as he informed Mendoza bitterly—had a leash on Mr. Torres-Domingo and assorted friends for some time. What the hell good did it do to pick up a minnow like this Ramirez, who just ferried the stuff across the border in small lots? If Mendoza was interested, they had known about the Maison du Chat for quite a while, and a usually reliable source of information had led them to expect the wholesaler on the premises tonight, to set up a deal with Neddy, Mr. Torres-Domingo being the middleman. At nine o'clock they'd expected him, and so it was very probable that he'd been, maybe, a hundred feet away from the kitchen door when Mendoza's bright boy had got a little too close to the game and flushed it early. And so their chances of getting him now, or even another line on him, were just about nil.

And if Mendoza could remember back seventeen years to when, God help us and if this good-looking redhead here would believe it, he and Mendoza had been in the rookie school together, Mendoza just might recall that one of the first things they'd been told was that there were different divisions within any big-city police force. And that one division was sort of expected to play ball with the others, seeing that they weren't exactly in competition with each other.

"Well," said Mendoza mildly to that, "I suppose I could have checked with you first, certainly if anything definite had showed up—but Ramirez was only one of those vague hunches, you know."

"Sure, sure, we all know Mendoza's hunches! Second sight he's got, maybe a crystal ball, I wouldn't know, our little genius Luis Rodolfo Vicente Mendoza! One look, and he says, that naughty fellow's got a stack of H. in his back pocket, and won't my good old friend Pat jump for joy to have a little of his work all done for him! Oh, he's a star, our Luis! Hey presto, and I've ended up with a couple of hired-salesmen punks I could've taken two months ago, instead of the real big boy—and our Luis thinks he does me a favor to give me this Ramirez!"

"Now when did I say so? It's the way the cards fall," said Mendoza philosophically. "These things happen. My crystal ball doesn't always show me the right picture—"

"That you can say twice," said Callaghan. "Got you in trouble before—got you a bullet in the leg in that Brawley business, and right now, by God, I'm sorry it wasn't in the head! And I'll never know how you hypnotize these respectable, high-class, good-looking women to go round with you." He looked at Alison there in the drafty corridor outside his office at headquarters. "You look like a decent God-fearing Irish girl."

"Only on my mother's side—she was a McCann," said Alison

solemnly. "And I think it's sheer surprise, Lieutenant—for any man these days who thinks he can still order us around, the dominant male, you know. By the time we've recovered enough to begin to talk back—"

"It's too late, I know." Callaghan shook his head at her. "You watch yourself. I've got another piece of advice for you, lady— whatever else you do with him's your own business, but don't ever get into a hand of poker with him. And seeing you've done about all the damage you can do tonight, Luis—on headquarters business, that is—I guess you can get out of my sight and take her home."

Mendoza rubbed his nose and said he wouldn't presume to teach Lieutenant Callaghan his job, but he did think that Ramirez—

"Oh, get out, scat!" said Callaghan. "He's on his way here now, I sent two men after him while you were phoning your bright little boy's wife. I can't hold him on anything, unless one of these two involve him or we find the stuff in his possession— both of which are likely to happen. Not that I give a damn about him, but thank you *so* much for pointing him out, and now good night to you."

Mendoza grinned at him, said, "*¡Uno no puede complacer a todo el mundo*—one can't please everybody! Be good, Pat— *hasta más ver*,"* and took Alison's arm down the hall to the elevator. "And now," he added, "*la familia* Ramirez is due for another shock."

"Yes, poor people. I must see them, to return half the tuition she'd paid, you know. I didn't like to blunder in the very day after, but I thought at the inquest I might have a chance to—"

"You haven't been subpoenaed, you notice. A very routine affair. Maybe twenty minutes—adjourned awaiting further evidence—that's how it'll go. Come if you like, but it'll be very dull, I won't be there."

---

*"See you around."

"I'd like to think that was a *non sequitur*," said Alison, "but I'm afraid you didn't mean it that way. I suppose that ex-football-star sergeant will represent you. I think I *will* go. I've never been to an inquest and it's an excuse to take the morning off. Besides, I do want to see the family, only decent."

Mendoza looked at her and shook his head, getting out his car keys. "Occasionally I agree with Pat—astonishing how I seem to acquire these high-principled women."

"That," said Alison sedately, "is a very premature verb." And twenty minutes later, at her apartment door: "Don't forget those stockings. Size—"

"Nine and a half, thirty-three inches, I'd guess it."

"Mmh, yes," said Alison, "and entirely too good a guess it is."

"Women, we never satisfy them—they don't like us too callow and they don't like us too experienced!" He laid a caressing hand round her throat. "I'd said to myself, very gentlemanly this time, maybe next time I'll kiss her good night, but I told you I'm always breaking resolutions...and sometimes even twice—or three times—if it seems like a good idea."

"Once was *quite* enough," said Alison rather breathlessly, pushing him away, "for three days' acquaintance!"

"So we figure it like compound interest, *chica*—I'll add up how much it comes to per week."

"Good night, *mi villano optimista*," said Alison firmly.

He smiled at the closing door; he never liked them too easy.

———

At about the same time that Alison Weir was struggling with the zipper of the oyster-silk sheath and reflecting that Lieutenant Callaghan's advice about watching herself was an excellent idea, Agnes Browne was standing in the cold dim rooming-house hall, shivering in just her slip and the cotton robe she'd tied round her when Mrs. Anderson called her to the phone.

"You *shouldn't've,*" she kept saying, almost crying. "Hitting a policeman like that, Joe, it's terrible, they might've arrested you—you shouldn't go losing your temper like that."

"Well, they got a nerve, snooping around you just on account you found a body! What the hell they after, anyway? You didn't have anything to do—Listen, Agnes, I don't get it, Rita says there was a guy came up to her after work, another cop, asking about you—I guess she told you—I just got in, had to work late, and when she—"

"Oh, dear," whispered Agnes to herself. "I—I know, she called me..." Rita was Joe's sister who worked the same counter as Agnes, it seemed funny to think if she'd got that job at Kress's instead she'd never've met Rita or Joe, and it'd been just chance really—and she couldn't wish she *hadn't,* but—"Oh, dear." Asking questions about how long had she known Agnes, Rita said, and like that. They must *suspect.* "I—I don't know what they're after, Joe, but no call for you to get in trouble account of me, it's my own—"

"You got nobody to talk up for you, I guess your friends got a right to—"

"You *mustn't,*" said Agnes in agony. "It's awful good of you, Joe, but you don't *know*—you—you better just not b-bother about me any more, because—" But she couldn't come out with it like that, over the phone, hear what he'd say, know what he'd think—she just hung up quick and went back to her room, shut herself in. It'd been bad enough feeling guilty all the while, worrying, but when it came to getting your friends in trouble— Agnes dried her eyes and blew her nose and thought forlornly, Well, that's that. And serve her right too. Tomorrow morning, go to *them* and tell the truth—shame the devil, like her grandma used to say—and have it done with, that was all. Whatever they'd do to her for it. And afterward Joe and Rita and the others that'd been nice, that she'd liked having for friends, they wouldn't want any more to do with her when they knew, but you couldn't expect different, she'd just have to take her medicine was all. Better go to the store first, tell Mr. Snyder she was quitting, she'd have to anyway—and it'd mean finding another room too, because Mrs. Anderson wouldn't—

And it was silly, go on crying like this, when it was all her own fault...

Twelve

The rookie who'd been riding the squad car that answered the call to Elena Ramirez's body was on night shift this week, and came into the precinct station on Main to check out at five past eight that morning, with his partner. They found the desk sergeant and a couple of the day men who'd just reported in guffawing over something on the sergeant's desk.

"We got a present from an anonymous admirer, boys—ain't she purty? I guess somebody figures we're not getting enough feminine companionship."

The rookie went up to look, and it was a doll—an old, dilapidated, half-broken-apart doll lying there. A big one, good three feet long. "Where the hell did that come from?" asked his partner.

"Vic found it propped up against the door when he came on just now."

"Like somebody'd sat it up there on purpose," said Vic. "The damnedest thing. Kids, I guess."

"Aughh," said the desk sergeant, "what some o' these punks think is smart! Here, Vic, stick it out back in the trash, will you? I—"

"Just a minute, Sergeant," said the rookie. He had a funny

feeling, looking at the thing; it was crazy, but—"Hey, Pete," he said to his partner, "does it kind of remind you of something? Look at the way it's got that one eye—I mean—it's the damnedest thing, but that dead girl over on Commerce, Saturday—you know. I mean—"

They all looked at it again and Pete said what about it, and the rookie said weakly, well, he'd just wondered if there could be any connection. "I mean, it's crazy, but maybe the boys downtown'd be interested—"

"In *this*?" said the sergeant. "Now that'd be something. I can just see myself calling headquarters, ask if anybody down there wants to play dolls."

"No, but—" The longer he looked at it, the funnier the feeling got. They had a little more backchat, the rest of them kidding him because that had been his first corpse and he hadn't acted as hard-boiled as maybe he should have; and the sergeant finally said, if he wanted to play detective so bad he could do it with his own dime and be sure and tell whoever he talked to it was strictly his own idea, none of the precinct's responsibility. They didn't think he'd have the nerve to do anything like that, but by then he was feeling stubborn about it, and he said all right, by God, he'd do just that, and got Vic to change a quarter for him and called downtown.

He got hold of Hackett after a little argument with Sergeant Lake, and in the middle of talking with him Hackett broke off to relay the news to Mendoza who'd just come in. The rookie hung on, listening to the lieutenant's exclamation in the background, and then jumped as Mendoza's voice came crackling over the wire: "Tell your sergeant I'm coming right around—leave it as it is, and stay there yourself!"

"Yes, *sir*!" said the rookie, but the wire was already dead. Ten minutes later Mendoza walked in and took a look at the doll before he remembered to throw a good-morning at the sergeant.

"*¡Vaya una donación!*"* he murmured very softly to himself, and his very mustache seemed to quiver with excitement. "Now what does this mean? But by God, whatever it means, it's the one—no odds offered!" He swung on the sergeant. "Let's hear all about it!"

There wasn't much to hear, when they got down to definite details. It had been sitting up against the left side of the double doors, in a position where it wouldn't either interfere with that door's opening or necessarily be noticed, in the dark; this was an old precinct station, and the doors were set at the back of a recessed open lobby at the top of the front steps, which was temporarily unlighted due to defective wiring. Consequently there was no *terminus a quo*;† the thing might have been there since midnight and gone unnoticed by the various patrolmen going in and out during the night; or it might have been put there ten minutes before Vic found it, though it was likelier to have been before daylight.

And of course every man there had handled the thing, but it was no good swearing about that now. Mendoza demanded a sheet of wrapping paper and swathed the doll in it carefully; Prints would have to isolate any strangers from the precinct men, that was all.

"So I've you to thank for this," and he turned to the rookie, who was nearly as surprised as the sergeant. "What's your name?" The rookie told him. "I'll remember that, you showed intelligence. What struck *you* about it?"

"Well, I—it's crazy, Lieutenant, but the way it looked lying there, it reminded me of that dead girl—the eye and all—it was just a sort of feeling—"

"Yes. You're a good man. Any time you want to get out of uniform, when you're qualified, I'll be glad to put in a word for you."

---

*"What a gift!"

---

†Latin, meaning no boundary or demarcation—no limit (here, to the time when the doll could have been left on the steps).

The rookie, who had heard a little more about Mendoza by this time, stammered incredulous gratitude; the sergeant was struck dumb; and Mendoza walked out with the doll cradled tenderly in his arms.

He could not resist showing it to Hackett before he delivered it to Prints; they looked at it lying there on his desk, mute, ugly, and enigmatic, and Hackett said, "I laid myself open—say it—I told you so."

"I'm magnanimous this morning. But that's the only thing I *could* say about it, boy—I'm just one big question mark about it otherwise. What the *hell* has it got to do with this?"

"Don't look a gift horse in the mouth. *Ya veremos*—I hope."

"Waiting for time to tell is just what we can't do, damn it. Take it down, will you?" While Hackett was gone he called Gunn's office.

"Morgan? He just got in—"

"*Bueno*," said Mendoza happily. "I want him. Now. Immediately. Sooner. Apologies to take him away from his job, but I need him."

Gunn said resignedly all good citizens had a duty to aid the police when requested and he'd shoot him right over. Mendoza looked up another number and called it. "Mrs. Demarest? Lieutenant Mendoza. I want to see you some time today. I think we've got the doll, and I want your identification—if it is. Also Mrs. Breen's... I don't know one thing about it except that I've got it—it just came out of the blue. Look, I won't ask you to come all the way down here, suppose you see if you can get hold of Mrs. Breen for some time this afternoon, and I'll bring it to your house. I probably won't get it back from Prints until noon, anyway. Right, then, you'll call me back."

Waiting for Morgan, he called Callaghan in idle curiosity about Ramirez. They had found an ounce and a half of uncut heroin in a plastic bag taped to the underside of the bureau in his room at the Ramirez house, he had been taken into custody, and yes, Callaghan agreed that the rest of the family looked innocent enough but of course a check had to be made. And was what he heard in the background evidence of how they usually examined witnesses in Homicide because if so it ought to be reported to the Chief.

"I'm just about to find out," said Mendoza, and hung up. Somebody out in the anteroom was shouting angrily; he could hear Hackett saying, "Now take it easy," and a woman saying something else. He opened the door in time to see a little dark fellow take a swing at Hackett which almost connected. Hackett, looking as surprised as a Great Dane attacked by a belligerent Peke, held the fellow off with a hand on the chest and went on saying, "Take it easy now—"

The woman was Agnes Browne, and she was saying, "*Joe!* Oh, you mustn't—please, Joe—"

"What's all this about?" Mendoza plucked Joe off Hackett and swung him around. "Now calm down, all of you, come into my office and let's hear about it—Miss Browne, or it's Mrs. Browne, isn't it—"

"No, it's n-not!" said Agnes desperately. "That's just what I came to tell you, sir—only I went to tell Mr. Snyder I was quitting first, and Rita *would* go and call Joe, and he has to come after and start all this ruction—he doesn't mean any harm, sir, please—"

"The hell I don't! I'd like to know what the hell you guys are up to, persecuting an innocent citizen what it amounts to and by God I'll see it carried to the Supreme Court if—you got no reason—just because she happened—"

"Oh, *Joe!* They *have.* I—I couldn't tell you, but now I got to—I came to confess and have it all done with, I know I've done awful wrong, sir, but please, Joe didn't know—"

Hackett said to nobody in particular, "I better apologize to Dwyer, I see how he came to walk into it." Joe stared at Agnes in astonishment and subsided, and Mendoza told them all to sit down.

"You want to confess what?" he asked Agnes.

She collapsed into a chair and began to cry. "I'm *black*!"

They all looked at her. Hackett said, "Well, I'll be damned. You see, Luis, I told you—it was that sort of thing, nothing at all. Now we know... You don't look very black to me, Miss Browne."

"I *am*—it's the *law*—I—I know I don't *look* so—my mother was half white, sir, and my dad more'n half, they didn't either, I'm about an eighth I guess or something like that, and everybody always said I could pass, and I thought I'd—but I've felt just awful about it, I've never done anything against the law before, sir, I swear I haven't! I—I don't know if that counts, makes any difference to how long I'd maybe have to go to jail—"

"Nobody's goin' to put you in jail!" said Joe.

"It's the *law*!" sobbed Agnes. "*They* know it's the law! And I gave a wrong address and all, I s'pose they found out and then of course they'd suspect something funny—"

"Well, now, I grant you we got some damn funny laws on the books," said Hackett, "but that's a new one to me, Miss Browne."

"It *is* the law, most states and I guess here too.* I know it was wrong, sir." She emerged from her handkerchief to blow her nose. "It says anybody with any black at *all* who pretends—"

"Oh, *that* one," said Hackett. "I forget now, does it say it's a misdemeanor or a felony?" He looked at Mendoza.

"I seem to remember it says misdemeanor," said Mendoza, "but offhand I wouldn't know whether the mandatory sentence is thirty or sixty days. A judge—"

"Now *listen*," said Joe.

---

*As recently as 1945, the California Civil Code, §60, provided, "All marriages of white persons with negroes, Mongolians, members of the Malay race, or mulattoes are illegal and void." "Negro" was defined as one-eighth African ancestry (other states still had "one-drop" laws making a person with *any* quantity of African ancestry deemed to be a "Negro"). The law banning interracial marriage was struck down in 1948 by the California Supreme Court in the landmark case *Perez v. Sharp*, 32 Cal.2d 711, 198 P.2d 17. "Passing" for white has never been in itself illegal in California; however, many racial minorities were prohibited from various activities, and so "passing" might result in a violation of the law. For example, a California statute (repealed in 1872) provided that "No black or mulatto person, or Indian, shall be permitted to give evidence in favor of, or against, any white person. Every person who shall have one-eighth part or more of Negro blood shall be deemed a mulatto, and every person who shall have one half of Indian blood shall be deemed an Indian."

"A judge might have a little trouble finding the latest precedent, somewhere around 1900 I should think."

"They leave all that stuff in to make life hard for law students," said Hackett. "There're some a lot funnier than that."

"Don't ridicule the law," said Mendoza severely. "If you ask me some of those ought to be looked up and enforced. There's another one that says it's a misdemeanor for a female to wear male clothing in public, and if you've ever walked down Broadway and seen all the fat women in pants—"

Agnes stared at them a little wildly and asked weren't they going to arrest her? "Agnes *honey*," said Joe, as if the sense of it had just penetrated, "you mean *that's* why you'd never go out with me, always acted so—Well, I'll be damned!" He leaned on Mendoza's desk and laughed. "You want to know something, I—I been in kind of a sweat about it because I figured it was on account I'm Catholic and you wouldn't have nothing to do—"

"Why, Joe! However could you think such a thing of me, I'd never—why, that's *un-American*, go judging people by what church—"

"Yes, I think there's a law about that too," agreed Hackett thoughtfully.

"Honey, one-eighth isn't so awful black, you know. Matter o' fact, you're a lot lighter-complected than me, and far as I know I got nothing but Italian both sides back to Adam. Though I guess at that a lot of us'd get some surprises if we knew everything *was* in our family trees like they say. You stop crying now, Agnes, it's all right, you see it's all right—"

"But—you mean you don't *care*—and they aren't going to arrest—"

"Well, I tell you, Miss Browne," said Mendoza, "the court calendars are pretty full, and we don't want to overburden the judges. I think we'll just forget it, but maybe Mr. Carpaccio here—it *is* Mr. Carpaccio?—would care to take the—er—probationary responsibility for your future good conduct, in which case—"

"That's a damn good idea," said Joe. "Come on now, Agnes, stop crying and come with me, you see they're not going to do nothing to you, it's nobody's business but yours… Don't I care? Listen, honey, you're the nicest girl I ever knew and the prettiest one too, and I couldn't care less if you're all colors of the rainbow. And no, Rita won't care either, I'd like to see her try— Besides, I read some place about a thing called Mendelian law, it says—"

"Take her away and explain that one thoroughly," advised Mendoza, shooing them out to the anteroom. "Yes, yes, Miss Browne, you're very welcome, thank you for coming in… Morgan, good morning, what kept you? Come in here, I've got a job for you."

———

Morgan wasn't enthusiastic about the job, took it on grudgingly, while taking Mendoza's point of view. "I've got no real reason to ask questions about this boy, and the school people would undoubtedly raise an uproar, want to know all about it, if a Homicide man walked in wanting to know all about one of their seventh-graders. There may be nothing in it anyway, and in any case not much to find out at the school, but it's obviously the first place to go for information about him. They may be a little surprised at your office wanting to know, but they won't be alarmed about it, and everybody's so used these days to being asked irrelevant questions by busybody government agencies, ten to one they won't think twice about it. Try to see his teacher—or all his teachers, if there are more than one— and his school records. I've jotted down some questions you might ask."

"All right." Morgan took the memo ungraciously. "I'll get

what I can for you, but I do have a job of my own, you know—
and things I've got to do today."

"I realize that." Mendoza also realized that some of the reluctance was due to the fact that Morgan didn't like him much
personally; that was just one of those things. Morgan being a
reasonably intelligent man, Mendoza didn't put it down to any
irrational prejudice, though he wasn't much concerned with the
reason if there was one. Probably not, just a matter of personal
chemistries; and he never wasted time trying to ingratiate himself with people who felt that way. He'd had the same reasonless
reaction himself often enough to know that it *was* a waste of time.
He merely thanked Morgan politely, saw him out, and deciding
he could not decently call down to Prints, to see if they'd found
anything interesting, before eleven, sat down to look over the
latest reports on his other current cases.

Before he had read the first three lines of what Sergeant
Brice had to tell him, another disturbance commenced outside
his door. He said resignedly to himself, "*¡Me doy por vencido!*"*
and went to investigate. As he might have expected, it was a del-
egation representing the family Ramirez, consisting of Papa,
Teresa, and Father Monaghan. Ramirez was being impassioned
in Spanish, and Hackett was patting his shoulder and repeating,
"*No se sofoque usted, amigo—está O.K., compreende?*"†

"Lieutenant—" Teresa clutched at his arm. "Please, you got
to believe none of us knew what my uncle was up to—"

"Never, never, never!" Ramirez whirled to state his case to
higher authority. "This villain, this bandit, to bring such disgrace on the family—I swear before God to you, never would
I have him in my house if I knew what he is guilty of! And now
you're thinking bad things for all of us, that we're all criminals—I swear to you—"

"Calm yourself, my son, I've told you the police will judge

*"I give up!"
†"Don't [choke/suffocate] yourself, friend—it's ok, understand?"

fairly, you must not worry. Lieutenant, I do hope there'll be no misunderstanding, I'm quite certain these people had nothing to do—"

"Yes, yes, yes," said Mendoza. "Ramirez—quiet! You've been in this country long enough to know that we're not ogres! Listen now. Your brother has broken the law and he will go to prison, but his crime isn't in my jurisdiction, understand? He was arrested by my friend Lieutenant Callaghan, and I have spoken with the lieutenant, who agrees with me that you people very likely knew nothing of the crime, although naturally he must investigate that. You understand that there must be investigation when a crime is committed. But if you've done nothing wrong, you have nothing to fear from the police."

"You *see*, Papa, I kept telling you it was all right, they'll find out we didn't have nothing to do with it, and Uncle will say too, he's not *that* bad, try to pull us into it! Thanks, Lieutenant, that was real nice of you, say that to this other cop—now don't take on so, Papa—"

They got Ramirez calmed down a little. Mendoza, suddenly struck with a not very hopeful idea, but you never knew and no harm to try, took Teresa down to Prints to look at the doll.

"No, I never seen nothing like *that* before... Why? Is it something to do with—? But how could it be?"

"Now there you've asked me something," he sighed. "Yes, it is something to do with it—that I can tell you now, at least I'm ninety-eight percent sure. But what, that's another question."

"It's—I don't like it," said Teresa, shuddering. "All pulled apart like that."

"Yes... I suppose you haven't got anything for me yet," he said to Carter.

"We've got a lot of dandy prints, Lieutenant—whether they'll tell us anything—" and Carter shrugged. "Let's see, you gave us the names of five of our own men handled it, well, I've got a couple of the boys checking records now, to eliminate those. At a guess, we've got two or three different people besides—I think. Tell you more when I know which to eliminate. We'll see if the strangers match anything in the other records, and have a look at the psychos on file first, way you suggested. You can have her back any time, by the way—we're finished with her."

"Thanks very much." Mendoza folded the paper round the doll and carried it back upstairs with him. He spent another five minutes on additional reassurances to Ramirez and the priest, got rid of them, unwrapped the doll on his desk, and said, "Now we'll just see if we can match up that little clue you were so superior about."

"What? Oh, that," as Mendoza tenderly slid the dainty strip of pink lace from its envelope. "Today's great thought, I'd forgotten—my *God*," said Hackett suddenly, "look at the time, I'll be late for that damned inquest, and it's old Curly too, he'll give me hell—have fun, *amigo*," and he snatched up his hat and ran.

———

The two women looked at it in silence for a minute and came out with twin reactions.

"Well!" said Mrs. Demarest. "What kind of a mother would go and let a child treat an expensive doll that way! Breaking things up just out of mischief, it's a thing I always saw *my* children got a good spanking for—just leads to trouble later on."

"A sinful waste—wicked," agreed Mrs. Breen, looking horrified. "A downright destructive youngster, must be, whoever's had it. I never saw anythin' like—"

"I've begun to think that might be an understatement—about who's had it," said Mendoza. "But is it the doll Carol bought?"

"Yes, *suh*, it is," said Mrs. Breen promptly, "or one just like it, because if I got to *swear*, well, of course I couldn't do no such thing. I just had the one in stock, not figurin' I could sell more'n that, you know, an' I couldn't guess how many of 'em the factory might of made, an' they'd be all just alike, except some was dressed in blue and some in pink like this here. But it's just exactly *like* the one Carol bought—or 'twas when it was new."

"Would there be some kind of a serial number on it, I wonder?" suggested Mrs. Demarest. "The factory maybe could tell what store they'd sold it to. Little cheap things, there wouldn't be, but a thing that was going to sell for twenty dollars—"

"Yes, it's possible. I haven't looked, the thing's in such a state I don't want to handle it more than necessary, and if there is a number the factory'll know where to look for it. That we'll find out. Now look at this." He brought out the three-inch strip of lace. "I'll swear to you this came off some part of the clothes, but it's not possible to fit it on anywhere."

They bent over it, over the doll, looking. "It's just like the lace on the underwear," agreed Mrs. Breen. "Same exact color. I reckon the factory could tell you for sure, 'bout that—but there's not an awful lot o' the lace left on, an' if it got torn off different times, well, there wouldn't be no fitting this piece where it was."

"I can't get over the way it's been—" Mrs. Demarest raised troubled eyes to him. "Can you tell us about it, Lieutenant, how you came to find it?"

Mendoza leaned back and lit a cigarette. "I'll tell you what I know—you tell *me* what it means! Carol bought this thing the night she was killed. That morning, a Mrs. Marion Lindstrom tried to persuade you," stabbing the cigarette at Mrs. Breen, "to sell it to her, and, when you refused, was insistent that you find out whether you could get her one like it, and left her name and address—"

"Real uppity she was," nodded Mrs. Breen, "as if I *could*, if I wanted."

"So. Carol was killed and the doll stolen. No evidence either way, as to whether the killer or someone else took it. Now, Mrs. Lindstrom lived just two blocks up from here, across Hunter

Avenue—and the next day, though it lacked a week to the end of the month and her rent was paid to then, she moved—unexpectedly and hurriedly. We can conjecture it was pure chance she ended up where she did, in a place called Graham Court, down the wrong side of Main. She'd have to take what was available right that day, if she was anxious to move at once—and what was available, of course, within the limits of what she could pay. All right. Time goes on, and last Friday night another girl is killed, within two blocks of this Graham Court. Killed the same way, and as was the case with Carol, there is absolutely nothing in her private life which gave anyone reason to kill her. She wasn't as bright a girl as Carol, she had very bad taste and not too much education, but she was an honest girl and well enough liked—and I don't suppose she wanted to die, you know."

"Ah, poor thing," said Mrs. Demarest.

"She was on her way home from a roller-skating rink, alone because her boy friend's father, who disapproved of her, had come and hauled the boy home with him. Fortunately they're out of it on evidence. This time the handbag was taken, found a couple of blocks away, but as far as we can tell nothing was stolen. Now, take a look at *me*," said Mendoza, sitting up. "I'm visited by a hunch—it's the same killer—and I've got no evidence whatever, that means anything, to back me up. Not until you told me about this doll. Then I've got Mrs. Lindstrom's name, and then I find out she's living in the same neighborhood this time too, and where does that get me? If I checked back on all the people living around there, I might find half a dozen others who'd moved there from *this* general neighborhood in the last six months. One of those things... *But*, where d'you think I found this little piece of lace? On the floor of that skating rink. There's some vague evidence about a boy or a young man who's been in the habit of sneaking into the rink by an unused door, and who—so the dead girl complained to several people—stared at her in a 'funny way.' I think he's the one, but that's mostly another hunch and I know nothing else about him, I've got no line on him at all. Except that *maybe* he dropped this little strip there one time—and that doesn't say it came from the doll. I say to myself, I'm woolgathering, all this doesn't mean one damned thing. And then this morning somebody leaves that doll carefully propped against the door of the precinct station down there—three blocks away from Graham Court."

"Well, that *is* queer," said Mrs. Demarest interestedly. "But this Mrs. Lindstrom, she wouldn't be the one—"

"There's not much to go on there either—yet. Her husband deserted her about a month before Carol was killed. There's a thirteen-year-old boy. All I know about him right now is that he's a big, strong boy—shot up early—big as a man, and probably strong enough to have done—what was done. I don't know if he did, or why he might have. I'm getting what I can about him, but"—he shrugged—"you can see I've got no real evidence to warrant a full-scale investigation."

"I don't know 'bout your rules for that kind o' thing," said Mrs. Breen, "but it shorely is queer, all that. Don't seem hardly possible, though, that a boy thirteen—and why'd she want a doll so bad, her with only a boy?"

Mendoza sighed and stood up. "I haven't even got an excuse to go and ask her that—and she'd only tell me it was for her favorite niece back east, anyway. I'm hoping the factory can identify this definitely, and in that case I'll want you both to make formal statements about it. Thanks very much, I'll let you know as soon as I can."

Thirteen

The phone call had come through, Sue said when she eventually got Morgan at the office after lunch, about eleven o'clock. It was the woman again, again sounding as if she were reading the message, refusing to answer questions, say anything else.

"I tried to—I thought if I could appeal to her, remind her of what she said before, what we—but she just gave a little gasp and said, 'Oh, I couldn't, Mis' Morgan,' and hung up. Dick—"

"Yes," he said, making meaningless scribbles on the note pad in front of him. Henry was there at his desk across the room, Stack right alongside under the other window; Morgan couldn't say much directly. "Go on."

And what it came to was—right back to Graham Court. Seven o'clock, Smith's message said, at Graham Court, the address and apartment number carefully read out. Morgan might as well come to him, ran the message (insolently phrased, sounding the opposite in the woman's soft voice), and he needn't think account of things going haywire last night he'd stopped meaning anything he'd said. He'd be waiting alone for Morgan at seven, and this had better be the pay-off, or else.

"All right," said Morgan steadily, "I've got that. Seven, that's early. I'd better not try to make it home first. Mean?—just more bluster, is all—don't worry, hon. You'd better expect me when you see me, O.K.?"

He put down the phone and went back to his open case book there on the desk, pretending to check notes, add a word here and there, but not really seeing anything on the page.

Two things said themselves over in his mind. *The apartment.* And, *Alone.* (Smith, of course, unknowing that he had any prior knowledge of the apartment, any other reason to be there.) It added up—for Morgan, and also to a couple of things that were no concern of Morgan's but interesting: that *alone* suggested that Smith had seen to it that neither the woman nor the boy had any idea how much money he was expecting, and that and the revealing of his home address suggested that very likely he was planning to decamp with the money, maybe at once.

What it added up to for Morgan the murderer was safety— maybe. Depending on where Mendoza's men were. He thought he might get some information on that point when he saw Mendoza an hour from now, with this stuff from the school.

From the time on Saturday night when the cold fact had penetrated his mind that the only real lasting safety was Smith dead, circumstances had been forcing on Morgan certain changes of his original plan he didn't much like. He looked at this one from all the angles; it was better than the street holdup in a way, and it would, of course, have to do.

You were always seeing something like that in the paper. A man shot himself, hanged himself, slashed his wrists in the bathtub: no known reason, no prior threat.

The tricky factor was the timing. If Mendoza's men were inside, it couldn't be done at all: they'd be too close, and not unlikely in a position to know at which floor Morgan stopped. But if they were outside, then—which way, before or after the Lindstroms? Before, he thought. Quick and quiet up to the third floor, and no backchat with Smith: as soon as the door was shut behind him in Smith's place, and Smith away from it. And no fooling around with any attempt to muffle the shot, a suicide wouldn't bother and there wouldn't be time. Gun in his hand: prints. Thirty seconds? There had to be a good chance he'd have time to be outside the door again, at least, before anyone else got there. There was a narrower chance that he could get halfway down the stairs before that. People exclaimed, talked a little, wondered, before they went to see. The ideal thing would be Morgan standing in the second-floor hall, just ready to knock on the Lindstroms' door, when doors opened and people came out saying, "Was that a shot?"

But Morgan halfway down (which was also halfway up) would do. *I'd just got to the Lindstroms' door when—I knew it was a shot up here, I started up to see—*

That was all he needed to say; none of his business, nothing to link him to an unexplained suicide.

Sue, of course no question here of passing it off as accident. It couldn't be helped. He'd got past worrying about the side effects; he was feeling now the way she'd said, Let's for God's sake get it done and over, any way at all.

Because, if he'd be honest with himself, he wasn't sure he could do it—that all this would come to any action in the end.

He had to do it, the only possible solution. He'd seen that clear on Saturday night.

Which of course was the point. If you got yourself wound up to a place where you were ready to do murder, you ought to do it right then while, so to speak, the spring was tight. He hadn't; he'd had three nights and nearly three days to think about it, and now he didn't know if, when the chips were down, he could really bring himself—

He touched the gun under his coat; he'd been carrying it because he was afraid Sue would find it if he left it around the house. He thought angrily, uneasily, Ethics be damned: what loss is that hood? He'd decided this, he was just being a damned coward, to think—

You got a little cowardly when you were thirty-eight, with a wife and child and a mortgage on the house and debts and a job that paid just forty-two hundred a year.

And once he'd thought, if he could feel he was to blame for getting into this mess—But of course he was, they both were, they'd known at the time it was a silly and dangerous thing to do.

Which brought him back to the woman, because he supposed—if you looked at it from all sides—and remarkable as it might seem, she wouldn't want to lose her husband, whatever kind he was.

People, thought Morgan tiredly: people.

The agencies' bright brisk assurances: we like to find *just* the right child for the individual parents: patience! The endless forms. The investigators: questions, questions. Time going by, and both of them afraid, *never*, and Sue—

And then, that woman. Just by chance sitting next to Sue in the lounge of a department-store restroom. "Such a lovely baby, Dick, I couldn't help saying—only a month old, and darling, she hasn't even named her, wasn't that interested—she—" Later they both thought, less lack of interest in the baby than preoccupation with the husband. Oh, obviously that curious mixture of obsession (that couldn't really be called love), dependence, and fear...

He was awful mad when he heard about the baby, he didn't want another kid, they take a lot of time and all, you know. And I can't go out to work now, with it to look out for. He's—my husband, he's back east, he's—well, he's sick, see, awful sick, in the hospital, and can't work. I'd just as soon—anyways, I guess it'd be better off with folks like you...

Yes, silly: dangerous. All that you forgot, confronted with the warm round armful that would be Janet Ann Morgan. A little sense you tried to use, you got the woman to *sign* a statement saying she was relinquishing the child voluntarily, and you told

Dr. Fordyce that Sue was nervous, didn't trust the agency's medical tests, wanted his report too. And Dr. Fordyce, very probably, could make a pretty shrewd guess at the truth, but he was an old friend and he figured, maybe, that it wasn't up to him to be an officious busybody. And all the tests saying just what Janny had been telling everybody since—*such a lovely baby*.

And now, Smith. Robertson, the woman said: Smith, Brown, Green, what the hell if it was O'Kelly or Bernstein or Gonzales... There he was, and he was the danger: it would all come to nothing if he were out of it, the woman was a nonentity with no force in her. So that left it right up to Morgan, and this was the only way he could see open to him.

When he came round to that point again, he got up and shut the case book. On his way over to Police Headquarters, he told himself that from another angle, it was safer really—if you came to murder—to do it cold, thinking. If you had to, if you could, if you could face the issue and take the only decision...

———

The waiter at Federico's saw Mendoza come in, and when he presented the menu also brought the two fingers of rye that was usually Mendoza's one drink of the day, and, five minutes later, the black coffee. They never hurried you at Federico's, and they knew their regular patrons.

Mendoza brooded over the coffee; he had something else to think about now, which was probably quite irrelevant, and that was Morgan.

Morgan, so much friendlier than he had been this morning, expanding on what information he'd got at the school, and then asking questions. Had Mendoza got anywhere on the Lindstroms, anything suggestive from the men watching the apartment, and just how did they go about that anyway, he'd think it was an awkward job, that they'd be spotted...oh, from a car, and tailing the woman when she—and only up to midnight, that was interesting...

Morgan, being affable in order to ask questions? And just why? Morgan—now Mendoza looked at him with more attention—strung-up, a little tense, putting on an act of being just as usual. So all right, he was worried about something, he'd had a fight with his wife, he was coming down with a cold or— quite likely—he'd felt a trifle ashamed of his barely courteous manner this morning and was trying to make up for it.

There were more interesting things to think about than Morgan. Over his dinner Mendoza thought about them.

The school, somewhat bewildered at being asked but polite to an accredited civic agency, said in effect that young Martin Lindstrom was one of its more satisfactory pupils. A good student, not brilliant but intelligent, co-operative, well-mannered and reliable. He had a good record of attendance and punctuality. He was somewhat immature for his age, not physically or academically but socially: not a particularly good mixer with other children, shy, a little withdrawn but not to any abnormal degree. Mrs. Lindstrom had never attended any P.-T.A. meetings, none of the teachers had ever met her, but that was not too unusual.

The tailers. Mendoza had debated about taking them off: a waste of time? Not likely to come up with anything, and there was no real reason to single these people out. In twenty-four hours she had left the place only once, between seven and eight last evening, the boy then being home; she had walked three blocks to a grocery store on Main and home again with a modest bag of supplies.

On Thursday she had an appointment at the county clinic. He toyed with the idea of putting a policewoman in there, to inveigle her into casual conversation, but what could he hope to get, after all? No lead, no line... He'd like to talk with her himself, judge for himself what kind of woman—See the boy, get some idea—Remembering Mrs. Cotter's graphic description, he reflected that Mrs. Lindstrom wouldn't be an easy woman to talk with, sound out.

The doll, his only excuse for approach, and not a very good one. He knew now definitely that it was the same doll: the factory had identified it by a serial number as the one sold to Mrs. Breen, and that was something: it might be a lot. Definite facts he liked: this was one of the few he had to contemplate in this business. But—as he'd said to Mrs. Breen and Mrs. Demarest— make it an excuse to see the Lindstrom woman: forget Elena Ramirez and go back to Brooks, say, you were inordinately interested in this piece of merchandise—and all the rest of it. She would only tell him some plausible tale of a niece or godchild, and that was that—no further excuse to pry at her.

He got out the little strip of lace and brooded over that awhile. He muttered to it, "*Eso no vale un comino*—not worth a hang!"* Both ends of this thing had come to a dead stop: blind alleys. There was nowhere new to go, on either Brooks or Ramirez. And yet at the same time he felt even more certain now that the cases were essentially the same case, that the Lindstroms were the link (or one of them), and that just a couple of steps beyond this dead end lay something—someone—some one more definite fact— that would lead him to the ultimate truth, and to a murderer.

He had also, for no reason, a feeling of urgency—a feeling that time was running out.

When he left Federico's he went back to his office. And that was for no reason either. He stood there, hat and coat still on, looking down at that doll on his desk.

He thought, It might mean this and it might mean that, but the one thing it meant, sure as death, was that somebody was trying to tell him something with it. And what he would like to think somebody was telling him was that the Lindstroms were definitely involved.

---

*The Spanish is so much more colorful: "Not worth a cumin seed!"

Suddenly he swore aloud, folded the wrapping paper round the thing, and thrust it under his arm. There were times you had to sit down and think, and other times you had to act, even if you weren't sure what action to take—there was a chance you'd pick up a new lead somehow, somewhere, if you went out and about just at random.

Take the excuse: go and see the woman, talk with her—about anything; something might show up, he might get the smell of a new line.

It was just before seven when he nosed the Ferrari into the curb outside Graham Court. Already dark, but the city truck had been around, finally, to replace the bulb in the street lamp a little way down from the entrance to the cul-de-sac, and he recognized the man just turning in there, walking fast.

Morgan. Small and rather dubious satisfaction slid through Mendoza's mind for a possible answer to this one little irrelevant puzzle: Morgan, perhaps, infected with boyish detective fever, using his own excuse to get at the Lindstroms?

If so, and if they were involved in this thing, the blundering amateur effort might warn them—or it could be useful, frightening them into some revealing action.

Mendoza got out of the car and stood there a minute at the curb with the doll under his arm, debating his own next move now—whether to join Morgan or wait until he came out.

———

Marty hadn't gone home after school, and he wasn't lying to himself about why: he couldn't. He was just plain scared, more than he'd ever been before his whole life. It had been bad enough this morning, he'd got out just as quick as he could, long before usual, and of course she couldn't come after to drag him back, make him answer questions. This morning had been pretty bad.

He'd had some idea what was going to happen right off, but

he just hadn't cared—then. The thing was, maybe like a silly little kid believing in fairies and like that, when he thought about
the afterward part (vague and eager) he'd thought, if it was
going to tell Them anything at all, it'd be right away, and maybe
even by this morning—sometime today—everything would—

Not like that. Maybe not even *some time today.* Maybe never.
And what might happen now, when he went home, he just
couldn't imagine how bad it'd be, or even *what* it might be. She
knew he had something to do with its being gone, with the door
always locked inside and all.

And besides Ma, what she'd do and say and ask—

This had been about the longest and awfullest day of his
whole life. He'd got up early, before it was light even: he hadn't
really got to sleep after he was back in from—doing that—just
laid there miserable and scared and wondering what would
happen now. And then getting out soon as ever he could, after
it started to happen. He hadn't really had breakfast, she'd been
too upset and he thought some scared too, to fix much, and
he hadn't wanted that; and she hadn't fixed his lunch to carry
either, so he didn't have any.

Times today he'd felt sort of empty, but not like being hungry. An awful day, other ways: all the ways it could be. He'd been
dumb in history class and Mr. Protheroe had scolded him, and
then in English class he'd felt so sleepy, couldn't lift his head up
hardly, take in what Miss Skinner was saying, and she'd been
mad. He was glad, sort of, when it was three thirty and school
was out, but another way he wasn't, because it was at least somewhere to *be.*

He didn't go home. He had the thirty cents Ma'd given him,
hadn't bought anything in the school cafeteria at lunchtime,
because he wasn't hungry then, but now he was and he bought
a ten-cent chocolate bar and ate it while he just walked along
going nowhere. Staying away from home.

He walked for a while, just anywhere, and sat on the curb

sometimes to rest; he started to feel like he couldn't breathe, from being so scared and not knowing what to do.

Because he had to go home *some* time. There wasn't anything else to do, anywhere else to go. It'd get dark, and he couldn't go on walking, sitting on curbs, all night.

Somewhere along one street, down near Main, he met Danny's ma. It was just starting to get dark then. She saw him, and she made him stop, and said, "Oh, you're the boy lives downstairs, aren't you? You know Danny, Danny S-Smith, don't you?"

"Yes, ma'am," said Marty, and he took off his cap like Ma and Dad both always said you ought to talking to a lady or when you came inside, to be polite.

"Oh, have you seen him anywheres? Was he to school today?"

"No, ma'am, I guess he wasn't, I haven't seen—"

"Oh, dear," she said in her funny soft little voice. "I guess he's for sure run off. I don't know what I better do about it. You see, his dad was kind of nice to him awhile, just lately, an' then he got mad at him, and I guess it sort of *turned* Danny—d'you suppose? Boys, they're funny anyways—never know what they're up to." It was like she was talking to herself. "I better ask Ray what to do. Only he said not to come home till eight anyways. Oh, well—" and she smiled sort of absent-minded at Marty and went past and he saw her stop and look at the ads outside the movie house there and go in.

He couldn't be bothered, think much about her or Danny.

It got darker, and then it was really dark and getting cold too, and his head began to feel funny, light, and he wasn't sure he could keep on walking, like, even if he sat down somewhere he might fall over.

There wasn't anything left to do but go home. And it'd be worse now, after a whole day... And worse too with Ma, because he'd stayed away so long.

It took a long time to get there, and he thought for a while he'd never get to the top of the stairs. And now he wasn't feeling so awful scared any longer—like he'd got past that—part of him was just feeling sick and so tired and wanting to get home because that was the place to go when you felt that way, and another part just wanted to have it all over with, whatever *was* going to happen.

He leaned on the door when he knocked and waited for her to come, and so when the door opened he almost fell down, and she grabbed at him. She hadn't called out sharp, way she always did, who was there, first before unlocking—but he hardly noticed.

"Marty!" she said, and there wasn't so much crossness in her voice as he'd expected, she sounded—almost like the way he'd been feeling—plain scared. "Marty, where you *been?*—I been nearly crazy all day—you got to say what you did, where you—go an' get it back! Marty—"

And that was the first time he ever remembered she didn't right away lock the door—but he didn't notice that much either, right then.

———

Gunn was starting a cold, and left the office early. As usual, he denied the vague stuffy sensation in the head, the little soreness in the throat, the general feeling of lassitude; he said he wouldn't dare have a cold after the way she'd been stuffing him with Vitamin C all winter. Christy, having been married to him for thirty-nine years next June, ignored that, stood over him to see he finished the glass of hot lemonade and honey, and said he'd better have something light for dinner instead of the hamburger, and why didn't he get into his robe and slippers and be comfortable, so far as she knew nobody was coming in.

Gunn said defiantly he felt perfectly all right, never better. "Of course," said Christy briskly, "but no law against making yourself *comfortable.*"

"I suppose you'll give me no peace until I do," said Gunn, relieved at being argued into it. And then the phone rang, and she said vexedly, There, if that was the MacDonalds wanting to play bridge tonight they could go on wanting—not, of course, because Gunn wasn't feeling well but because she didn't feel like it herself.

He had his tie off, in the bedroom, listening to her murmuring protests at the phone, when she came to the door and said crossly it was somebody who insisted on speaking with him, wouldn't take no for an answer. So he went out and picked up the phone.

"Mr. Gunn?" said a male voice, confident, courteous, used to doing business over the phone. "I've got a little deal for you, sorry to disturb you at home, but I'm glad I've finally got hold of you—your office let me have your number. You don't know me, I'm Earl King, King Contracting out on Western—but your office sent a memo to me, and I guess a lot of other places, about a fellow named Lindstrom, wanting to know if he'd applied for work or been hired, under that name or any other—"

"Yes?" Gunn sat down beside the telephone table.

"Well, I've got him for you. It was quite a little surprise to me, I tell you, because of the kind of thing it is—deserting his family—if you'd asked me, I'd have said he was the last man. He's been working for me nearly six months, one of my steadiest men, and under his own name too. When—"

"Well, that's fine," said Gunn. "We're glad to know where he is, and in the morning—"

"Wait a minute, this is just the start. When I got your form letter asking about him, well, there wasn't any doubt it *was* him, name and description and all. But I tell you, it staggered me. I couldn't help feeling there must be something on his side, you know, because of the kind of guy he is. And I didn't want to go and haul him off the job in front of the other men, make a big thing of it. What I did, I met him at the job half an hour ago when he'd be through for the day, and tackled him about it. No trouble at all, he broke right down, said he was glad it'd come out and he'd thought it would before this, and anyway he'd been feeling so bad about it he couldn't have gone on much longer—"

"That's fine," said Gunn, yawning. "Glad to hear it. He's decided to go back to his family? So that's that." Surreptitiously he swallowed, testing that soreness at the back of his throat.

"Well, not quite," said King. "Now the dam's broken, he's been telling me a lot of things, but more to the point he insists on seeing you—you're the one's after him, so to speak, and he's in such a state—well, he's one of those terribly honest fellows, you know, can't sleep if they forget to pay for a cup of coffee at a drugstore counter—you know what I mean. He's got to get it all off his chest right away, to you."

"In the *morning*," said Gunn, remembering that Mendoza would also be interested and want to see Lindstrom, "if he'll come—"

"I can't talk him into that, Mr. Gunn. He's in *such* a state—not wild, you know, don't mean that, but—Look, I can't help feeling so damned sorry for the guy, he's sort of desperate—keeps saying he can't rest till he explains how he came to—you see how it is. Look, if you'll agree to see him tonight, I've said I'll drive him over there. I know it's an imposition, but—there's one thing about it, too, I don't know but what it'd be just as well for—Well, I think you'll be interested, and if—"

"Oh, hell," said Gunn. But this was, in a way, a funny sort of job, and you ran into these things sometimes. Strictly speaking it was Morgan's case and he ought to be the one to handle this, but let it go. At least it didn't mean going out again, and an hour should take care of it. "All right, bring him here if it's like that. Have you got the address?"

"Just a minute, I'll take it down... That's quite a little drive, don't expect us much before seven, O.K.? Thanks very much, Mr. Gunn, I hope this isn't interfering with any plans—I appreciate it. He's really a nice fellow, I can't help feeling he—Well, we'll see you about seven then, thanks again."

Gunn hung up and said "Hell!" again. Christy wasn't very pleased either, said she thought he'd given up being on twenty-four-hour call when he retired. But she got dinner a little early, and they'd eaten and Gunn was sitting in the front room in his robe and slippers when the doorbell sounded, while she cleaned up in the kitchen. He'd left the porch light on; he went and let them in, brought them into the living room.

King, fortyish, nice-looking, responsible-looking fellow. And Lindstrom, a big man, tall and also broad, still in his work clothes, and yes, the very look of him making you think, The last man. A steady type, you'd say—mild blue eyes behind steel-framed glasses, square honest-looking face, big blunt workman's hands twisting his white work cap.

"Come in, sit down, won't you?"

Lindstrom burst out, nervous, apologetic, "It's awful good of you, see me this way, and Mr. King too, drive all this far over—I got to thank you—I just got to tell, explain to you, sir, I—I don't mind whatever you got to do to me for it, it was a terrible wrong thing, I knew that all the while, I felt so bad after—but I—"

"No one's going to do anything to you, Mr. Lindstrom. It's just that when a family is deserted, you understand, the county has to support them, and we try to find the husband to save ourselves a little money." Gunn smiled, to put the man more at ease. "It costs the county quite a bit, you know. Even in a case like your wife's, where there's only one child—"

Lindstrom looked down at his cap; for a minute it seemed as if his big hands would tear it apart, straining and twisting. "That's what I—you don't *understand*—I—" He raised desperate, suddenly tear-filled eyes to Gunn. "I—we—got two boys," he said. "Two. The—the other one, Eddy, our oldest one, he's—not right. Not noways. She wouldn't ever hear to—even when that doctor said—But she allus kep' him hid away from ever'body too, account of being—shamed. Secret, like."

Fourteen

Morgan stepped inside the dark, smelly front hallway of the apartment building and shut the door after him. This was it, here and now. And it was the damnedest thing, he'd expected it to feel like going into action, but instead—a little ludicrously—he felt exactly the way he had when he'd been in that senior play in high school. Walking out on the stage, all the lights, painfully conscious of every breath he drew, every slightest gesture, and yet somehow divorced from himself so that he moved with a stranger's body, spoke with a stranger's voice.

This was it, this was it. Start now. Remember—and as he went up the first half-dozen steps, sudden sharp panic stabbing at the back of his mind (the way it had been that time on the high-school auditorium stage, oh, God, suppose I forget—) that he'd forget just the one detail of his plan that would bring the whole thing down like a house of cards on top of him.

Think about what you're doing. You'll be all right, you're getting keyed up to it now, you know what you've got to do, you've *decided*, and now time's run out, you're on—move!

Quick, because you've been watched in, every second counts now, the timing is the important factor here. You'll be all right, you can do it.

He went fast up the stairs. There were sixteen steps, and a tiny square landing, uncarpeted, and then you turned up six more steps to the left, to the second-floor hall. The door to the Lindstroms' apartment was just across there, and the next flight right around from the top of those stairs, left again. He got to the landing, and his breath was coming too short—God, he'd never do it, out of condition, another flight and he wouldn't have strength to aim the damn gun—But he had to hurry, he had to—

A woman screamed ten feet away in the dark hall. And screamed. And the third scream shut off sharp and final, cut off as with a knife.

After that it was mostly reflex action for Morgan. The only conscious complete thought he remembered having was, Not destiny I should kill Smith: every time something happens to stop it. That in his mind while the screaming sounded, and then he was across the landing and plunging up the six additional steps, and in the hallway—behind that door there, no noise now, no screams, and then other sounds, and a boy's frantic voice, *"No, don't, Eddy, don't, please—"*

He expected the door to be locked, he pounded on it to let them know someone was here, coming. Afterward he remembered it wasn't until then he realized it was the Lindstroms' door—and now, no voices inside but a queer grunting, thrashing-around noise that raised the hair on his neck, and he put his shoulder to the door, shouting warning.

It was not locked, it swung in under him, almost threw him head foremost. Feet on the stairs below: a voice calling something.

He didn't see the woman, not then. Only one lamp on in the dingy room, a body on the floor, a big dark figure crouched over it, with hands reaching—

"What's going on here, what—" He was halfway across the room; he stopped, seeing the woman then, twisted limp figure sprawled across the threshold of the bedroom; he looked away from her, dry-throated, saw the big figure had straightened to come at him, lumbering. In the full light then, coming with guttural mouthings, and Morgan saw what it was, saw—

Blind, instinctive, he clawed for the gun in his pocket. The butt caught in the pocket lining; hands took hold of him and slammed him back against the wall and he thought all the breath was knocked out of him, he couldn't—Animal gruntings, a fetid breath hot on his face. He tugged desperately at the gun and it came free, the pocket tearing loose, as he went down full length on his back, and hands lifting, holding, smashed his head down against a chair leg.

Dark exploded inside his head, he was blind, he was done, but the gun in his hand, and he jammed it into what was on top of him, just at random, and pulled the trigger.

———

Johnny Branahan had been riding patrol cars for nearly twenty years; he was growing a spare tire around his diaphragm and he wasn't quite as quick on his feet as he'd been when he was a rookie. He wasn't a particularly ambitious man, or the brainiest man in uniform, but he was a good cop, within certain limits: he did the job he was supposed to do the way it was supposed to be done, and he wasn't one of those did just as little as he could get away with, either. He was conscientious about studying the lists of hot cars and wanted men.

The call came over at six minutes past seven, and they were quite a way off, so even with the siren going they were the fourth car to get there. An assault, it was, by the code number, and must be a three-star business, some sort, with four cars called in. The ambulance was already there, and quite a crowd—honest to God, you'd think they grew up out of the ground, let anything happen—

Wilkinson and Petty, Slaney and Gomez, handling the

crowd: he spotted them as he braked the car, and Gomez caught his eye and called to him as he and his partner got out. "Upstairs, Johnny—second floor, the lieutenant's up there."

"Right," said Branahan. He was puffing a little when he got to the top of the stairs; it was the apartment right there, door open, and he could see the white-coated interns inside, just lifting a stretcher.

"This one's a D.O.A. too," said one of them. "We'll come back for those—O.K., boy, let's get the show on the road." Goldstein and Costello were handling the smaller crowd up here, tenants, trying to get in to see the blood, see the corpses, honest to God you wondered what got into people—

"All right, folks, let the doctors through, now—"

As the interns came out with the first stretcher, the crowd parting reluctantly, he caught a glimpse of another man in there, one of the downtown men, Lieutenant Mendoza from Homicide. Quick work, he thought, and moved back himself to give room to the interns at the top of the stairs.

That put him at the foot of the stairs to the next floor, and out of the corner of his eye he saw a man crouched halfway down those stairs, and got a flicker of movement as the man retreated a little way, farther into the dark up there.

It wasn't brains made Branahan go up after him, any conscious process of reasoning. It was just that as an experienced cop he knew there must be something funny about anybody who didn't come rushing up to join the crowd when anything like this was going on.

He started up the stairs, and above him heard sudden movement, and then the fellow began to run—light and fast—up toward the next floor; so then of course Branahan ran too, and caught up with him at a door the man was fumbling at, and swung him around. It was damn dark up there, and he had his flash out ready; he shot it in the man's face and said, "Hold it, brother, let's see what you look like."

The man swore and swung on him, so Branahan belted him one on the side of the head with the flash, and the man staggered back against the wall. Branahan took a second look and was pleased; he'd had reason to remember this name and face on the wanted lists again, because he'd picked this hood up once before, five-six years back.

"Well, if it isn't Ray Dalton," he said. "Up on your feet, boy. Hey, Andy, up here! I got a deal for us! It's just a damn shame, Ray, you so homesick for California you couldn't wait to head west—but New York's kind of mad at you on account you spurned their hospitality. You oughta learn better manners, Ray—No, you don't, me bucko, just hold it now," and the bracelets clicked home as Andy came pounding up the stairs.

———

By nine o'clock the excitement was about all over; they were tying up loose ends there at the General Hospital. If you could say anything like this really ended, or ended satisfactorily, maybe this had. The woman was dead, and the murderer was dead; the boy wasn't badly hurt; Morgan had a slight concussion and could go home tomorrow, they said.

The reporters had come and gone, after the usual backchat with the nurses about flash-shots and noise. This would make the front page tomorrow morning, just once, and not as a lead story; people would talk of it a little and then soon forget it.

"Also," said Mendoza to Hackett, lighting a fresh cigarette, "we can't claim to have done much about winding this up, can we? Just the way the deal ran—sometimes you get a hand you can't do a damn thing with."

"That's the way it goes sometimes. But I don't know, Luis— you'd linked this up, in the process of time—"

"I think so, yes. It only needed somebody with official excuse to get into that apartment for any length of time, you know—sooner or later such an outsider would have heard or seen something to rouse suspicion, and then the lid would have blown—with what we had already."

"One hell of a thing, who'd have—And damn lucky in a way it ended like this, nothing worse. I've got no sympathy for that woman, that I'll say—she got what she asked for. But when you think what it must have been like for that kid, for the husband, all these years—" Seven years, the husband said, since they'd come west away from home where everybody knew.

"Mother love," said Mendoza, and laughed. They had quite a lot from the husband about that, by now: incoherent, poured out in sporadic bursts jumbled together with self-apology. *I knew it was awful wrong of me, but I got to a place where I just couldn't stand no more. An' I thought, if I wasn't there, it'd be bound to come out—they'd make her put him away somewheres—account it was getting where she couldn't handle him herself, all I could do to manage him, times, he was so big, you know.* They were silent awhile, thinking about it.

Mother love, maybe: also pride, shame, ignorant conviction of guilt. An obsession: if he was to be put away, questions, forms, people knowing; and also habit, also familiarity, saying the doctor back home was wrong, no danger, poor Eddy just like a little kid, he'd never—A little kid twenty years old, six-feet-four and stronger than most men.

Ashamed of him, but refusing to send him away. And quite possibly aggravating the whole mental state by the unnatural secret life she forced on him in consequence—on all of them. Moving in or out of places by night, watching, waiting, so that none would see. Keeping him in by day, close-watched: if she had to go out, the husband home from work, the boy home from school, to keep watch. Taking him out like a dog for exercise after dark, keeping to unlighted side streets. Training him like a dog, no noise inside the apartment. Building three lives around the one unproductive life, everything else subordinate to looking after Eddy and keeping Eddy a secret from everyone else.

I figured she'd have to give it up, if I wasn't there. He got into, well, like rages they was, times—any little thing'd set him off, wanted to smash things, you know, an' she couldn't handle—Same time, he knew lots o' things you wouldn't expect, an' it was like that doctor said, when he got to be fourteen, fifteen, you know, getting to be a man, like, he—It got harder, he kept wanting get out, away, by himself, an' then when you'd bring him back, say no, he got just terrible mad, couldn't see why—

Of course Lindstrom had argued with her. Not the kind of man to be very articulate. Not the kind of woman to listen, reason, understand clearly what she was doing and why.

And I never did think he'd ever turn on any of us—on his own Ma! Didn't seem possible, if I'd thought that I'd never in this world gone off like I did. I knew it was awful bad for Marty, sleeping same room and all, 'twasn't fair—but she wouldn't never listen. I just got to a place where—

Mendoza dug his cigarette into the tub of sand in the corridor there and repeated, "Mother love."

"People," contributed Hackett rather savagely. The pretty blonde nurse came out and said they could see the boy for just ten minutes, if they wouldn't let him get too excited, he'd been in shock after all and needed rest and quiet.

The boy had tight hold on his father's hand, sitting up in bed looking at them a little uncertain, a little scared still. "We don't bite," said Mendoza, smiling down at him. "There's just a few little questions we want to ask and then we'll let you go to sleep."

"Yes, sir. I—I *want* to tell you—how it was, it was my fault, I know that—let him get away, when I knew how he was, he'd maybe get in trouble. But I—but I—That first time, it was all account of that doll, it was awful silly but he wanted it so bad, he saw it in the store window, there was a light left on even when it was shut, you know, and times I took him out, nights, we went past a couple times and I couldn't hardly get him away from it, he—"

"He took funny notions like that," said Lindstrom. "Don't you get excited, Marty, I'm right here to watch out for you now, and all they want to know, I guess, is about—about today." He looked still a little dazed and shaken, but his voice was reassuringly stolid.

"But I *want* to tell—about everything, have it over… Ma, she'll be awful mad—I made things happen like they did." He hadn't been told about his mother yet; there was time. "I—I was scared to tell her, first, that time—over on Tappan—and then I had to, account of knowing what he'd done. Ma said— she told him she'd buy it for him, see—the doll. She'd saved up the money—"

"Waste, waste," muttered Lindstrom. "Foolish, but she'd do such, whatever he—"

"And then I guess she couldn't, somebody else—And that night, I was out with him, he ran off and I couldn't catch up—I looked everywhere, I went to that store but they'd taken the doll out of the window a while before, he wasn't—And when I f-found him, he *had* it, a great big box and inside—I thought he'd stole it, I *shouldn't't've* let him get away like that—"

"You take it easy now," said Hackett, soothing; he glanced at Mendoza. They could both reconstruct that one, Brooks, now. Eddy peering in the shop window, seeing Carol come out with the doll. *His* doll, that he'd been promised, that she had no right to. Following, working up into anger at her thievery.

"I—when I heard—about that girl, and I remembered there was a little spot on his shirt, like blood—I *had* to tell Ma, but she wouldn't listen, she wouldn't believe he'd—She said I'd just forgot, she had so bought the doll, and I was making up bad stories—"

Mendoza sighed to himself; he had heard that animal mothers too always gave more attention to the runt of a litter, the sickly one... "I'd like to hear something about the skating rink, Marty. This girl, this time."

"Yes, sir. That was even more my fault, 'cause I knew how bad he could do, then. I *shouldn't've*—but Ma'd got kind of sick, she was doctoring at the clinic and couldn't go out with him any more nights, I had to every night. And sometimes it was kind of hard, things I wanted to do with other fellows, like movies sometimes—you know—I—he got away a couple times more, and once when I found him he was at that place, he'd found a sort of little back door that was open and he was getting in, and I had to go after, I had an awful time getting him to come away—he liked the music, and he liked to watch them going round and round. And—Dad, *you* know how when he liked anything he'd be good and quiet, just sit there still as could be, hours sometimes—I thought it was all right! I—I went with him a couple of times, and he never moved, just sat there watching and listening, see. So I thought, he'd do like that long as that place was open at night, never bother nobody, nobody knew we was there at all. And, Dad, it wasn't like cheating to sneak in without paying like that, because we wasn't *using* it, I mean didn't go to skate. I thought I could just, sort of, leave him there and it'd be all right, he'd just sit and never do nothing. And I did, a lot of times, I went off and to a movie or somewheres, not to see it all through but mostly, you know—and came back to get him, and he was fine, right where I'd left him."

"And at the rink," said Mendoza softly, "he saw a girl, a pretty girl who looked like his beautiful doll... How'd I know that? Why, I'm a detective, Marty."

"He was—funny—about the doll," said the boy with a little gasp. "I mean, I guess he sort of—loved it—but same time, he did things to it—bad things. Yes, sir, it was like that—at that place, he saw this girl, he got terrible excited about it, kept talking about her—I mean, what—what he meant for talk, he couldn't ever talk real plain, you know. It was really that, sort of, that'd tell you what he was like, because just to look at him, he—"

Yes; not until you looked twice, saw the eyes, the lumbering walk, or heard the guttural attempts at speech, would you know. Otherwise, to the casual look, just a big young man, maybe a little stupid.

"Once down on Commerce, when I was with him, I saw her too—he—tried to go up and talk to her, I got him away then. And I guess she was a little scared, remembered me anyways, I mean what I looked like, even if it was dark—because a couple days after, in the daytime, I saw her in the street again, and she made like to say something to me, but she never—Danny was with me, he—"

"You're doing fine, but don't try to tell everything, just take it easy."

"He wanted—to skate with her, round and round, to the music," said the boy faintly. "I shouldn't never have left him there that night. I got sort of scared about it in the movies, I thought I'd better—and he was gone! I looked everywheres, but it was so dark and I didn't dare call at him very loud, people— And when I did find him, it was right *there*, that lot where—I didn't know then, I didn't, I never saw *her*! He had a lady's handbag, I didn't see that until we was down the street a ways, and I thought he'd stole it. I just dropped it, like, didn't know what else—he didn't mind when I took it, he—"

So that built up Ramirez for them. He saw the boy she was with taken out, and the girl left alone. So now was his chance to go skating round and round with his pretty doll who'd come alive for him—and that was all, probably, he'd followed her for: to tell her that, ask her. And the girl, confronted there in the dark, alone, in the empty lot, with the animal mouthings, the eager pawings, losing her head, struggling to get away—And that was all it had needed.

Mendoza said, "All right, Marty, that's all for right now. You just try to stop thinking about it. Go to sleep and don't worry any more."

"He was just wild, find the doll was gone, 's morning." The boy lay back tiredly on the pillows, his eyes closing. "I think even Ma was real scared then—so was I—and tonight, well, she'd been telling him all the while I'd—get it back for him— and when I said I couldn't, he—"

"Yes, we understand all that. Don't worry about it now— everything's over."

As they turned to the door Lindstrom said rather desperately, "Please, sir, I got to ask you—will they—will they do anything to—to my boy or me for being to blame about this? I mean, I want to do what's right, I ain't trying to get out of anything, but—"

Mendoza turned back to him. "There's no legal responsibility involved here really, now the boy's dead, Mr. Lindstrom. I couldn't say, it's an academic question, under other circumstances very likely the D.A. and the grand jury might have decided to call it criminal negligence. As it is, I scarcely think so. Certainly not the boy, a minor couldn't be assumed responsible... I might add, however, that at any time these seven years *you* could have taken action, if and when it seemed—indicated. A word to any of a number of agencies—police, county health, doctor, hospital—"

"She made us *promise!*" burst out the boy. "She made us promise on the *Bible!*"

Mendoza looked at them a minute more, smiled, said good night, and followed Hackett out to the corridor. "Any comment?" he asked, very soft and amused.

"*Nada,*" said Hackett heavily. "Just—*people*. Leave it there. Are we wound up here?"

"I want to see Morgan."

Fifteen

"The gun," said Mendoza.

"Damn lucky—I had it on me," repeated Morgan. He was all there, himself, sitting up smoking a borrowed cigarette, not much of a bandage to frighten his wife when she came; but he'd had just enough sedation to slow his mind somewhat, at the same time loosen his tongue.

"I don't deny it. You've saved everybody quite a bit of trouble—including the expense of a trial. It's only a small point, Mr. Morgan, and maybe you'll think I'm being unnecessarily careful. But as of the moment, California law says you don't need a license for firearms unless you're carrying them on the person or—I needn't quote the whole thing, that's the relevant part. License, Mr. Morgan?—and not that it's any of my business, but how did you come to be carrying a loaded gun on a visit to one of your cases?"

"It's all shot to hell now," muttered Morgan, "all for nothing—and you know, I don't think—I don't think I could've done it anyway." He looked at Gunn, at the other side of the bed—Gunn, who'd had to get dressed and come out after all. "I'll tell you," he said, "I'll tell you—didn't go there to see Mrs. Lindstrom, Mendoza. I went to kill a man. A man named Smith."

They heard about Smith in disjointed phrases. Gunn's round, amiable face got longer and more worried by the second. "Oh, you damn fool, Dick—can't have been thinking straight—should've come to me, gone to the police, he couldn't—"

"Oh, couldn't he! Can't he! I remember enough law—Extortion? The law doesn't take your unsupported word, does it?"—turning on Mendoza, who shook his head. "What could I do, what else could I—? Well, there it is—wasn't intended, I guess—and now we're right back where we were. God, I don't know—"

"Smith," said Mendoza. "Description?" And when he'd pried that out of Morgan, "Yes, well, he won't be troubling you for a while. His real name's Dalton, he's a small-time hood on the run from parole in New York, and we picked him up tonight in the middle of the other excitement. He's got two years coming back east."

"Oh, God, you don't mean it—he's—all this for—"

"Take it easy, Dick," said Gunn, sitting down, looking almost sick with relief. "That doesn't mean you're out of the woods, but it makes it the hell of a lot easier. If the woman's so—tractable, the way you say, there shouldn't be any trouble. Put it through nice and quiet, get her to see a lawyer with you, there shouldn't be any contest, just a routine thing. Dalton wasn't after Janny, only the money, he wouldn't—"

"You think—no hitch, do it like that? If we—oh, God, I hope so, we've both been about crazy—" Morgan sat up and clutched Gunn's arm. "You said Sue's coming?—want to tell her—tell her it's all right, or almost—"

"Sue's coming, you lie down. I called Christy, she's gone over to stay with Janny, and Sue'll be taking a cab down, on her way right now, probably."

Mendoza stood up. "There'll be an inquest, of course, but purely formal. You needn't worry about it. Self-defense, justifiable homicide. Which is a very damned lucky outcome for you,

Morgan. You don't know how lucky. If you want the Luger back, you'll have to apply for a license."

"Oh, well, keep it, I don't want it. I—I feel *fine*," said Morgan, and laughed. "Wish Sue'd get here. You can have the damn gun. Glad now—didn't use it—or the way I planned, anyway—"

"Just as well." Mendoza looked down at him, smiling very faintly. "I'd advise you, Morgan, not to get in a situation again where you start thinking about murder. In the first place, it never solves any problems, you know—only creates more. And in the second place, from what you told me of your plans for this one, it wouldn't take a full-fledged lieutenant of detectives to spot you for X about half an hour after the corpse began to cool. However, as it is we're all very happy you happened to be in the right place at the right time—and congratulations on the rest of this working out for you." He nodded to Gunn, still looking amused, and went out.

After a minute Morgan said, "Damn him—that's—when I thought I was being so clever, too...but I suppose he's right, at that. Just—something about him—puts my back up, is all."

Gunn sneezed, said, "Oh, hell, it *is* a cold," and took out another cigarette. "Well, you know—Luis," he added soberly, "maybe he's just what they call overcompensating, for a time he was only another dirty little Mex kid in a slum street. You know? Tell you one thing, Dick, he's a damned good cop—if a little erratic now and then," and he grinned. He found a packet of matches, looked at it without lighting the cigarette. "He's also a very lonely man. Which maybe he'll find out some day."

Morgan moved restlessly. "Give me another one of those, will you? I wish Sue'd come..."

———

"Philosophizing?" Mendoza came up behind Hackett in the lobby.

"Yeah, I guess you could say I was," said Hackett, who'd been standing stock-still, staring vacantly at the wall. "I guess so. You know, this whole thing—it just struck me—what for? What's it mean?"*

Mendoza laughed and shrugged. "*¿Quién sabe?—¡Sabe Dios!*† Nice to think it means anything."

"No, but it makes you wonder. You look at it and you can work up a fine righteous wrath against that damn fool woman, against the ignorance and false pride and plain damned muddle-headedness that's killed three people—four, if you count him—and all unnecessarily. But was it? The way things dovetail, sometimes—Morgan just happening to be there, and with a gun on him—because if he hadn't had, you know, I don't think he could have handled that one alone, I don't think any two men—Without the gun, maybe Morgan dead too. And maybe it was all *for* something, Luis—what we don't know about, never will. To save the boy—maybe he's got something to do here, part of some plan. You know? Maybe," and Hackett laughed, "so Agnes Browne could get all straightened out with her Joe. Maybe so the Wades can keep their nice high-class superior-white-Protestant bloodline pure."

"Comforting to think," repeated Mendoza cynically. "That's why I'm a lieutenant and you're a sergeant, Arturo—every time I formulate a theory, I want evidence to say it's so, or I don't keep the theory. *¿Comprende?* On that, there's no evidence. If you want to theorize, *chico*, maybe it all happened so I could meet this pretty redhead! Change, please, if you've got it—*¡Date prisa, por favor!*"‡

Hackett took the quarter and gave him three nickels and a

---

*Compare Sherlock Holmes's remark, after concluding an ugly case of double murder: "'What is the meaning of it, Watson? What object is served by this circle of misery and violence and fear? It must tend to some end, or else our universe is ruled by chance, which is unthinkable. But what end? There is the great standing perennial problem to which human reason is as far from an answer as ever.'" Doyle, "The Cardboard Box," 73.

---

†"Who knows? God knows!"

---

‡"Hurry up, please!"

dime. "You watch yourself with that one, boy—I got a hunch you don't get something for nothing there."

"All these years and you don't know me yet. Wait and see. *Hasta luego*—eight o'clock sharp, we've a lot of routine to clear up." Mendoza went over to the row of public phone booths.

When Alison answered the second ring he said, "Luis. Would you like to hear a story of human foibles and follies?... Yes, we've got him, it's all over. But for the routine. I'll be with you in twenty minutes, you'll be interested to hear all about it."

"Well, yes, but it *is* rather late—"

"Night's still young, *chica*. Twenty minutes," he repeated firmly, and hung up on her reluctant laugh.

Hackett was gone. Mendoza stood on the steps, lighting a cigarette, and the dead man in the freight yards wandered through his mind. The next thing, now. Tomorrow. A couple of rather suggestive little things, there: might yield the ghost of a line to look into... When he came out to the street, somebody in a brash new Buick had sewed him up tight in the parking space; it would take some maneuvering to get the Ferrari out. He swore, getting out his keys; no denying at all that a smaller car—He might just look into it, no harm in looking. Maybe that Mercedes...

He slid under the wheel and started the engine. Meanwhile, Alison. He smiled to himself; he expected to enjoy Alison...

READING GROUP GUIDE

1. Does Agnes Browne behave in a realistic manner? Do you know people like her?

2. Dick Morgan will do whatever he has to do to protect his family. Does he make good choices? What were his alternatives?

3. How do you think Lt. Mendoza feels about his ethnic heritage? How does he relate to Mexican Americans whom he meets? Does he relate differently than the white police officers?

4. What do you think about Mendoza's relationship with Alison Weir? The events of the story take place around 1960—how would their relationship be different in today's society?

5. What should Marty Lindstrom have done differently to save his family?

6. Does the author's depiction of the families in the

neighborhood feel realistic? How might they be different today?

7. Some of this story is about the relationships among young teenagers. How do you think this differs today from what the author depicts?

8. Do you think race relations in America have changed materially since the time of this book?

9. After reading this book, do you want to read other police procedurals? Other books by this author? Why or why not?

FURTHER READING

ADDITIONAL BOOKS BY THE AUTHOR:

Blaisdell, Ann [pseud.]. *Nightmare.* New York: Harper & Bros., 1961. A standalone, made into the Hammer film *Die, Die, My Darling!*

Egan, Lesley [pseud.]. *Against the Evidence.* New York: Harper & Row, 1962. The first Jesse Falkenstein mystery.

Linington, Elizabeth. *Greenmask!* New York: Harper & Row, 1964. The first Sgt. Maddox mystery.

Shannon, Dell [pseud.]. *Knave of Hearts.* New York: William Morrow, 1962. Another fine Lt. Mendoza novel.

For a complete list of Linington's works under the name Dell Shannon, see:

Heising, Willetta L. *Detecting Women 2.* Dearborn, MI: Purple Moon Press, 1996.

ABOUT LININGTON AND HER WRITING:

Bailey, Frankie Y. "Elizabeth Linington." In *Whodunit?: A*

Who's Who in Crime & Mystery, edited by Rosemary Herbert, 119. Oxford: Oxford University Press, 2003.

"Elizabeth Linington." In *Encyclopedia of Mystery and Detection*, edited by Chris Steinbrunner and Otto Penzler, 247. New York: McGraw-Hill Book Company, 1976.

King, Margaret J. "An Interview with Elizabeth Linington," *Armchair Detective* 13, no. 4 (Fall 1980): 299–307.

POLICE PROCEDURALS:

Dove, George N. *The Police Procedural*. Bowling Green, OH: Bowling Green University Popular Press, 1982.

Wall, Donald C. "Police procedurals." In *The Oxford Companion to Crime and Mystery Writing*, edited by Rosemary Herbert, 342–46. Oxford: Oxford University Press, 1999.

OTHER NOTEWORTHY POLICE PROCEDURALS:

Connelly, Michael. *The Black Echo*. Boston: Little, Brown & Company, 1992. The first Harry Bosch mystery.

McBain, Ed. *Cophater*. New York: Permabooks, 1956. The first 87th Precinct book.

Uhnak, Dorothy. *The Bait*. New York: Simon & Schuster, 1968. The author's first novel, preceded by her nonfiction book, *Policewoman: A Young Woman's Initiation into the Realities of Justice* (New York: Simon & Schuster, 1964).

Wambaugh, Joseph. *The New Centurions*. Boston: Little, Brown, 1970. Wambaugh's first book about the L.A.P.D.

ABOUT THE AUTHOR

Barbara Elizabeth Linington, who wrote fiction under the pen names Anne Blaisdell, Lesley Egan, Egan O'Neill, and Dell Shannon as well as her own name, was born March 11, 1921, in Aurora, Illinois, a small city about forty miles west of Chicago. Her parents moved to Los Angeles when she was seven, and she attended Herbert Hoover High School and Glendale College in the L.A. suburbs. Linington began writing in high school, but her first novel was not published until 1955, when she was thirty-four. It was titled *The Proud Man,* an historical novel about Shane O'Neill, prince of Ulster in sixteenth-century Ireland. She published two more under her own name and, in 1956, a third, *The Anglophile,* under the pen name Egan O'Neill. She tried to publish a fifth historical novel, but finding her fiction out of touch with the liberal politics of the day, Linington turned to crime fiction.[*]

Her first mystery novel, *Case Pending,* was published in 1960, under the pseudonym Dell Shannon. According to Linington, when she sold that novel, she was under contract with Doubleday for her last historical novel, *The Kingbreaker* (1958),

---

[*]In an interview quoted in "Elizabeth Linington," in *Encyclopedia of Mystery & Detection,* edited by Chris Steinbrunner and Otto Penzler (New York: McGraw-Hill Book Company, 1976), 247, Linington recalled, "It was on the national patriotism theme, but the leftist liberal publishers wouldn't buy it, so I swore I wouldn't write another historical until they published that."

and so they wanted her to use a pen name. When she wrote *Case for Appeal* (1961), about police captain Vic Varallo of the fictional California town of Contera and later the Glendale Police Department, publisher Harper wanted still another pseudonym, to avoid confusion with the Dell Shannon books. Lesley Egan was born. Linington also wrote another series under that name, featuring Jesse Falkenstein, a Jewish lawyer-detective and his future brother-in-law Sgt. Andrew Clock of the Los Angeles Police Department (L.A.P.D.). Under her own name, she wrote about the detective squad at Hollywood's Wilcox Avenue police station, the lead character being the Welsh cop Sgt. Ivor Maddox, a great fan of mystery fiction himself.

Linington's crime fiction is, with one exception—*Nightmare* (1961), written as Anne Blaisdell—in the subgenre known as "police procedurals." These typically focus on multiple cases being worked by various officers in a single location. Linington explained in an interview in 1980 that most of the cases she used were real. "I have a stack of back detective magazines," she said, "*Master Detective, True Detective,* and so forth. When I'm plotting out a case, I sit down and go through these things. You have to change them around a little bit, you know." For some of her series, she said:

> I had to do an awful lot of research on the L.A.P.D. when it looked as if I'd be writing police procedurals, and you know learning police techniques... I know all about the precinct stations and everything. And of course you have to keep up with the newest techniques they have... I found out how they operate and, you know, their salary schedules and police examinations...for plain-clothes detective and sergeant...the kind of things they have to know...criminal slang, and that sort of thing. I've got notebooks filled with stuff.[*]

---

[*]Margaret J. King, "An Interview with Elizabeth Linington," *Armchair Detective* 13, no. 4 (Fall 1980): 300, 301.

Linington wrote so prolifically, averaging three books a year during the 1960s through 1980s, that she amassed eighty-eight titles, and mystery critic Allen Hubin hailed her as the "Queen of Police Procedurals." Linington credited her output to highly organized writing methods. For many years, she would hand-write out a chapter, then type it up in the morning, revising as she went along. Then she would read over the first five chapters and make herself notes, and after making emendations, would go on to the next five chapters. Later in her life, suffering from back pain, she gave up doing her own typing. She stuck to a strict schedule, however, taking about two-and-a-half months for each of her books: two months of "gestation" followed by two weeks of intensive writing.

Politically, Linington was a conservative, a longtime member and staunch supporter of the John Birch Society. She viewed the Society as representing a real cross-section of the American public, with members of every creed, color, and economic status. However, she broke with the Society late in her life because she disagreed with its embrace of organized religion, something she vigorously opposed. Linington never married, but she wrote warmly of romance, marriage, family life, and children, making her police characters realistic and likeable. Frankie Y. Bailey, assessing her work, said, "There is a clear opposition of good and evil and a marked sensitivity to the suffering endured by the victims of crime."*

Nominated three times for the Edgar Award, bestowed by the Mystery Writers of America (MWA), Linington wasn't part of the community of American crime writers. "I'm not really in touch with any of them," she said in 1980.† She dropped out of the Hollywood chapter of MWA because, in her view, it was mostly TV writers and script writers, with whom she had little in common. In her sixties, Linington had had enough of the big

---

*Frankie Y. Bailey, "Elizabeth Linington," in *Whodunit: A Who's Who in Crime & Mystery Writing*, edited by Rosemary Herbert (Oxford: Oxford University Press, 2003), 119.

†King, 302.

city and moved to Arroyo Grande, about two hundred miles up the California coast from Glendale. She wrote more than twenty books there, dying in 1988. Two more of her mysteries were published, under the Dell Shannon byline, posthumously.

THE RAT BEGAN TO GNAW THE ROPE

An award-winning mystery from C. W. Grafton—father
of prolific mystery writer Sue Grafton—that will keep
readers guessing until its thrilling conclusion.

Short, chubby, and awkward with members of the opposite sex, Gil Henry is
the youngest partner in a small law firm, not a hard-boiled sleuth. So when an
attractive young woman named Ruth McClure walks into his office and asks
him to investigate the value of the stock she inherited from her father, he thinks
nothing of it—until someone makes an attempt on his life.

"First published in 1943, this outstanding hard-boiled whodunit
from Grafton (1909–1982), the father of MWA Grand Master
Sue Grafton, introduces Kentucky attorney Gil Henry.... Series
editor Les Klinger's annotations enhance the text. The superior
prose and logical but surprising plot twists amply justify this
volume's reissue as a Library of Congress Crime Classic."

—*Publishers Weekly*, Starred Review

For more Library of Congress Crime Classics, visit:

sourcebooks.com